REDEMPTION ROAD

REDEMPTION ROAD

a novel

TONI SORENSON BROWN

Covenant Communications, Inc.

Cover image *Sunset at Serengeti Plains, Tanzania* by Photodisc © Getty Images.

Cover design copyrighted 2006 by Covenant Communications, Inc.

Published by Covenant Communications, Inc.
American Fork, Utah

This is a work of fiction. The characters, names, incidents, places, and dialogue are products of the author's imagination, and are not to be construed as real.

Printed in the United States of America
First Printing: August 2006

11 10 09 08 07 06   10 9 8 7 6 5 4 3 2 1

ISBN 978-1-59811-180-4

For the real Grace and for Taylor Lee, who first paved the path

Author's Note

If you've never been to Africa, come along for an adventure that will take you into the very heart of a wondrous continent called both dark *and* dawn. *For those of you who know and love the African people and soil as I do, let's journey together, touching on ground sacred long before our arrival, knowing that it will remain so long after our footfalls fade.*

This is a story of choices and consequences. It is a tale of heartbreak and healing, of romance and return. It is a story ordinary enough if you believe that one solitary soul, tattered and discarded, is still worth saving, and that the road to redemption winds through a forgotten village even in the darkest part of the darkest place on earth.

"Bless thy faithful people and keep them from disease and pestilence,
from poverty and want, from conflict of any kind,
and from political oppression."

—Gordon B. Hinckley, August 7, 2005, Africa

CHAPTER 1

A troupe of vervet monkeys has taken up residence outside in my apartment courtyard. I can't see them, but I can picture their small, gray bodies and all-black faces. I've gotten used to their cries and grown appreciative of how they eat the scorpions that crawl across the walkway. Back home in Utah I had a cat that kept the mice away; here in Africa everything is different.

When I get the bad news, I am standing at my kitchen window listening to a mother monkey scold her children. Bad news has a way of stopping time, of heightening every sense so that the moment is never erased—not completely—no matter how we try to scrub our minds and scrape the pain from our memories.

The morning is uncharacteristically cool. People think that Africa is the land of the scorching sun; for the most part, that's true. Here in Kenya, the country straddles the equator so that we have both the unrelenting heat of the savannas and the unchanging cold that tops Mount Kenya with a perpetual cap of white. Soon the sun will push up the temperature, but for now a faint breeze comes through my shoebox of a window, swirling a fresh layer of fine, red dirt and the ripe scent of rotting garbage. The slums of Nairobi are miles from my city flat, but they are also miles in breadth and width, endless heaps of refuse. The aroma is thick, a mix of both garbage and burned petrol from the teeming city.

Wind works at the once-white piece of lace hanging at my kitchen window. Over the months that I have been in Africa, every white thing I own has taken on the colors of the land—not the vibrant mamba greens and rich dyed reds, but the grays and browns of compost long gone dry, the stain of ancient blood; it's the color of African earth. My curtain is dingy. My bare feet slap the cool stone floor. I'm supposed to wear shoes or at least flip-flops at all times—hookworm, you know. But I've never been prudent, never precautionary. In my hand I hold an avocado; dimpled black and green, it is ripe and ready to be my morning meal. In my right hand I grip a shiny, sharp *panga,* a local hand-crafted machete-like knife, that I am about to plunge into the avocado when the telephone rings. "Rattles" is a more accurate description.

Before I lift the receiver I know that I will hear my sister's voice on the other end of the line. Twins have a gift for knowing such things.

"What's wrong?" I ask.

Silence.

"Laura, what is it?" A feathery sob sounds all the way from Utah.

"Is it Mom? One of your kids? It's not Dad's heart again, is it?"

"No. Lana, this time . . . this time . . . it's me."

"You?" My heart stops. Nothing has ever been wrong with Laura. She is the strong, straight arrow. My life is the one that has zig-zagged out of control. I hold my breath and wait as the pads of my bare toes press into the rough grout of the stone floor.

"I just got out of the shower," Laura says.

"Okay."

Fear quivers in the sound of her breathing. That same fear crawls up my spine and pulses in my head. Outside my window the mother monkey screeches, a car door slams, and my sister's words make no sense.

"I found a lump in my right breast."

"What?"

"A lump."

A razor rips through my own chest. My hand shoots to my right breast, and I feel heat.

"It's a *lump,* Lana—a big one. I'm standing here wrapped in a towel, calling you in the dark. You're the only one I could think of."

A very different pang hits me. My only sister, my identical twin, and I have not spoken in months. It has been years since we talked about anything more significant than what lesson she was teaching in Relief Society, our mother's latest addition to her flower garden, or what Laura was thinking of naming her latest infant. At thirty-two, she is the mother of six. I was married once, but I have no children.

"How can I tell Ethan?" Laura asks. "This is going to break his heart."

In my mind I see my brother-in-law's kind, dark eyes. He and my sister share that crazy, over-the-moon kind of love. Laura's right . . . this news will devastate him. I look down and realize that I have squeezed my avocado so hard that green flesh has oozed through the torn black skin. The shiny *panga* is on the floor next to my bare foot. *When did I drop it?*

"You have to tell him," I say. "You can't wait."

Nothing.

"Laura, breathe."

"It hurts. I've never been this scared."

"I know," I say, even though I have no idea how she feels; my twin telepathy is overridden by my anguish. "I wish I was there to hold you."

I hear her gulp. "Like during the thunderstorms when we were little?"

"Something like that." My voice breaks.

"Lana, I know what you're thinking, and *don't*. Don't go back there. All that is in the past."

"I'm not thinking anything. I don't think about it . . . do you?"

"Never."

"Me neither. Okay, where is Ethan now?"

"In bed. Everyone is asleep here. I cleaned the house then showered, and that's when I . . ."

"Listen to me, Laura—a thought just hit me."

"What?"

"You're still nursing David, right?"

"Daniel."

"Sorry, Daniel. How old is he?"

"Two and a half."

"Okay. So we both know I'm a lousy aunt," I say, feeling farther and farther from her. "I guess he's eating solids, then."

"Don't try to be funny, Lana. Nothing is funny right now." Her tone tightens, and the space between us stretches thin.

"I know. I was just thinking that maybe you have mastitis like you did when you were nursing Brigham." Brigham is Laura's oldest child, the one I remember best.

"I'd forgotten about that."

"Well, don't jump to the most dire possibility. Maybe there is a logical explanation for your lump."

"Like *cancer*," she says, and the word is as sharp and deadly as the blade on the stone floor.

"I'm the pessimistic twin, not you."

Laura sighs into the telephone, jagged and dry. "Oh, I wish you hadn't put such a distance between us."

I fight the feeling of offense that rises inside me. "This is no time for junk from our past. Let's stay focused, okay?"

"Okay."

Thinking that maybe all my years in therapy haven't been an utter waste, I say, "I need you to do two things for me, all right?"

"What?"

"Promise me that you will go wake up Ethan and tell him what you have told me. Also, give me your word that you'll see a doctor *tomorrow*. Don't let them make you wait. Be assertive for once in your life."

Another span of total silence. I try to picture my sister at this moment, damp and dire, quivering in the shadows of her tidy suburban home, her shag carpeting vacuumed in neat, straight rows. I try to envision her foreign world, with children's artwork and family photos stuck to the refrigerator door like medals, but all I can see is a fat black fly dancing across the wasted browning flesh of my avocado. I cannot take my eyes from its performance. Up and down, buzzing and bobbing. Then the whole world goes still; even the mother monkey outside ceases her high-pitched chatter. I blink, and the fly is gone.

I blink again, and an image of my sister flashes against the screen of my mind. I haven't seen her in months, but last time I did, no one would take us for twins. She's tried to keep her hair blonde and shoulder length, like when we were teenagers. The weight of birthing six children has made her rounder, fuller, and older-looking than she is. Me? I've cut my hair short and dyed it dark. I run, and there's not an ounce of baby fat on me. While Laura is soft and round, I'm edgy and willowy.

"Lana?" she says.

"What?"

"I'm sorry."

"Sorry for *what*? It's just like you to apologize for discovering a lump in your breast."

"No," Laura says, "I'm sorry for burdening you with this."

"You are *not* burdening me."

"I know you have your own problems."

I snicker. "I've always had problems; that's no secret. But you're my kid sister, and I'm glad you turned to me first."

"You haven't called me your kid sister in years. It makes me feel safe."

"Two minutes and seventeen seconds. I'm that much older, and you'd better not forget it."

I manage a shallow breath and try to swallow the lump that has lodged in my parched throat. It is the size of the avocado pit. "Just do the things I've asked, okay?"

"I will. I'll call and let you know as soon as I know anything for sure."

"Good. Are you going to tell Mom and Dad?"

"Not until I get the doctor's report."

"I think that's wise. Mom's going to freak, you know."

"I know, and I can't even think about what this will do to Dad. He's such a worrier."

I half chuckle. "You should read the emails he writes me. Dad's convinced I'm going to contract AIDS or TB or any one of a thousand African diseases. He knows them all."

"Dad loves you so much."

"Uh-huh. He's never given up on me."

"None of us have, Lana."

My heart goes suddenly cold. "Yeah. Whatever."

"I mean it. Dad talks about you and Africa all the time. He's taken a real interest in the country since you moved there."

"Africa is a continent, Sis, with fifty-four countries."

"I'm sorry. I'm not thinking. I just want you to know that you're still very much part of our family. Dad says there's an LDS meeting-house somewhere in Kenya, even a mission based in Nairobi; maybe you could . . ."

"I don't mean to change the subject," I say, interrupting her and very much meaning to change the subject, "but let's get back to you. Promise me that you'll see the doctor and let me know."

Laura's voice goes gentle, almost pleading. "I'll go see the doctor tomorrow, but will you make me a promise too, Lana?"

"What?"

"Promise me that you'll say a prayer, just for me."

My spine goes straight and stiff, and without hesitation I say, "I promise I'll say a prayer."

We both know I'm lying.

CHAPTER 2

Depression has a stranglehold on me; its fat fingers pinch and squeeze and threaten to choke the last bit of air from my lungs. We are familiar foes, depression and me. There are times when I do battle with the blackness by slipping on my running shoes, kicking up my heels, and putting space between us. Today I borrow a van—a *mutate*—from the hotel for which I work, and with my sister's health crisis riding shotgun, I head out of town to visit Mama Grace. Her smile is the antidote for all that is grim.

Mama Grace is a true friend, one of those people who elevate me just by being near her. She was born in Botswana, but came to Kenya when she fell in love with a boy who was from the lake town of Kyushu. The romance ended tragically, but Mama Grace's love for Kenya proved undying. It was here in Nairobi that she discovered her grandest passion of all: teaching. For the last thirty years she has worked in a variety of educational programs; education is stressed here, but it costs money and there is little money in the pockets of those who need it most. So Mama Grace worked and saved for years to purchase a piece of real estate no bigger than my parents' backyard in Utah. Her dream is to turn it into a school for the street children of her village.

I met Grace the first week I was here. My job with Hotel Harambee is mainly public relations. It's up to me to create a thriving relationship between the hotel and the community. I'm good at the concept even if everything African is new to me. Since the word *harambee* is Swahili for "let's pull together," and since it is Kenya's national motto, right away I saw the wisdom of a community service project.

"We should help build Mama Grace's school," my assistant Nygoya suggested. "It will be a very good thing to do."

Grace's school, it turned out, was a pile of rubble on a scrap of bald land in the slums outside the city.

"To get there," Nygoya explained, "take the main road out of town, go through the second-class district, then keep going and going. When you feel it in your bones that you are in the heart of hell, make a right turn and you will see a little hand-carved sign announcing *Redemption Road*. Mama Grace will be the woman with a Bible in her right hand and a passel of children at her skirts."

"She's a religious woman?" I asked.

Nygoya's rhino-sized head bobbed. "Mama knows God."

"Um."

Nygoya's mouth opened and the room filled with laughter. She's an immense woman. Her muscular arms make me recall those Book of Mormon pictures of Nephi crossing to the Promised Land. Nygoya used to be a game warden on a local wildlife reserve; rumor has it she was a crack shot and quick on the trigger. She is fond of wearing camouflage clothing and a tilted beret. Her head is shaven to the scalp, and if it were not for her fake eyelashes and Red Delicious lipstick, she might be taken for an overweight man. Her tone was serious when she said, "A warning word . . . you cannot approach Mama Grace without an offering."

I was already acquainted with the way so many officials here work—by bribery. Bribes are as thick as mosquitoes during the rainy season.

"It seems odd that we have to offer shillings to help Grace build her school."

Nygoya frowned. "Mama Grace does not want money. She wants books. When you wish to see Mama Grace, you must bring a book for her library. It can be old, it can be battered, but it must have words and pages. She is most fond of picture books for children. *Bring me a book,* is Mama Grace's mantra, *and I will teach you how to read it. Come with a respect for education, and we will learn together.*"

"Okay," I said, intrigued. "I'll meet her and we'll take it from there."

Nygoya rubbed her mouth with the back of her hand, smearing lipstick like red blood across her chin. "Once you meet Mama Grace, you'll be hooked like a fish."

She was right.

Today my offering is a copy of Mem Fox's *Koala Lou*. I think the children of Kenya might get a kick out of seeing a koala. It does not take much to make these children happy. Orphaned, poor, and often ill, African children are the happiest and most grateful children I have ever known. They make it easy to understand why Grace wants to help them, so in my bag I carry several books I've ordered off the Internet for occasions like today, when I need to pay entrance into Mama's school.

Driving through Nairobi reminds me of the utter chaos and not-so-good will in the parking lot after a BYU/U of U football game; it's crammed and crazy. I dodge in and out of weaving traffic and blaring horns, then make my way from the city into what's called the second-class district, past the Third World Meat Market with its sun-baked, fly-swarmed animal carcasses swaying like hanged convicts, ripe for cutting down.

I try not to look.

The paved road ends when I take a turn by a billboard that reads *Choose Abstinence, Choose Life*. Africa is a continent stalked by diseases and plagues. AIDS is the latest, perhaps the most frightening monster of all to strike. Tuberculosis is also baring its ghastly fangs. I'd read about the horror, I'd seen news photos, but until I was here among the people affected, I had no understanding—none at all.

Shanty Village, as Nygoya calls this place, begins when I see a young girl, not more than ten, with a baby tied to her back. Her eyes are dark, staring sockets. The infant molded to her spine is small and limp. The girl watches me, unblinking and desperate. I slow down and reach across the seat for my bag. I know not to come here empty-handed, and I grab a handful of hard-tac candy.

"Sweets," the girl pleads.

I smile and offer her the simple treats. She accepts with both hands—the way all African people accept and offer gifts.

"As ante sane," she says, glancing down.

"You're very welcome. Is this your baby brother?"

"My sister." She smiles, meeting my gaze.

"Where is your mother?"

The smile vanishes. "There." She points to what I took for a pile of garbage. On closer observation I see that it is a sort of tent structure made of cardboard and corrugated metal. "My mother is tired. She is very tired."

I want to get out and help, but already other children—scores of them, barefoot and just as desperate—are racing toward my van. On my first trip here I came with my boss, Mr. C, along with Nygoya and a host of hotel employees. This is the first time I have come to Shanty Village alone, and now I hear Nygoya's warning ringing in my ears: "Never come alone. Never come when it is dark. You are a *mzungu,* and if you are alone, Shanty Village is not safe for you."

I feel no fear, but it is a fact that mine is the only white face around. I hand the girl a bottle of water. "*Magi* . . . for your mother," I say, pushing on the gas pedal.

I pull away, leaving behind dozens of disappointed children. I try not to look back—it's too heartbreaking—but I cannot help glancing in my rearview mirror, and when I do, I see that the girl is sharing her meager handful of treats. Bittersweet tears fall down my cheeks and drip off my chin; they are wasted like the tears of a melting popsicle. One thing I cannot get used to about Africa is the endless need and my inability to fill it.

On my first visit here Nygoya was firm. "You will see sights that will bring tears to your eyes. Save your crying for later when the children cannot see you. Never let the children see you cry. Your tears will only infect their wounded lives."

Depression tightens its chokehold on me, only this time on my heart. There is not enough candy for all of the hungry children. There is *never* enough.

Soon both sides of the narrow, dirt road are lined with shanties and an endless train of needy children. Black faces. Hopeful smiles.

"How are you?" they shout. "How are you?"

"I'm fine."

I smile. They smile. I wave. They wave.

It would be easy to get lost here, for this is not a single village, but a million shanties stretching in all four directions. To the people who call this area home, there is order: village chiefs, markets, even a place to get a manicure and your hair plaited. There are bars and brothels. The poverty is savage, the filth seething. There is no running water. No electricity. A narrow rut in the red dirt road flows with human waste. I won't tell you what it smells like: there are no words. I will tell you what it feels like: I'm being swallowed by a monster. I'm Jonah in the big fish's belly. I'm being devoured, soon to be decomposed. There is no way out except through God's grace.

Africa's Grace will have to do since, as far as I can tell, God long ago abandoned this place and these people. But then, what do I know about God and His business?

I spot the little hand-carved sign that has become a welcome beacon over these past months: *Redemption Road*. I'm moving so slow it is not difficult for the parade of children to keep up with my van. When I stop in front of Grace's school, which, even after our hotel's help, is still only four concrete walls with part of a roof, I am surrounded by dozens of children, blatantly curious about why a *mzungu* woman would be here. What have I brought to ease their hunger?

Accidentally, I bump the horn and Mama Grace's thin body appears in the open doorway. Wrapped in a green cotton *kanga*, she spreads a flat palm above her eyes to shield herself from the harsh afternoon sunlight. The jangle of her bracelets makes me think of Santa's sleigh bells. I feel immediately welcome.

"Lana! Is that you?"

I get out, making sure my bag is tucked securely beneath my arm. Thievery here is understandably rampant, but I don't see any thieves; all I see are children and Mama's brilliant smile. Her eyes are ebony, polished to gleaming. Her nose is wide, her lips full, and her skin is as black as her eyes. To me, she is the picture of Africa.

Mama Grace rushes forward to wrap me in one of her bone-crushing hugs. She is a frail-looking woman with the strength of a lion. Her hair is cropped short with high bangs cut severely across her forehead like she whacked them with a pair of her rusty scissors . . . which she most likely did.

"I brought you a book," I say, reaching into my bag.

"Not yet," Mama Grace says. "Come in and you can place it on my shelf yourself."

The children around us chant: "Bubbles. Do you have bubbles to blow?"

"No," I say, turning to the crowd. "No bubbles today."

"Do you have stickers?" they ask in English painted thick with an African accent I've come to cherish; it's both sweet and savory, and every word carries flavor. "We love stickers."

I feel guilty. "No. I'll bring stickers next time."

Mama Grace guides me by my elbow. Just as we are about to step inside, a round black object, big as a tire, comes bounding toward us with cheetah-like speed.

It *is* a tire.

It hits me from the rear. Mama Grace manages to grab the doorway and hold on, but my knees buckle and I go down hard. The tire bumps over me, bangs against the wall, and then falls sideways. Confused, I look up from the hard dirt and through a forest of dusty black spindly legs just in time to spot the body of a small boy unwind and emerge from inside the tire.

He whoops and breaks into a furious little warrior dance, turning circles and drumming on his black balloon of a belly. "Hee, hee!"

I stagger to my feet, brush myself off, and take a deep look at the wisp of a child who has just assaulted me. He can't be more than five years old. Dressed in nothing but a ratty gray T-shirt that exposes his distended belly, and a pair of trousers two sizes too small, the boy smiles at me with absolute triumph etched across his face.

The stranglehold on my heart is gone. My windpipe is no longer blocked. I can breathe, and I do. Gratefully, I fill my lungs with dusty, overcooked air. That smile, wide as a river and just as fertile, winds its way into my heart. His eyes are dark, but how they beam light!

Like he is made of rubber, the boy bounces toward me, touches my arm, bounces back. Then in a flash he takes off, splitting the crowd, rounding a corner, stopping to look back to make sure I am watching. Grinning.

Mama Grace shakes her head and tries to hide her amusement. She gives my ribs a nudge. "The game is called tag. You are supposed to chase Jomo now."

I know tag, and I chase the boy Grace calls Jomo.

"That way! That way!" the children scream. I run the way they point.

"I'll get you!" I call, and a cheer roars through the street.

I see him now, up ahead and slowing his pace so that I can play along. I run faster, darting this way and that. I almost trip over a goat, and the children laugh with jubilance. A few women stare at me with wonder. What a sight I must be!

Still, I run. I chase this little boy with all my might, for something deep within me whispers loud and clear: *Jomo is one African child that I cannot allow to slip away.*

CHAPTER 3

Once I'm out of breath and defeated at tag, I take refuge in the budding school. There is not much shade, and the air is still now, but beneath the cover of Grace's roof I sit with my friend. I choose a chair so that my back is straight and my feet touch the floor, while Mama Grace folds herself up in some sort of yoga position and arranges herself on the floor, the folds of her colorful *kanga* billowing around her. A feeling deep within me senses that I am treading on holy territory.

To an outsider watching us, the scene might appear barren and needy. Beneath us is a gray concrete floor cracked in so many places the jags remind me of lines on a map. The walls are made of cracked concrete blocks that are mortared together unevenly. There are piles of worn books organized by level and subject. Grace has the alphabet written out in black bold marker on a flat sheet of cardboard that once may have packaged a refrigerator. Her chairs and tables are mismatched and scarred. I make a mental note to see what I can do about getting Mama Grace a real chalkboard, child-sized desks, and school supplies like crayons and number-two pencils—the basics that are void.

"The needs are always greater than the supplies," Mama says, observing my mental inventory-taking. "For so many, many years I taught for other schools. Now, thanks to your hotel's help, I will be head teacher for my own school. I am most grateful."

I shake my head. "I was just thinking how I might be able to help more."

"Oh, Lana, your heart is good. This book helps. It is the only koala book in my whole library. *As ante sane.*" She flips through the pages and smiles at the illustrations.

My whole heart wishes that I could build her a real library with endless books, computers, and all the supplies the children here need and deserve. Jomo's little head and gargantuan smile pops up at the glassless window, disappears, pops back up. He is ready for another game of tag, but I'm still short of breath.

"*Sakini,*" Mama tells him, then turning to me, she winks. "Jomo is no ordinary street boy."

"Does he have a . . ." I struggle to recall the Swahili word for family.

"*Umbari,*" Mama Grace says.

"Yes, *umbari.*"

"Jomo has a sister who looks after him."

I feel relieved. So many of the children have no one.

"Tell me what you know of Jomo," I say.

She laughs. "He's a robber, that one."

"A robber?"

"He stole your heart, didn't he?"

I have to laugh too. "Yes, I suppose so, though every child here tears at my heart."

A shadow fades her smile. "Our life here is very different from yours, Lana. The first time I met you, I thought to myself, 'What's a frail little American woman like her doing here?'"

"Frail?"

"I misjudged you. You have proven yourself very strong. Very generous. Still, it is impossible for you to know what it means to be African."

"I don't presume to be African. I only want to understand so I can help."

"Yes, your heart is strong, but little Jomo has never known a father. His mother was taken long ago."

I know enough to know what *taken* means. She died of AIDS.

"You are right, Mama Grace, I don't understand. How can a child who has known so much sorrow and so much want be so happy?"

"You can steal from the body, but it is much harder to steal from the soul. God in His goodness gave Jomo a happy soul." She looks at me with an intensity that makes me look away. "Lana, you know of God, don't you?"

I nod but say nothing. My first day in Nairobi was like going to Bible school. Here, everyone paints their homes and their automobiles and their businesses with messages of God. Bible verses plaster the sides of taxis. People speak openly of God's goodness. They pray on the streets. They are not ashamed or afraid to be bold in their faith. At our high school graduation in Provo, land of God's chosen, Laura's petition to offer a prayer was defeated for fear of "offending someone."

"Have you traveled, Lana? You look to be gone."

"Oh, I'm sorry. I was just thinking. Tell me more about Jomo."

"He is not a regular comer. He resides a good distance from Redemption Road."

Then an idea leaves my mouth before it has gone through my brain. "Do you think I could take him home with me?"

Her smile leaves completely. "Jomo is no stray dog."

"No. No. I'm sorry if it sounded like that; I mean . . ." I do know what I mean; I have too many emotions swimming around inside my head, inside my heart, to sort through them.

"You are a true *rafiki*," Grace says. "Your heart is good, but I can tell that it is troubled. Lay your worries here," she invites, pointing to her bare feet.

I unload at Mama Grace's feet, unburden my heart. I tell her how I ache to help the street children of Nairobi, how I feel so inadequate. I tell her about Laura and how I wish I could reach halfway across the world to comfort my only sister. I don't get to the true center of my pain. I can't.

Mama shakes her head sympathetically. "I am sorry for your sister. Finding a breast lump is much like finding a leopard at your heels."

"It could be nothing," I say.

"Is your sister's nature to overreact?"

"No. Laura is levelheaded. I'm the one who generally leaps to the most negative conclusions."

"That does not sound like the Lana I have come to know. You are very levelheaded. My school would not be so complete without your levelheadedness."

"I wish we could do more . . . faster, too."

Her eyes sparkle. "Africa runs on *hakunamatata* time."

"I know. *No worries.*"

"All is well," Grace says. "I am most grateful for you and your hotel."

"It was all Nygoya's idea."

"She was once my student."

"I know; she told me. Nygoya is a great *rafiki* to us both."

Children sing and call from outside; a horn blares in the distance. I'm ready for another game of tag with Jomo.

Mama Grace sighs. "I have been blessed with many great friends. One day you must meet Gavin. I have told him about you."

"Have you told me about him? I don't remember anyone named Gavin."

"Gavin is like a son to me—my *mzungu* son."

"What does Gavin do?"

"He is a safari outfitter. He loves wildlife; he loves Africa. Like you, Gavin brings me books and tales from the veltlands." Grace reaches to touch my arm. "Lana, worry drowns your face. I am sorry about your sister."

"It's just that I think God made a mistake."

Her eyebrows lift. "How so?"

"*I* am the one who has broken God's commandments. He should punish *me,* not my sister."

"The God I know does not make mistakes. He does not punish. He loves and lets us choose, like a good parent." She reaches for her Bible. It is big and black, and the cover is worn to tatters. "Deuteronomy," she says, like I should know what she is talking about.

"It's a book in the Bible, right?"

"Yes, Lana. I have discovered that there is great power in God's word. There are answers to life's hardest questions." She licks the side of her thumb and begins turning pages. Her Bible is marked up like a coloring book, and I smile, remembering from my childhood how I used to red-pencil my Book of Mormon. That was a lifetime ago. I haven't even seen a Book of Mormon in years.

"Ah, yes. Here it is: Deuteronomy 30:19." I expect her to read aloud to me, to give me a lecture, but she reads the verse silently, closes her eyes, smiles, then closes her Bible. "Yes, there is healing power in God's word. Now tell me, what else is weighing on your heart today?"

We talk of my childhood. I don't mean to divulge much, but find myself pouring out memories like water from a kettle. We talk of the sweetness of new romance, how it turns sour with time. Like always, I stop short of any memory too sharp, too jagged.

Jomo's little face appears at the window. *"Jina lako nani?"* His infectious laugh drifts though the open window like fresh air. He says something, pointing to me.

"I should understand Swahili by now, but I don't know what he's asking."

"He wants to know what you are called."

"Lana," I say, searching my mind for a way to reply in Swahili. *"Jina Langu ni* Lana."

"Lana." The way Jomo says my name sounds like the beginning of a melody I want to hear again and again.

"You want to play more?" he asks, shifting to English. "I want to play more. You are a fun *mzungu.*"

My heart smiles.

I am amazed at how street children like Jomo, unschooled, are almost always trilingual; they usually know Swahili, English, and their own tribal language. I am anxious for the day Mama Grace opens her school to these children so they can learn even more. I turn to her and watch as she unwinds her legs and stands.

I ask Mama Grace, "Would you mind if I went back outside and played with Jomo and the children? I have some sweets in my purse I'd like to give them."

She shakes her head. "Go on, Lana. Out there is where you belong."

Hours later when I am lying in bed I think about how my day unfolded; like the wings of a strong bird, it lifted me to places I had not been, permitting me to see things I had not witnessed and to feel things I had not felt for so long. In spite of Laura's worry and Jomo's poverty, I feel elevated.

Sleep comes slowly, carrying me away, back to a time when my life was surrounded by rugged mountains and caring people who sheltered me from the storms of life. In the end, they could not keep me safe from myself. Somewhere in the back of my head I hear my mother's voice, tired and disapproving. I see my father, his shoulders stooped from disappointment. I hear my sister praying: ". . . and please bless Lana so that she will make right choices. Watch over her, Father, and keep her safe."

A monkey screeches outside my window and I bolt upright in bed, back to the present. My room is pitch black except for a sliver of blue moonlight that drifts through a crack in my blind. It is Mama Grace's voice I hear next: "Deuteronomy 30:19."

I do not own a Bible, so I slip out of bed and go to my laptop computer. I turn it on and wait for an Internet connection. While I wait I make myself a cup of *chai,* African tea that is supposed to be very healthy.

When I make my connection I type in a search for the King James Bible online. Deuteronomy 30:19 reads: *I call heaven and earth to record this day against you, that I have set before you life and death, blessing and cursing: therefore choose life, that both thou and thy seed may live.*

A different voice, one that is distant and yet familiar, fills my head: "Choose life. Choose blessing over cursing."

The truth moves through me. "We always have a choice. Always."

Impulsively, I write Laura an email. It is short and to the point. "Choose life," I write. "Choose blessing over cursing." I type in the Biblical reference. It's not exactly a prayer, but closer than I've come in a very long time. If only I could be there to see the look on Laura's face when she realizes *I'm* quoting scripture to *her.*

CHAPTER 4

My father always taught me to exert my energy, my resources, only on those people and things within the circle of my influence; anything else is futile. My mother taught me that life is a garden; we reap what we sow. For a woman who has lived as many years as I have, my circle is too small, my garden too sparse. With stinging remorse, the reality hits me now in the early afternoon of my life when the seeds planted in my youth should be blooming bright and full, when the slipping sun's warmth should be seeping deep, nurturing my soul. It is a time when I should be reaping the firstfruits of my life's harvest. My circle should be full of color and sustenance.

Instead, I am alone in the vast barrenness of Africa.

When Laura and I were young, we dreamed of creating circles both wide and deep. Our father, the mechanic, would fix anything in our lives that might break. Our mother, the gardener, would help us cultivate and cull our futures until they grew both rich and sweet. Late at night my sister and I stayed awake drawing our individual circles, whispering of temple weddings, white dresses, grooms with dark hair and blue eyes. We concocted stunningly handsome returned missionaries capable of carrying us all the way through eternity. We numbered and named our children. Laura's would play sports, mine would play music.

Laura never let that dream out of her sight. Now she's reaping a bumper crop: a devoted husband, a quiver of children, a stable home, parents who are proud of her, and friends everywhere she turns. It is hard to feel sorry for my sister in light of all that she has.

Somewhere along the way my vision blurred and led me in a different direction: a weakened faith; two failed marriages; no child to rise up and call me Mother; acquaintances, but few friends. It is hard to feel sorry for myself in light of all that I have done wrong.

I stand on a street corner in the heart of Nairobi. Thousands of people from all walks and ways of life surround me. If every face, a different shape, a different shade, is a child of God, how can each child—when there are so many—be important? How can God keep track of every person? How can one as unworthy as I matter?

A horn blares, and someone shouts as a rogue taxi careens up onto the walkway. People scatter, and the strong arm of a stranger yanks me out of harm's way. The front end of the taxi clips a street vendor's small grill, and smoke and burning ashes scatter all around us. Small, charred pieces of meat are quickly grabbed by thieving hands, and the man is left to start over—but has nothing to start over with.

"*Yote*," he mutters.

Yote means "all." He has lost all he has.

I stoop to help and see myself offering a handful of shillings.

"I have nothing to offer in return," the man says, shaking his head. His skin is dark and withered, the whites of his eyes yellow. He has no teeth, and his robes are black from smoke and filth.

"Take it," I say, "I don't want anything in return. You can buy fresh meat to start over."

His trembling hands clamp over mine. "Thank you, thank you, thank you."

"You're welcome."

I move on down the road, through a crowded sea of people. I cough on the smoke that I breathed in, on the bitterness and shame of defeat that fills my body. In that one unguarded moment the brutal truth washes over me, and I know in my heart that I *am* reaping the seeds I have sown: rebellion, disobedience, selfishness. They make for nothing but strangling, noxious weeds, and even those have withered to brittle, lifeless vines.

Then the smiling face of a woman passes in front of me. In her arms is a small, bleating goat. Something about her reminds me of Mama Grace, and I hear Mama's voice: "Choose life."

Desperation replaces my despair. I want to choose life. I want to expand my circle, to replant and cultivate my life's garden, but how?

I keep walking, winding my way through the masses. I'm on my afternoon break from the hotel; I have no destination, no purpose, except to walk and think. It has been days since Laura called. This morning she emailed to report that she has finally scheduled a doctor's appointment. They will get her in "as soon as possible." If I were there I would drive her to the office and camp on the doorstep until the doctor examined her. But I am not in Utah, and it does no good for me to chastise her timidity across the distance.

So we wait.

"I'm not sure I understood the meaning of that scripture you sent me," Laura wrote. "Of course I'll choose life. Is that what you meant?"

I emailed back and tried to explain, realizing how woefully inadequate I am at presenting such deep truths. "Come to Africa," I finally wrote. "I'll let you sit at the feet of Mama Grace; she can teach you."

Wishing Laura were by my side, I meander down Market Street and step around the woven mats and blankets that mark one vendor's territory from another's. Kenya is the definitive cultural and ethnic melting pot. Freed from colonial rule in 1963, it is home to a twisted mix of people. Most of the faces are dark. The clothing is both modern and ancient. I see blue jeans and T-shirts, black veils over faces, silk kimonos and elaborate saris, turbans swirled high. I see cornrows and Afros, Asians and Indians. *Wazungu* like me stand out. Children deftly dart around the merchandise, knowing how to read people and faces. They wear little more than their beautiful brown skin. I've come to see myself as pale here in a land that is so rich and ripe with nature's varying shades of browns and blacks.

I think of Jomo. Mama Grace was right—he has stolen a piece of my heart. I miss him and look forward to the weekend so I can go back to the village for another game of tag. I have never known such energy, such joy. Once I caught hold of him, I did not want to let go, not ever; I wanted his spirit to infuse me. I took hold of his hand, and he gave my fingers three tight squeezes. A pent-up emotion deep within my heart burst, making it impossible to stop tears from spilling.

He looked up at me with sudden sorrow. "I am sorry. Did I squeeze too tight?"

"No. No. It's not that."

"You are sad?"

"No. These are happy tears."

"I do not understand."

"Me neither."

For months, but especially in the past few days, an old, hard part of my heart has been turning like a wheel rusty from disuse. It hurt. It terrified me. I knelt down and took Jomo in my arms. I tried not to squeeze him too tight, but oh, how I ached to encircle him, to freeze that moment, to never let go.

Two young teenage boys on bicycles nearly bowl me over, and I am back to the present.

Piles of pineapples, tomatoes, avocadoes, yams; rows of carved wooden giraffes and elephants; jewelry that glimmers in the amber sunlight—it's all there, sold by anxious shopkeepers who live or die by a four-by-four-foot square. Voices call and plead, and I pluck out a Swahili word here and there that I recognize.

Absentmindedly, I pause in front of a leathered old man grilling maize. He holds out a charred white cob and nods with anticipation. "Of my *shamba*," he says.

I search my mind for the meaning of the Swahili word. I know it and try desperately to grab it from my brain's dictionary. When it comes, the man demonstrates vivid surprise that I understand.

Shamba means "family farm." "You grew this corn yourself?"

The man smiles proudly and nods. I offer him a few extra shillings and walk away feeling . . . different, like the air is somehow cleaner and easier to breathe. I tell myself that in some small way I have widened the circle of my influence. I made an ancient African man smile. I did not eradicate his poverty. I did not change his life. But I made him smile.

Now . . . what can I do for Laura? For Jomo?

CHAPTER 5

"So you've fallen in love with an African man." Nygoya leans back on a chair in my office with a cup of steaming *chai* in one hand and a wide grin across her face. Today ostrich feather earrings, dyed blinding pink, dangle from both ears. Her enormous combat boots are unlaced, and I notice that her socks match her earrings. My office is not large, and Nygoya's presence seems to fill every inch, to push the walls back and expand the space. "What will your parents back home in America say to that?"

I smile. "They'll say I've improved my taste in men."

She laughs a deep belly laugh, sloshing tea from the top of her cup and spilling on her hand. She does not seem to notice. "What is this handsome boy's name?"

"Jomo."

"After Jomo Kenyatta, no doubt."

Jomo Kenyatta was Kenya's first president; his statue sits in the city center, and streets and schools and children are named after him. He has been dead since 1978, but the people honor him still. A portrait of him hangs in the lobby of our hotel.

"Just Jomo?" Nygoya asks. "Most Kenyan children carry three names."

"Why three?"

She drinks the dregs of her tea, sets the cup on a side table, and leans down to retie one of her boots. "A Christian name, a given name, and the name of the child's father."

"A *Christian* name? Jomo is a street boy."

"That does not mean Jesus is not his Savior."

I feel reprimanded, like I've just had my hands slapped. I look at the map of Africa on the wall directly behind Nygoya's head and share a recollection with her. "When I first arrived in here I was surprised to see the side of my *matatu* painted with the name of Jesus. Since then I see Jesus' name painted on walls and cars and buses. Even in the slums Jesus is everywhere. It's like religious graffiti."

Her black boots slam down, and she leans toward me, growling, "There is no greater name."

"I know. I respect that. It just surprised me that Christianity is so . . . so . . ."

"Celebrated."

"Uh-huh. That's the perfect word."

"Is Jesus not celebrated where you come from?"

A million memories flash through my mind: family home evenings. Bedside prayers. Primary lessons. Young Women activities. Tithing envelopes. Commandments. Endless sacrament meetings. Guilt. *Where was Jesus in all of the religion?*

I try to answer my friend, feeling like I'm suddenly under fire. "No. I mean yes. Jesus is the center of my religion."

She bats fat, thick eyelashes at me. "What religion is that, Lana?"

"Officially it's called The Church of Jesus Christ of Latter-day Saints."

She sits tall, and her eyes widen. "You are *Mormon?*"

I squirm, confused at how Nygoya could make that connection. "Um . . . sort of. I was raised Mormon; I'm not really um . . . not . . ."

"I know a Mormon, Mama Dale, who is a nurse at the baby center. You are nothing like her."

I feel insulted though I know Nygoya did not mean to insult me. "Religion isn't really my thing."

She stands, hands pressing against her ample hips, and looks at me with something akin to pity in her expression. "I had better get back to work. I am escorting a group of Australian guests to the giraffe refuge. Seems they don't have many giraffes in the outback." She laughs, but the sound is forced.

I follow her to the doorway, frustrated and plagued with a need to defend myself. "I know my answer sounded pathetic. The truth is, I'm not sure how I feel about spiritual things."

"You feel guilty. It doesn't take a brain doctor to see that."

"Okay, I'll give you that; I'm an *expert* on guilt."

She clicks her tongue. "That doesn't sound like a skill to boast on. We'll talk later if that is okay. After all, you are my boss."

"Sure. Later."

I don't feel like Nygoya's boss. I feel like her student, and the subject is life; it's the same way I feel about Mama Grace. I'm a student, and Africa is my classroom. But right now there is a stack of hotel work on my desk vying for my attention. I just begin to sort it when I hear footsteps outside my door. I look up to see my boss, Mr. C, standing there in his perfectly creased yellow shirt and purple tie. He is tree tall, black as midnight, and serious about making our hotel an asset to Nairobi. "*Jambo,* Lana."

"*Jambo, bosi.*"

"*Habari?*"

"Things are fine. Busy."

We discuss a few pending hotel matters before he asks, "And how is Mama Grace's school coming along?"

"I was out there a few days ago. She is very appreciative of what has been accomplished, but work appears to be at a standstill."

Mr. C frowns. "I am saddened to hear that. We must see that her school is finished as soon as possible, before the rains come. It is unfortunate that we can devote only a few hours here and there. I wish our employees were more dedicated to service. It seems in their off hours they would rather lounge than labor."

I hand him a list of things I've come up with—supplies that are needed, projects to be completed, ideas for making the school outstanding. I also include a list of public relations possibilities to help the hotel receive positive press from helping the school.

He scans it and looks at me with a smile. "You have grand vision."

"I realize the hotel can't do everything, but if we pull together . . ."

He laughs. "*Harambee!*"

"Of course. Please sit."

"It is not necessary. I wish to tell you how much I appreciate your willingness to study and learn of Kenya and our people. I receive many compliments about you—a few complaints, as well."

"Oh?"

He waves me off. "*Sijambo*. No problems. Those who complain say you are not easy to bribe. They say you have honor that cannot be corrupted for any amount of shillings."

I sit silent, not knowing how to respond.

"The hotel's bookings have risen sharply these past months. I attribute those numbers to your arrival. You are a fine employee, Lana."

"*Asante.*"

"One more item: this day I received sad news. Simba Sighters, the safari outfitter our hotel has been affiliated with, has closed business."

"*Kwa nini?*"

"It seems *bosi* Steve grew careless at a watering hole, showing off for one of his tours in a pool swimming with *mamba*." His head moves slowly from side to side.

"A crocodile ate him?"

"That is the report. They found only *bosi's* hat, I'm afraid."

"I'm sorry to hear that. I met Steve. He seemed nice."

"The man was a fool; forgive me for saying so. He took crazy chances just to show off, sneaking up on sleeping lions, dipping his bare toes where *mamba* swim. In the end, craziness always kills."

Mr. C reaches into his jacket pocket and hands me a paper. "This is the name of a new safari outfitter—Moja. It comes highly recommended, and I would like you to arrange an evaluation meeting."

"Yes, *bosi.*"

When Mr. C leaves, I glance down at the paper. A name and telephone number are scribbled in red ink. The name is Gavin McQueen. A bell goes off in my head; I've heard that name before . . . where?

CHAPTER 6

There is no word from Laura, but my father emails me regularly. I can tell from his latest message he doesn't know about the cancer scare—yet.

Hello Princess:

How are you? For the past months I've been worried about you every single second, but last night after your mother and I got home from the temple I felt a peace come over me, an assurance that no harm is going to come to you while you're in that forsaken place. I still don't understand your love of a land so filthy and desperate. I hear tuberculosis is claiming more African lives than AIDS. You are current on your immunizations, aren't you? I cringe to think about the medical facilities there. Don't forget to take your malaria pills. You sleep with thick mosquito netting, don't you? I can't get a visual image of you in Africa, no matter how I try. I know. I know. You're going to tell me not to worry, that the African people are wonderful. I can't help worrying. And I want you to know that I've set a goal for myself: I'm going to study about this land that you love so much and learn a bit more about the people. How close are you to Nigeria and Ghana? There are temples in those places, you know. Miracles if you ask me.

Brigham is coming over this afternoon with his Scout troop. I'm going to teach them all how to change a tire. Laura has had the flu, and so I think your mother and I will take the kids for the weekend.

Your mother sends her love, as do I.
Dad

I lie down on my narrow bed in my narrow apartment, close my eyes, and try to create my own visual. I see my parents' kitchen. Mom is standing at the stove, stirring something with a long wooden spoon—fudge maybe. Dad is seated at the table with a carburetor gutted on a piece of newsprint, parts scattered everywhere. It is impossible for me to picture my parents apart . . . the two truly are one.

I think about marriage and what it can and should be. A weight of sheer loneliness presses down on my heart, and I have to fight the feeling of depression, always there waiting for an opening.

There are tribes in Africa that marry their daughters off as young as twelve. Boys enter into a manly rite of passage about the same time. I was eighteen when I got married, old enough to make it legal and young enough to believe I could make it work.

"Don't marry Nick," Laura told me.

"Why?"

"He's twenty-six. He's been around."

"So?"

"So, I know you. You won't be happy."

"You don't know me at all. You don't know what goes on inside my head, what I do when you're not around to whisper right from wrong in my ear. Laura, we are not the same!"

"Lana, I can't forget the night he shoved you against the wall. I can still see the bruises on your wrists. You've still got marks on your back."

White-hot anger seethed through me. "I didn't ask you for your help. You didn't need to come running and stick your nose in where it wasn't welcome."

"It was needed, though."

"Nick's got a temper; so what?"

"So what if one day . . ." Laura's voice trailed off. She stood by the window in a room we'd shared all of our lives, looking out at the Wasatch Mountains splotched gray and green. The smell of fresh-cut grass wafted through the open screen. "I don't want to fight with you."

"You *never* want to fight!"

"I'm just saying that you can't trust Nick. What's a marriage without trust?"

I was indignant. "Nick is a returned missionary."

"He got *sent* home, Lana—that's not the same thing as returning honorably."

"You are the most judgmental witch on the planet!" I flung a shoe at Laura, who didn't even duck, so it hit her in the face and bloodied her bottom lip. I wasn't sorry.

"*Please* don't marry him." Even now I can still see the tears she tried to hide.

"Why do you think you have the right to run my life? You don't. Neither do Mom and Dad. Besides, none of you know Nick at all."

It turned out I was the one who didn't know Nick. I didn't know he was violent, vulgar, that he had an addiction to pornography and pretty girls. Six months into the marriage, Nick met a red-headed dental assistant named Destiny. I divorced Nick, who promptly married Destiny. The last I heard, they were happy and raising two carrot-topped sons.

"People change," my mother told me, trying to quell my bitterness. "Anyone can repent."

"Yeah, anyone."

I roll over on my side, aching from the pain of so many drowned memories struggling to resurface. I hadn't thought about Nick in months. It's not just him; my entire life is weaving back in tattered threads.

My parents were not expecting twins. They were prepared for "one whopper of a baby," as Dad puts it, but not two. When Mom delivered dual daughters, she promptly passed out from the shock and woke to find herself the mother of two very *different* girls.

Born first, I was anxious to get out and get on with life. I weighed a full pound more than Laura. My lungs were fully developed and capable of keeping everyone at Utah Valley Hospital awake and alert. Laura could barely whimper.

Laura, being deprived by my greediness even in the womb, was thin and frail. While I eagerly gulped at my mother's colostrum-swollen breasts, Laura lacked the strength to nurse. She spent her first days under glass, hooked to tubes and wires, nourished by powdered formula fed through a glass bottle and a rubber nipple.

Mom's heart naturally pounded a little harder, a little faster, for the weaker daughter. She did not choose to love Laura more; she had no choice in the matter.

Dad, though, championed *me*. He applauded my forthright ways, my brave grip around his index finger. I have a photo of him next to my mother's hospital bed. He wore a short-sleeved blue work shirt, a smudge of black grease on his shoulder. My infant pink fist circled his finger. He looked down at me with wrenching pride and glory. I suppose Laura was tucked away in the ICU at that rare moment of separation. In the fuzzy background is the face of my mother. Her sad, disappointed eyes are turned to me. I know that worry distorted her features; she had to be frantic about her absent baby girl. Laura was down the corridor, warming beneath a lamp like a burger at McDonald's while I was basking in the undivided attention of my parents.

As we were born, so we grew.

Me first.

Laura lagging behind.

Only she did not follow me everywhere. She was never one to venture beyond the borders our parents set.

"Do not go down the stairs."

Dad tells the story of how I bounded down headfirst, breaking my collarbone at the age of eleven months. Laura sat obediently at the top of the landing, watching and wondering at my wailing.

At three, I stole a roll of postage stamps from Dad's garage and posted my own forehead, arms, and stomach. "Mail me away," I said.

Dad chuckled. "Where do you want to go?"

"Africa!"

"Why there?"

"They have lions." I roared and drew back my lips in a terrifying curl.

Mom peeled the stamps from me one at a time.

My stampless sister stood by, confused at my crazed behavior. I roared at Laura until her whimpering swelled into a full-blown cry.

When we turned five and entered kindergarten, Mom requested that Grandview Elementary separate us.

Principal Harman was perplexed. "Most mothers of twins want to keep their children *together*."

"I'd like to see Laura have a chance to blossom outside of Lana's shadow. My girls are very different from one another."

The principal nodded. "I understand."

The truth is, back then, none of us really understood.

While Laura opted to attend BYU-Hawaii, I found myself back home, divorced and devastated. I was humiliated and hurt. For months I was a husk of my former self. I shadowed Dad around at the garage. He tried to teach me how to change oil and tune an engine. Mom tried to teach me how to quilt and how to decipher between a flower and a weed. They were lessons my parents had failed at teaching me all of my life.

After my divorce from Nick, I got a job working at the Sundance Ski Resort in Provo Canyon. It gave me confidence and a little money, but my parents insisted I attend church. I promised the bishop that I would turn my life around. I wasn't lying, not on purpose; a part of me wanted to change, to be more like Laura. In the end I was miserable. My parents were miserable.

"I gotta get out of here," I said.

Mom and Dad held the door open wide.

I moved to Salt Lake to attend the University of Utah, concentrating on general education classes. Laura wrote from Hawaii that she had received spiritual confirmation that she was to serve a mission. We were only twenty, but even then Laura was sure of the road she wanted to take.

She came home and went to BYU, majoring in early childhood education, studying for her future mission. She took a Spanish course hoping to be called to South America.

When Laura's mission call came to Billings, Montana, I threatened to vomit on her Mary Janes. "At least they could send you to some exotic faraway place."

"I'm thrilled," she said in a resigned voice.

"No, you're not."

"I'll make it work."

"I know you will."

I got a job working the night desk at the Salt Lake Ramada. Dad bought me a used Chevy Monza. I dyed my hair black, cut it extra short, and wore red to the rival football game between the U and BYU.

Mom was mortified to sit with me in the stadium. "There is a spirit of rebellion on that campus," she said.

I scoffed. "Mom, Gordon B. Hinckley went to the U."

"Well, that was a long time ago."

"Maybe the spirit of rebellion isn't on the campus; maybe it's in me."

"Maybe so."

By the time Laura returned honorably from Montana, I was a junior. I'd found my niche in public relations, with a minor in accounting. I pulled down good grades and earned enough money to feel independent. By the time Laura was sealed to Ethan Hunter in the Salt Lake Temple, I had graduated. Nine months later when Laura gave birth to my nephew Brigham, I was working at the Hilton in London, pacifying disgruntled guests.

"I don't know why you have to live so far away," Mom complained. "We hardly ever talk anymore."

"We're talking now."

"Lana, I swear I don't know you anymore. Did something happen that I don't know about—something that gave you such a sour outlook on life?"

"Mom, I'd love to keep chatting, but I've got work to do. I'll talk to you again soon."

"Lana, I have the feeling that you didn't just move away; I think you've run away. Am I right?"

"I gotta go now, Mom. My boss is on the other line."

Life back in Utah went on just the way it was supposed to. Dad became bishop of the ward, and Mom stood by him, beaming. Laura filled her house with children, and I traveled the world, making friends and making money that I didn't have to spend on anyone but me.

There were guys, but nothing I allowed to grow serious. I convinced myself that I did not need anyone in my life. I was a complete person without a partner.

For years, I had myself convinced that I was happy.

What's happy? That's a question I couldn't answer until I met a little African boy named Jomo. He has no reason to smile, and yet he never stops smiling.

Lately I've caught myself smiling every time I think about him.

CHAPTER 7

It's the weekend, and Mr. C, Nygoya, some other hotel employees, and I have spent the day working on Mama Grace's school. It has been more of a vacation for me than work.

Nygoya has my digital camera and is trying to record the progress of our project.

"Stand there and pose," she orders me.

I act silly and do a flamingo stance. Mama Grace runs up behind me, and I topple to the ground. "Take the picture," Mama Grace shouts, laughing so hard she wheezes.

I've never seen her act so carefree and joyful. I want the day to last forever, but it doesn't. Mama goes back inside, Nygoya keeps taking photos, and I sit there as an arc of little girls tug at my hands and pull me toward the skeleton of an old rusted chair. There is no padding, no cushion—only a deformed frame. They want me to sit outside in the alley by Grace's school so they can braid my hair.

"It's too short," I say.

"*Tafadhali,*" they beg. *Please.*

"Are you sure Jomo isn't around?" I ask, scanning the crowd for the umpteenth time. "I would really like to see him."

Most say they don't know Jomo, but one girl tells me that Jomo is with the big boys at the far end of the village, riding bicycles.

I raise my eyebrows. Bicycles are rare and treasured, usually reserved for only the more privileged. I am happy for Jomo if someone has blessed him with a bicycle. I should have thought to do that for him.

My body is exhausted. I'm covered in mud and muck from the streets. Scrapes and scratches mar my bare skin. Dried sweat engulfs me in a thin layer of salt and stink.

"I need a shower," I say to the girls, realizing as I do that these young girls have most likely never known the wonder and comfort of warm water spraying down, washing them clean.

Finally I sit on the edge of the chair and tell the girls, "Go ahead. Have fun."

They giggle and dance and immediately attack my hair. The tugging and pulling feels wonderful, for they are gentle experts at their craft. One little girl with dark narrow eyes and a nasty scar on her chin begins to hum as her fingers fly deftly, pulling and twisting my short locks. I swear I know the song, but it can't be.

Her feet are not bare like most of the girls, but clad in rubber flip-flops . . . castoffs from some charity group—not the right size . . . they never are. Her own hair hangs in perfectly straight braids down her back, so fine and intricate they are a work of art.

"What is the name of that song?" I ask.

"My name is Benda," she says, grinning, showing a broken front tooth.

"*Jambo*, Benda. What is the name of the *song* you are humming?"

She grins wider, not understanding, and the tune rises louder. My mind is playing tricks on me. I am sure the melody is one I used to sing when I was seven years old, something about "Give said the little stream . . . Give, oh give, give, oh give." How could that melody wind itself all the way from the mountaintops of Utah to the ridge-back slums of Nairobi?

I begin to hum along, and the girls all giggle. Time winds back, and I am seven years old again, feeling nothing but the luxury of laughter rising from the tips of my toes to the twisted whispers of hair that stick out like feathers from the top of my head. I lean my head back, hum at the top of my lungs, and lose myself in that redeeming moment.

That is when a red pickup truck bounces down Redemption Road and stops in front of Grace's school—in front of me. A man in a blue baseball cap honks a melody of his own. He unfolds himself and steps out, tall and blond. Another *mzungu*.

"*Jambo!*" he says, and all the children squeal and leave me to surround him. From the back of his pickup truck the man lifts a box just as Grace and the rest of the crew come out from the school.

"I see you're making progress," he says to her.

Mama Grace throws her arms around the man's neck, nearly toppling his box. "Gavin!"

I observe as handshakes and introductions are made. The box is opened and oranges are passed around. If gold nuggets were ladled out, the children could not be more delighted. The man performs by taking three oranges and doing a quick juggling act, allowing one orange to hit him on the top of the head. The children crumple in laughter.

I sit back and watch until Grace grabs me and yanks me to my feet. I'm always surprised at her strength.

"Gavin McQueen, make yourself acquainted with Miss Lana Carter."

"Habari za mchana," he says with a crazy accent that is part Queen's English and part Swahili with a twang that makes me think of Texas.

I'm not sure what he said: either something about the afternoon or fire ants. My Swahili needs work. Still, I can't help smiling. "Nice to meet you."

He looks me squarely in the eyes and says, "I understand you tried to call me." A small boy clings to his leg, and Gavin lifts the child effortlessly to his shoulders.

I'm confused. I have never met this man in my life. "You must have me mixed up with someone else."

Mr. C raises a hammer and nods at me. "No, no. This is Mr. McQueen from Moja Outfitters."

The name clicks. The man clicks. Mama Grace's Gavin is also Mr. C's safari outfitter.

"Y . . . ye . . . yes," I say, stuttering, "our hotel is looking for a safari outfitter to link up with."

"Great!" Gavin, ducking so the little boy's head doesn't get bumped, leads me into the school. "I just got back from a Killi tour. I'm anxious to see all the progress you good people have made for Mama Grace."

There isn't much to show, but Mama makes every inch seem like a yard. She is proud and grateful, giving all of the credit to us. I notice how Mr. C sits a little taller, his spine a bit straighter. He is a proud man with a good heart; parts of him remind me of my father, and I wish the two of them could meet. Worried thoughts of Laura suddenly rush to the front of my mind. It's been almost a week, and I haven't heard anything more about her health.

Mama Grace scurries about the cramped quarters like a toy unwound. She is proud and grateful for every point of progress. "Look at the books Lana has brought me." She goes to a pile and holds up a small stack of picture books; she then holds out two flat palms to Gavin.

The tips of his ears redden as he jumps up and rushes back out to his truck. He returns with a thin, blue book, dog-eared and scuffed. "Quotes from Mother Teresa," he says, cracking a smile.

Mama Grace accepts the book with gratitude. "I much admire Mother Teresa's teachings."

"This book has stories about the lives she touched in India."

"I look forward to reading it. *Asante.*"

A loud, cracking noise sounds above us. All heads crank upward.

"It's only me," says Nygoya, whose bounteous body is wound around the exposed rafters like a recently fed anaconda. She's dressed in workmen overalls and a blinding purple blouse. "This roof needs work before the rains comes." When she spots Gavin she lets out a squeal. "*Bosi* Gavin! You are returned!"

Nygoya drops down, and the walls wave like an earthquake has hit. She and Gavin speak in breakneck Swahili. It's obvious they are well acquainted.

I pretend I'm not interested. I go to the front door and ask the street children about Jomo—again. I was looking forward to seeing him, to playing tag, to learning more about the child who has won my heart.

Gavin's laughter turns my head. It echoes like thunder. His presence raises the energy level in the room. When he turns to talk with Mr C, Nygoya nudges up to me and works me back into a corner. "He's single."

"He is?"

She licks her lips and nods.

I feel like a schoolgirl, whispering in the corner about a new boy just enrolling. "Thanks for the heads-up, but I'm not interested . . .

not that way. Mr. C wants me to check out what kind of safari outfitter Gavin is."

"I see what you're checking out." Her laughter bellows like a startled animal.

I feel my cheeks go hot. "Stop it! I'm not interested."

"Yes, you are."

"No. I'm not."

"Yes, you are."

My jaw clenches, and my voice lifts—higher and much louder than I intend. "I am *not* interested in Gavin McQueen!"

Every eye in the room darts to look at me, to see my pale *mzungu* face flush the bright red of a vervet monkey's backside.

CHAPTER 8

When night falls in Africa, it falls fast. There is no slow-setting sun because the horizon line is one flat, endless line. We still have some sunlight left, and I excuse myself to go outside to bask in my burning humiliation. There is a small spot against the side of Mama Grace's school. I go around and make myself comfortable with my back against the concrete and my bottom on the hard earth. The same little girls who plaited my hair follow me. They are eating the peels from the oranges Gavin gave them. Here, nothing goes to waste. Here, everything is appreciated and used. I dread going back home to America, the land of plenty. I don't want to fall into my old ways of excess and ingratitude.

I like the changes that are happening from my inside out. I can't explain them, but my time in Africa has brought me glimpses of sheer joy. How can I stretch those moments into hours, those hours into days?

The girls ring around me. We laugh. We talk. The little girl, Benda, who seemed to hum a familiar song, is gone. I tell myself I was mistaken about the song.

"Someday soon you girls will be able to go to school here at Mama Grace's."

They look dubious.

"We have no money for uniforms."

"Or books," another girl says.

I don't know how to respond. Maybe, I think, the hotel can help support a scholarship fund. The need here is so enormous. It dawns on me that of the dozen girls who surround me—ebony-eyed, beautiful children—odds are that six of them are infected with AIDS.

Suddenly I feel guilty for being so jovial. Here, death has a stranglehold on the innocent. Back home my sister is going through hell. What right do I have to laugh out loud?

The girls sense my shift in mood and wander off. I feel my body relax, and soon my eyes close. The sun beats warm and steady; flies buzz and children giggle. Through a glassless window I hear Gavin and Mama Grace recounting memories.

"Once Gavin brought by a sick lion cub for me to nurse back to health," Grace recalls.

He chuckles. "It was only for one night—just until I could get it to a proper shelter."

"It was the longest night of my life," she says, laughing.

Gavin says, "Tell them about the time you sent for me, telling me you needed a substitute for a season."

"What about it?"

"I didn't know you meant the *whole rainy season!*" He laughs and slaps his bare, tanned knee. "I learned more during those three months than I ever did in boarding school."

By eavesdropping, I glean that Gavin is older than me by seven years. Widowed, though no one goes into the details. He was born in Oklahoma (so much for the Texas twang), came to the Dark Continent with his parents, and has lived in nine of Africa's fifty-three independent nations.

I can't help craning to learn more, but the subject turns to lumber and the need to insulate the upper story to keep the school as climate controlled as possible. I smile to myself, feeling the ever-present sun beating down on my weary body. I drift off and wake to find myself sheltered from both heat and blinding light.

Someone is standing over me, holding up a piece of corrugated metal as an umbrella. At first it is just a silhouette, but then I see the big eyes and wide grin.

"Jomo!" I shout, struggling to my feet.

"Your face sweats." He fans me with the metal, making a swishing sound, sending a small swarm of flies away for the moment.

I wipe my sun-baked brow with the back of my hand and reach out to hug Jomo. He sets the square piece of rusted metal down and allows me to embrace him. It's like hugging a bag of twigs. Except for

Jomo's tight, round stomach, the boy is skin and bones. He hugs me back, though, stronger and tighter than I expect him capable of.

I pop my head through the open window. "Hey, everyone . . . Jomo is here! Are there any oranges left?"

Gavin is seated on the floor, telling stories. He looks up at me and squints. "Who's Jomo?"

Mama Grace huffs. I don't understand it, but she seems displeased with my affection for Jomo. Perhaps she doubts my sincerity, but in time she'll realize my desire is only to make Jomo's life better. Ever since I met him I've been silently planning ways to make a difference in his life, to provide for him the things that every little boy should have: shelter, education, clothes, and food. And an unbounded supply of love.

I can't explain my feelings; neither can I deny them.

I walk Jomo around to the front of the school, where he is introduced.

Nygoya lifts him off the ground, and I'm afraid her bear hug will crack one of his fragile little ribs. He giggles, his legs dangling in midair, and looks at her with wonder.

"You are big, like a rhino," he says.

Most women would be offended, but Nygoya only laughs. "I like that, a rhino. Have you ever seen a black rhino?"

"No," he says. "I have never seen even a *simba.*"

"What?" Gavin says, prying Jomo free of Nygoya's squeeze. "You're an African boy who has never seen a lion?"

Jomo shakes his head. "Not one living."

"Perhaps one day I will take you on safari—"

"Enough of that!" Mama Grace cuts Gavin off. "This boy is hungry." She takes an orange from the pocket of her *kanga* and holds it out to Jomo.

"*Asante Sane,* Mama."

"Now go back to your play. We have work to do here."

I don't understand how Mama Grace can turn a cold shoulder to Jomo. He is the most engaging little boy I've ever met. I walk him out front to our hotel van. It is locked tight because thievery here is understandably rampant. I take the key from my pocket and unlock the door. Jomo climbs in hesitantly and awkwardly; the orange is still in his two-fisted grip.

I leave the door wide open so he will feel safe. I sit in front and allow him the entire back seat. He keeps touching the vinyl, petting it curiously.

From my purse I take a small protein bar and a bottle of water. "It's all I brought," I say. "Next time I'll do better."

He eats the bar, even licking the wrapper. My heart breaks as I watch Jomo fold the shiny paper into a neat square. Here, nothing is wasted. I vow I will do better . . . . I'll do whatever it takes to improve Jomo's life.

"Tell me about your sister," I say.

"She is called Anyango."

"That's a beautiful name."

"It means *rafiki*."

"Ha—*friend*. And Anyango, she cares for you?"

He nods. "My sister, yes, she cares very much for me."

I look at Jomo with scrutiny. He wears the same ragged clothes he had on days ago. His feet are bare and filthy. His extended stomach is a sure sign of malnutrition. There is a scab on his right knee and an oozing scrape on his elbow. I offer him a Band-Aid from my purse, but he has no idea what to do with it. I show him, gently pressing it over his elbow. "Does that hurt?" I ask.

He shakes his head. "I fell from the bicycle. I am learning to ride."

"Someone told me that. Do you own a bicycle, Jomo?"

"No. The bicycles, they belong to Malik."

"And who is Malik?"

"He is *bosi*."

"Malik is your *boss*?"

Jomo's eyes dart downward. "No. Malik is my *rafiki*. He lets me ride his bicycle. He, too, cares for me."

I have a million questions to ask Jomo, but I can tell he has grown hesitant.

"I will come again," I say.

"When?"

"Soon. And I will bring you a surprise."

He squints. "What is a surprise?"

"A gift. I will bring you a gift."

He smiles, and a thud sounds against the side of the van. I look out to see three boys, older than Jomo, on bicycles.

Jomo scurries out of the van. "Malik!" he says, smiling at the boy in the center and rushing to his side.

"Malik!" Mama Grace's voice sounds, and I turn to see that everyone has come out of the school to see what's going on. Mama does not look happy.

"Jambo," I say, approaching the boys, "you are Jomo's *rafiki?"*

Malik can't be more than fourteen, but he is strong, and there is leeriness in the way he looks at me. I assume he is suspicious of me—a strange *mzungu*; Malik is Jomo's protector.

"Yes, I am called Malik. I am Jomo's *rafiki.*" He looks down at Jomo and rubs the boy's tight black curls. Jomo looks relieved. He offers Malik the orange.

"No," Malik says, grinning now at Mama Grace, "the orange belongs to you. It is not necessary to share it."

Jomo climbs on the back of Malik's bicycle and they turn to leave.

"Wait!" I say, "I, too, am Jomo's *rafiki.* My name is Lana."

Malik sighs. "Jomo told us of you. You are a teacher like Mama Grace?"

"No. I'm not a teacher. I work at a hotel in Nairobi."

Malik nods. "I must go now. I have work to do."

"Work?"

"Yes. I work in my *baba mdogo's* bicycle garage. Jomo helps for money."

"I see. Well, I'll be here again next Saturday. Please come by again."

"I will be here," Jomo says.

They turn, and Jomo lifts his hand to wave. He is still gripping the orange.

Gavin's hand softly touches my shoulder. "How did you meet Jomo?"

I smile at the memory. "You could say he bowled me over."

Mama Grace chuckles, and I'm glad to see her bad mood has lifted. *"Rolled* you over is more accurate." She then tells everyone about Jomo's tire entrance, how he toppled me to the ground.

We laugh and talk until the mosquitoes grow so thick we are forced to separate.

Mr. C turns to me. "You and *bosi* Gavin will be working together to join our hotel guests with his safari tours."

Nygoya nudges my ribs. "I hope that will present no problem."

"No problem," I say, blushing like a teenager. I wedge my way into the van and realize that Jomo left his bottle of water.

We drive away, leaving Mama Grace standing in front of her half-constructed school with Gavin's arm looped over her shoulder.

I look at Nygoya. "What did Malik mean when he said he works in his something *baba* . . . something—"

"He works for his father's young brother. The man operates a bicycle shop in another village."

"Oh. I'm just glad Jomo has someone looking out for him." Though it has grown dark, there are still children around the van, hoping for one last handout. A sense of melancholy descends, robbing me of my earlier joy.

Nygoya gives me a sideways stare. "Cheer up, my *rafiki*, I do believe you made a fine impression on *bosi* Gavin."

"What is that supposed to mean?"

She lets out a bellowing laugh. "I think it was your fancy hairdo."

My hand flies to the top of my head, where I feel a hundred little tufts of errant hair. Again, I am humiliated at the impression I've surely made on Gavin McQueen, but what does it matter? The last thing I need complicating my life is a man. Happiness returns, and I can't keep my own laughter from billowing out and joining with Nygoya's. A genuine friend never lets you take yourself too seriously, and Nygoya is my true *rafiki*.

CHAPTER 9

I work the next day—Sunday—eighteen hours straight, trying to keep my mind busy, trying to do a job Mr. C will be proud of. I print out two personal emails: one from Laura and one from my father. They both give me information to ponder.

I take a taxi home. My apartment seems cold and empty. There's not much to eat, and I settle for a hard-boiled egg and half of a ripe mango. I lie down, meaning to re-read my emails, but I fall asleep only to dream of Jomo. In my dream, he is clean; he is laughing. His little fingers twine around mine, and when I look down at him I see he wears a truly white shirt and dark pants. Shiny black shoes that hurt his feet. I kneel to untie them and realize where we are—inside an LDS chapel. Jomo is the only Black child in Primary. "I'm Trying to Be Like Jesus" pounds from an unseen piano.

Jomo beams. "Mama Lana," he says, giving my hand a hard squeeze.

I wake up, shaking and afraid.

Alone.

The blanket I pull up to my chin does not chase away the cold seeping through me. I am unable to fall asleep again and cannot turn on a light because the power has been switched off until morning. It happens when Kenya's rainfall is low and electricity is stretched thin. The nocturnal sounds of Nairobi scream and howl. The screech of brakes turns into the screech of a panther. The sound of a horn is the trumpet of an elephant, ready to charge. Monkeys outside in the trees leap and scream; they are my only alarm system. A fast-moving shadow crosses in front of my window. A bird? A robber?

What is real? What is imagined?

Without moving I lie with my eyes slammed shut and wonder at the chapters of my life. How much was prewritten by the hand of destiny, and how much of it did I write with my own decisions?

I am a sinner.

My sister is a saint.

Those are facts.

So why, then, is she the one who is stricken? For the first time in so long there is a flicker of light, of direction in my life. I don't deserve it.

"You missed your target, God," I say aloud against the blackness. "I'm here. I'm the one you want to punish. Come get me. Leave Laura to raise her family. Come get *me*."

Sleep won't come, and so I creep out of bed, grab a flashlight from my nightstand, and read my emails: the one from Laura first.

> Dear Sis:
>
> Don't worry. No news is good news. The doctor thinks it might be nothing more than a lump. He's going to biopsy it, and I'll keep you posted. Being in touch with you again means more to me than you can know. You are my strength, and I think about you all the time. Dad is going crazy looking up information on Africa. Don't be surprised if he shows up on your doorstep one of these days. I'll be in touch. Keep praying for me.
>
> Love, Laura

No news isn't necessarily good news. A foreboding shrouds me like a wet robe.

Dad's email is the one that really has me perplexed.

> Greetings Princess,
>
> I have a confession to make. It surprised even me, and it pains me to make it to you now. I have held some misguided feelings of bigotry in my heart. Until you ended up in Africa I had no idea how I really felt.

I read and re-read that paragraph. My father a bigot? No way. He is the most open-minded, openhearted man I have ever known.

I am not sure where I got the idea that Black people are somehow inferior to Whites. I know it's not true. God says so right in the Book of Mormon: "he *inviteth* them all to come unto him and partake of his goodness; and he *denieth* none that come unto him, black and white, bond and free, male and female; and he remembereth the *heathen*; and all are alike unto God" (2 Nephi 26:33).

I'm not struck by the word *black* as much as I am by the term *heathen*. It applies directly to me.

Lana, I want you to know I'm working through my feelings. I want to rectify any wrongs I might have committed. I'm doing this for two reasons: I love the Lord and don't want to cause injury to any of His children. Next, I love you and want to understand your devotion to the African people. I am repenting, and I hope you don't mind my sharing with you the things I learn. I welcome your thoughts—you've never been one to hold back.

All is well in Zion.

Love, Dad

All is *not* well in Zion. My father just doesn't know it yet.

I don't have to think about where Dad might have picked up any hint of bigotry. The Utah I grew up in is a White state. Theory went through the LDS culture that Blacks had been less valiant in the premortal life. I must have heard that a thousand times, but never from my father or any prophet. How I wish people who believe that theory could meet Mama Grace, Nygoya, and Jomo. I never dreamed my father bought into it. If he had those feelings, he never let on. In fact, he taught us to accept and love all people, regardless of skin color or religion.

I lie awake until morning comes—thinking. There is no dawn here, just sudden light. I meet the day with a mental list of tasks to accomplish, and I move through the morning with speed and purpose. I have many tasks at work, and I want to shop for some items for Jomo—maybe even a bicycle of his own.

There are bugs in the tap water—invisible, but alive and deadly, millions of microscopic parasites whose job it is to rob me of my health, my strength, my very life. I have to boil the water a full ten minutes before I can even brush my teeth.

If Mom were here, she would delight in making a spiritual analogy between Satan's army and African parasites. I hear her voice fill my head, see her eyes glow like bulbs. The conversation plays out in my mind as if the two of us are here in my Kenyan flat with birdsong and monkey chatter out my window.

Her finger wags in my face. "Lana, just because you don't see them doesn't mean they aren't there. Evil spirits whispering to your spirit, prying your fingers from the safety of the iron rod."

I scoff. "How can they pry my fingers if Satan's followers don't have bodies?"

Mom huffs. "I'm speaking metaphorically. They are after your spirit, Lana, working overtime. If you weren't such a strong-willed leader, so capable of greatness, Satan wouldn't bother with you. He wants you because you are one of the Lord's elect."

"You don't know me very well."

"I'm your mother."

"What do you know about me?" I ask.

She's frustrated now. Mom hates to be pinned by her own words, and she tugs at her apricot-colored curls. "Like I said, you are capable of greatness."

"Take an unfiltered look at me, Mom. There is nothing great about me. I've failed at everything that really mattered in my life."

Her eyes dart away, confirming my self-judgment. "That's not true," she says to the floor. "You've done very well in your career. You've traveled this whole world. You've got a master's degree, for pity's sake; that's something to be proud of."

"It's not what matters most, is it?"

Now her voice softens and pleads in the same tone that Laura uses when she is leading me toward a favor.

"If you don't like the direction of your life, it's not too late to take a different road."

"What are you getting at?"

"I'm talking about repentance."

At this point my imaginary conversation goes silent. I cut the fire on my burner, and though my water has only boiled for six bug-killing minutes, I use it to scrub my teeth until my gums bleed brilliant red.

CHAPTER 10

At work I am distracted. Laura will not leave my mind. Jomo will not leave my heart.

I catch up on everything Mr. C has assigned me, attend a few meetings, and then look for busy work to quell my churning angst. Mid-morning I receive an email from Laura.

> Dear Lana:
> You should know that Mom and Dad know. They'll be there with me for the biopsy. All in all, they are acting very calm. Mom went right to the temple; it's where she finds her solace. Dad, on the other hand, headed out to his garage. Did I tell you that he's rebuilding an old boat? When you get home from Africa we'll all go waterskiing at Deer Creek like we did so long ago. I guess if you waterski in Africa, you get swallowed by an alligator.
> I'm worried about Ethan. He's a wreck. He walks around with his head bowed all of the time. None of us have your strength. Even from the other side of the world we can feel it. I love you, and I'll keep you posted.
> Laura

I struggle about how to reply: "There aren't alligators in Africa . . . crocodiles. Come, and we'll go on a safari together. I haven't even been yet." What else can I say? I'm doubting my own feelings. Is my uneasiness a true connection with my sister? Am I sensing her worry, or am I struggling with only my own fears? "I'm glad Mom and Dad know," I write. "Their love for you will be your strength. Laura, everything will be fine." How I wish I felt that confidence.

Two days pass, and I find it difficult to concentrate. I feel helpless and so far away. Not so long ago I would have filled my empty time at the local bars. Even before Laura and Jomo, I'd lost my interest in all the things that used to bring me excitement and meaning. Now all I want to do is work, help Mama Grace, and play hide 'n seek with Jomo.

I search the Internet for any and all information on breast cancer—just in case.

I wander during my lunch break and find myself drawn to children's clothing. Guessing at the sizes, I buy Jomo new clothes: a bright yellow shirt, jeans, and sneakers. My mood brightens at the thought of him receiving my meek offerings.

I call home and talk to my parents' answering machine. Mom's voice promises to get back to me as soon as she can. When I don't hear anything from her for twenty-four hours, I call Laura's house. I hear my sister's voice make the same exact promise: "Please leave your name and number, and we'll get back to you as soon as possible." I don't know who else to call.

I don't know what else to do. My mind imagines all sorts of dramatic and painful scenarios. It's not like me to lean to the negative, and for a remedy I wander down the hallway to Nygoya's office. She has an elephant gun mounted to her wall that is longer than the front of her desk. Rumor has it she wrestled it away from a poacher. "Would you like to ride out to Shanty Village with me?" I ask.

She looks up from her computer screen; the top of her shaved black head reflects the green light like she is wearing a green beanie. "Why?"

"I don't know," I say, shrugging. "I'm bored."

"Would you like to go out dancing this night? It is Ladies-Get-in-Free-of-Charge night at the Biting Croc."

"No, thanks. I'd just like to check on Mama Grace."

"Is anything wrong?"

"Not that I know of."

Nygoya blinks, and I see she's testing a new shade of sunshine yellow eye shadow. "When you first came to Africa you were more fun, Miss Lana."

"Really?"

She bites her bottom lip. "Perhaps *fun* is a wrong word to use. You were wilder. Now you are tamer. What has changed you?"

I lean against the door frame and smile. "I was just wondering the same thing."

"Aren't you planning on going to Mama Grace's this coming Saturday?"

"Yes."

"I can go with you Saturday, but I cannot go today. Today is my lecture day."

I frown. "I'm sorry. I forgot."

Her bottom lip slips out fat and pink. Once a week Nygoya visits local schools to lecture on the evils of poaching.

"My feelings are injured," she says with a deep, dramatic tone. "How can you forget this important part of my job?" She tugs at a huge gold cross she wears around her neck. "I teach children about the evils of poaching. Poaching is very evil."

"Yes, and I'm sorry," I repeat.

"You are forgiven." She waves her palm at me, and her frown turns upward. "Have you heard from *bosi* Gavin yet?"

"No."

"He'll be in contact with you. I believe he became smitten when he met you and your fancy hair design."

I laugh at the memory. "You're imagining things. If we do make a connection it will be because Mr. McQueen wants the business Hotel Harambee can send his way."

"He is an excellent safari outfitter. The man knows Africa. Gavin was born in the USA but has lived here most of his life."

I nod. "I'm not thinking about Gavin or work. I just want to go for a ride and clear my head."

"Your thoughts are worried?"

"I'm okay."

"You should not travel to Shanty Village alone."

"It's the middle of the day. I'll be fine."

She lowers her head and gives me a hard stare.

"I've done it before," I say confidently.

"Assure me that you will leave before darkness falls." The way she says it is more of a command than a suggestion.

"I will."

"Safe journey, then." She hands me a book to give Grace, a volume of African fables. "I'll have to borrow this from her library," I say. "It looks like a good book."

"I have never known a *mzungu* so interested in Africa."

"I love this land."

"You are also loyal to the USA. I see the flag you keep in your office."

"I am proud I am an American, but I'm glad to be here in Africa. One country makes me appreciate the other even more."

"I have been to your country," she says, tapping a sharpened fingernail on her desktop.

"Really? I didn't know that. You never mentioned it."

Nygoya laughs. "I am a woman with many mysteries."

"I'm sure you are. Tell me about your visit to America."

"I was young—twelve years of age—when I went with an exchange program to the USA. We toured your Washington, D.C. One day I will visit your Hollywood, California. I want to meet movie star Angelina Jolie. She loves Africa very much."

I smile. "I think she would like you, Nygoya. You both do much good in this world."

Nygoya lowers her voice to a hoarse whisper. "I will tell you one of my mysteries."

I wait, intrigued.

She points her thumb up at the elephant gun. "I hate poachers."

"That's no secret."

Her massive, bald head bobs. "Yes, the mystery is that I once shot two and a half poachers." She aims a finger pistol at me as the green glow from her computer screen reflects in her eyes.

I am shocked. "How did you manage to shoot two and a half poachers?"

"Bang. Bang. Half a bang."

I perch myself on the edge of her desk, uncertain if she is teasing or telling the truth. "Tell me more."

Nygoya stands. "We will speak of mysteries later. Now I must go teach school children the dangers of poaching. There are rhinos to save."

CHAPTER 11

Instead of taking the hotel van, I ride a local bus out to Shanty Village. It's not really a bus, but more of made-over tourist van. Right away I'm tempted to take my camera out of my bag and snap a few shots so I can send them home to Laura. She would find them unbelievable and entertaining. The floor of the van is worn clear through in spots. I can see the black road whizzing past, then the red dirt kicking up from the hole between my feet. A man seated across from me clutches a scabby, pink-eyed goat. Chickens flop and cluck as the bus slashes forward, the driver ignoring one of the few traffic lights in the city.

Most of the people and animals have gotten off by the time we leave the second-class district. The driver, a rail-thin man with a huge head, gives me a slant-eyed stare. "You are headed for Redemption Road?"

"Yes."

"You have been there before?"

"Yes."

"It's not a short journey."

"No."

The driver turns, and I can see that his cheek is scarred. It looks like a knife once tore through it. "You know someone who lives there?" he asks.

"Mama Grace."

He sighs. "She is the soul mother of Africa."

"That she is."

"You are Mama Grace's *rafiki*?"

"I hope so. I work for the Hotel Harambee. We are trying to help finish Mama Grace's school."

The driver looks satisfied. "Then I will feel safe in taking you to her."

While we bump along I have a feeling that Mama will not approve of my little scouting expedition. The truth is I am not coming to visit with her as much as I am to locate Jomo. The clothes and sneakers I bought him are in my backpack. I can't explain my immediate and intense concern for this child. How can I convince Mama Grace that all I want to do is make Jomo's life a bit brighter? She has never known the abundance I have. She cannot understand my motives. She simply thinks I'm interfering, singling one child out from millions.

It dawns on me that I am a stranger in a strange place. Mama Grace cannot understand what it is like to be White, American, and blessed with more than enough. Even if I stayed in Africa the rest of my life, I could never really know what it is to be African, to see through Mama's eyes.

I scoot to the front of the bus, wrapping my fingers around a pole to keep from losing my balance. I tell the driver, "Actually, I have also come to see another *rafiki,* a little boy named Jomo. He lives at the top end of the road. Would you mind taking me there first?"

He frowns. "The top end of that road is not a good district. It is plagued with evildoers."

"Evildoers?"

"Yes. Brothels and bars. No churches. No schools. Men without souls reside there."

"I'm told that is where Jomo lives. He is just a boy."

"He lives with his family?"

"A sister, I think." I shift my weight from one foot to the other. The questions make me uneasy because I realize how out of place I am, how unprepared I am. "Jomo told me that he has an older sister who cares for him."

"It is a fact that here there are not many traditional intact families. Nearly 50 percent of our country is infected. I am proud to say I have been tested. I am negative." The driver places his long-fingered hand over his heart, like he is pledging allegiance.

It is unusual to hear an African speak so frankly and openly about AIDS.

I don't have a response. In spite of my hunger to learn all I can of Africa, I am still clueless about many of her ways, and in my ignorance—sometimes my *arrogance*—I give offense without meaning to. I've learned it's often best to keep quiet.

We pass out of the city onto the dirt roads of the village. A woman on the opposite side of the bus sits with her head down, her gnarled hands crossed over a walking stick. I try to imagine the life she lives. The bus slows as we pass a group of women balancing bundles of wood on their heads. A young man pushes a handcart filled with water barrels, which he will sell one drink at a time if necessary. How many miles has he covered this day? Tomorrow and the tomorrow after that will be the same for these people. I want to provide Jomo with a brighter option.

The driver stops to let the old woman off. I stand to help her and look out toward a shanty where two children engage in all-out battle over a shriveled piece of watermelon rind.

Reality marches up my spine, and I am reminded just how far away from home I have traveled.

Back in Utah in Laura's suburban neighborhood, two-story houses line the streets, and children play on plastic swing sets and carpets of cut green grass. When Laura's children are hungry she jumps in her SUV and drives down the street to a grocery store stocked with more food than most African children will see in a lifetime. My sister is a skilled cook; she watches cooking shows like some housewives watch soap operas. It is impossibly easy for her to assemble a delicious, nutritious meal in her chrome and granite kitchen with a polished hardwood floor beneath her feet. Here, in the red dirt streets of Nairobi, children are fortunate if they receive a bowl of *wali*, the Swahili word for rice, or a piece of bread—*bofulo*. Three square meals a day is an unfathomable concept.

Back home, Laura's kids turn on the tap to gorge their bellies with safe drinking water. Here the children drink boiled water fetched from the same rivers and streams where both people and animals wash away their waste.

Knowing Jomo lives a life so sparse, so savage, splits my heart down the center.

The driver cranks his head to look at me. "I will agree to take you partway up Redemption Road. If I go too far, the way narrows and I am unable to turn my *matwana* around."

It's true. Though his *matwana* is not as big as our hotel van, the road offers little turn-around room. "I am grateful for whatever you can do."

"Do you still wish to visit Mama Grace?" he asks.

"Yes."

He scratches the side of his head. "How will you return this night?"

My body tenses. "I'll catch the next bus back to the city. I know where there is a stop at the edge of the village." My words are a joke. While there is a bus stop there, there is no regular schedule, no guarantee.

"If you have the proper money, I will wait for you."

A feeling of relief washes over me. The truth is I have neglected to think my return trip through. Like so much of my life, I've made this trek on impulse.

The end of the road where Mama Grace has set up her school is very different from the upper road. As we move northward the road narrows, the shanties grow smaller, so close together that most of them overlap like shingles on a roof. A few people sell wares spread out on woven mats: carvings, jewelry, fruits, and vegetables. Dark eyes stare at us, wondering at our presence. The air is thick with smoke from small cooking fires and pungent with the waste of so many people and animals.

A pack of mongrel dogs, ribs sticking out and tails dragging, crosses in front of us. The driver stops.

"This is as far as my bus goes," he says. "I will turn around and wait here."

"I don't know how long I'll be."

"Perhaps I should meet you at the other end of the road, at Mama Grace's school."

I pause to think. "If you could stay *here* for a little while, I'll look for my friend."

"Very well. Come back before dark. I do not wish to stay here after dark. It is not safe."

"I understand." A wad of shillings is passed from my hand to the driver's. I hold back enough to motivate him to stay put until I find Jomo.

CHAPTER 12

There is no shortage of people to ask for help. Children are all around. I dole out sweets, one at a time, asking if anyone has seen Jomo. It dawns on me that most of these children, who live as close as blades of grass, who see each other every day, do not know one another—not in the sense that neighborhood children back in Utah know each other.

But then the skinniest boy I have ever seen steps forward. "Jomo lives there," he says, pointing at what looks like an endless row of identical shanties jetting off in an opposite direction.

"Where?"

"There," the boy says, jabbing his finger in the air, "at the end. Jomo lives *there*."

A narrow trench in the road winds like a snake, forcing me to keep stepping over a river of raw sewage. Flies are thick, and the children seem older, louder. I walk in the direction that he points, looking back to make certain my driver has not left. I wave to him, but he does not wave back.

Suddenly a bicycle appears in front of me, cutting me off. Another bicycle and another slash in front of me, spewing dirt and wet filth. Someone laughs. I look at the boys and recognize Malik.

"Jambo," I say, relieved at the familiar face.

Malik looks at me with the eyes of a stalking lion.

"Jambo," I say again. "I'm Lana, Jomo's *rafiki*.

"Why are you here?" he asks, as his friends flank in closer. "You do not belong here."

"I came to see Jomo. Do you know where I can find him?"

Malik glances at his friends; he is obviously their leader. As I study him, I take him for fourteen, maybe older. His features are hardened and lean, and his eyes are old and dry, the eyes of age. I wonder at all that he has been through in his life.

"Why do you want Jomo?" Malik asks with clear suspicion.

"I mean him no harm. I've brought him some small gifts."

His friends laugh, the sound of wild animals, hungry and savage. I can't stop myself from backing away as fear creeps up my spine. I step in something damp and thick. Malik smiles.

One boy climbs off his bike and moves toward me. His forehead is scarred—like a razor blade has ridden down it a thousand times. I wonder at his life; what kind of existence have these African street boys known?

Two dirt-caked hands go out, and the boy says, "Show me the gifts."

The thought that I am being robbed races through my mind. There are other people around, curious, but if I were attacked, would they help? I doubt it.

Malik shakes his head and clears his throat. "This *kichaa* is Jomo's *rafiki*. She is also acquainted with Mama Grace."

I nod, not knowing what Malik has just called me. "We've been helping to build her school."

Now Malik laughs.

Another boy pushes his bike forward, and I suddenly feel completely enclosed. My heart pounds in my throat. Sweat drips down the back of my neck.

The boy, this one younger and broader, says, "I *hate* that school."

How could anyone hate Mama Grace's school? Still, it's evident to me that this boy knows hate, is intimate with its dark power.

"I don't understand," I say. "I'm only here to help." Even to me, my words sound hollow and untrue.

"*We* will help *you,*" Malik says. "Jomo lives here in our village. He is one of us."

My breath comes easier. "*Asante.* Are you part of Jomo's family?"

"Here, we are all family."

The boy with the scarred forehead is so close to me I can smell him. "Jomo lives *there*—on the *choo.*" He nods to a small building that reminds me of a decrepit telephone booth. A line of people wait in front, hopeless faces, questioning my presence here.

I stare back, aghast. "Isn't that a public restroom?"

"A toilet house—a *choo,*" the boy says, and they all laugh.

I can barely force the question out. "Jomo lives in *there?*"

Malik pushes his way in front of the boy. "No. Jomo lives up." He aims a finger at the top of the structure.

The horror of what I am seeing seeps into me slowly, like poison. There is a mat, the dregs of an old blanket, some woven baskets, turned on their sides. *This is what Jomo calls home?*

"Where is Jomo now?" I ask.

"He is not here. He is riding. My uncle provided him with a bike."

"That's wonderful. Do you know where he's riding? I'd really like to meet with him today."

Suspicion burns in Malik's dark eyes. "Here, Jomo belongs. You do not belong here."

I swallow and watch as a Herculean fly crawls over Malik's face, around his eyes, up his nostril and back out again. Malik barely flinches. He drops his chin, and I realize I am being threatened.

"I care about Jomo." My hand goes over my heart.

"Why? Jomo is only a street boy."

Another boy demands, "What do you want from Jomo?"

"Nothing."

"You wish to buy him, to take him home to America?"

Yes, my heart says. "No. No. I just want to be his friend—his *rafiki.*"

The boys snicker and close in even tighter. Malik's hand reaches for my backpack. I spin and realize that I am surrounded—not by a few, but by dozens of boys, most of them without bikes, but with hard, sharp eyes that burn hatred. Where did they all come from? The drum of my heart pounds in my head. I try to glance down the road to see if my bus driver is still around, but I cannot see anything but dark, staring eyes and groping hands.

"Jomo!" I scream.

Laugher rattles all around me as arms and legs creep so close they touch me.

"We mean you no harm," Malik says in a commanding voice that helps to quell the mob. "We only want to protect Jomo."

"You don't need to protect him from *me,*" I assure him. "I can see that you are like a big brother to him, but doesn't he have a sister who watches out for him?"

Malik opens his mouth to answer, but a woman's voice rises above every other sound. She wails, and in a single wave the boys turn away from me. Down the center of the narrow path, a full-grown ostrich runs toward us, followed by a hundred shouting, crazed children, wielding sticks and throwing rocks at the terrified bird.

I feel sick.

The boys that had me surrounded forget I am there. They run, climb back on their bicycles, and move to the head of the pack, right behind the ostrich. I know that a bird that size has the capability of killing a man with one powerful kick. But this bird is wounded, worn out; its left wing hangs down, as if broken. Dark blood covers its neck.

Malik glares at me as he reaches behind him and pulls out a *panga.* He gives a terrifying warrior shriek and shoots off on his bicycle.

I try to swallow the fear that has me choked. My heart thunders. I do my best to search the crowd for Jomo. I don't see him, but he could be in the middle of the crush.

A horn sounds, and I think of my *matwana* driver. The doomed ostrich has veered off in his direction.

In a numb stupor I walk back down Redemption Road. The driver, harried and angry, gives me a lift to Mama Grace's school.

"You were gone much time. It is not safe for me to be here when the sun sleeps."

"I apologize."

"You did not locate your friend?"

"No."

His anger softens. "It is difficult to locate someone here."

The bus swerves, and I lurch forward. In the road lies one of the stray dogs I saw earlier. It is on its side, heaving, eyes rolled back, tongue out. No one is in sight, but the shaft of a spear protrudes from the dog's rib cage.

"Stop!" I say. "The poor thing is suffering."

"No," says the driver, moving around the dying animal. "Do you not understand? This place is not safe."

"No one is left. They've all gone after the ostrich."

"There are people all around us. Just because you cannot see them does not mean they are not there."

I think of the parasites in my water. I think of Satan's followers. I look around. The streets appear empty, the shanties appear deserted, but I know the driver is right. In the shadows, out of sight, are men, women, and children watching us, waiting for our next move.

I do not know the fate of the ostrich; I can only guess. But the sun seems brighter as we roll closer to Mama's school. She is outside roasting chunks of pumpkin on a small wire grill. She looks up at me with milky eyes and no smile.

"Lana."

I pay the driver another handful of shillings. "I won't be long. Will you please wait?"

"It is going to be dark soon."

"Ten minutes. No more."

"Ten minutes will cost you."

"I'll pay later."

"I will wait."

I do my best to explain to Mama Grace about my solo presence here on a weekday evening. I do not dwell on the past half hour, on the horrors I have witnessed. "I just had to come find Jomo."

"You encountered Malik?"

"Yes."

"He is the *akida*—the leader of the village boys." She spits in the dirt, and within seconds flies have sailed down to suck up that sordid bit of moisture. She coughs, and I note how tired she looks. The whites of her eyes are yellow, lined with red veins. Her shoulders stoop, and still she does not offer me even a flicker of a smile.

"Are you ill, Mama Grace?"

She turns blank eyes toward me but does not answer. We ease ourselves down on a hunk of broken concrete she uses as a stoop. "Lana, it is not wise for you to come here alone like this."

"I realize that. I just had to do it."

"You are a woman who does what she feels led to do."

"Yes, I hope so."

"At any cost?"

I assume she is talking about my safety. "I can take care of myself. I have Mace in my backpack."

"And hand sanitizer, also, I suspect."

"Yes."

"And a plastic bottle filled with safe water."

"Yes."

"So you think that you are prepared for the dangers of my village."

"I think I must find Jomo."

She sighs, and I think that Grace has lost weight; the skin around her neck sags, and she appears older somehow. "You appear to be the exception to John 10:13."

"You know I don't know that scripture."

"It is about the hireling and the sheep."

"You mean how the shepherd goes after one lost lamb?" I ask, searching my mind.

Mama Grace looks pleased. "I mean how the hireling usually flees when there is danger to the flock, because he is only a hireling. You do not flee, but run to the danger in search of a lost lamb that is not your own."

How can I tell her that Jomo feels like my own?

"Lana, I know you are a woman with a good, kind heart. You care about Jomo, but your caring can cost dearly."

"I have money."

She shakes her head violently. "It is not the cost to you that matters. What will your friendship with Jomo cost *him*?"

"I don't understand."

"No, you do not understand. You are not one of us. You are white. You come from a bountiful land. You *cannot* understand."

"I understand that I want to help one little boy, to make his life a little brighter. I can do that, Mama Grace. I have to do that."

She turns a piece of charred pumpkin with the end of a stick. "And what is your proposal for Jomo?"

"I can provide food and medical care; I can pay his tuition when your school opens. And I can pay for a better place for him to live." I shudder thinking of Jomo sleeping atop that outhouse. "Please, Mama, let me try to help make his life a little better. *Please.*" I don't realize I am crying until Mama's hand reaches out to dry my tears.

"What of Jomo's sister, Anyango?" she asks.

"I will provide for her also."

"You have money to do this for not days, not weeks, but years?"

I nod. I have never known the kind of urgent, smoldering yearning that fills my entire body. I can and I will help Jomo and Anyango.

Mama Grace bows her head. Somewhere a bell clangs, a rooster crows.

"Very well," she says, standing, her knees cracking. "I am not Jomo's family so I cannot speak for them. You may have to seek permission from our village chief. Jomo and Anyango may refuse your help."

"Please give me your blessing so I can try."

"Yes, I will." She raises her voice and calls out in a language I do not understand. Within a minute a passel of children have gathered around her. She requests they search for Jomo. Most do not know who he is, but when I tell them that he is the little boy who sleeps atop the public toilet, that he is probably riding a bicycle, they tear off running, with the promise of sweets when they return with him.

We wait in strained silence. I give her the book offering from Nygoya, and she takes it inside to place it on her shelf. When she returns, she looks happier. "My library is growing like a beautiful garden."

Ten minutes pass, and the driver blows the horn. I beg him for ten more minutes.

"It will cost you," he says, and I sense a threat in his tone.

"I will pay."

"Yes, you will pay."

And then I see him. Jomo comes riding toward me on a small silver bicycle, pedaling so fast his legs are a blur. He gives me a wide, open-mouthed grin.

"*Jambo!*" he cries, aiming right for me like he did when he came rolling toward me in the tire.

Mama Grace attempts to hold me back, but loses her grip as I rush to meet Jomo. My backpack swings and nearly hits her.

Jomo jumps from his bike right into my open arms. I hardly know him, but in that space of a heartbeat, he has laid claim to the deepest part of anything good I have left in my soul.

Mama Grace stands beside me, shaking her head. "You have found your lone lamb."

The driver blows the horn again. Mama Grace pacifies him with a piece of charred pumpkin while I take Jomo inside the school to give him his new clothes and shoes. He puts them on right over his old rags—the same gray shirt and pants he wore the first time I saw him. He is unsure how to put on the shoes.

"I never had *viatu*—shoes for my feet," he says.

I fight back tears. "I'm sorry I forgot socks."

"What are socks?"

We have only a few minutes, but in that time I tell Jomo of my heart's desire. I pour out one plan after another. I tell him how I will pay for him and Anyango to attend Mama Grace's school as soon as it begins operation. I tell him that I will find a new place for them to live.

His little brow knits. "We have a place to live."

"I have been there," I say. "Malik and his friends showed me where you live."

At the mention of Malik's name, Jomo's smile brightens. "Malik got me a bike to ride. He watches over me."

My heart aches. "I want to be the one to watch over you—if that's okay." I kneel so we are nose-to-nose, then I take him in my arms and hold him until he pulls away.

The horn sounds again, and I know it is time to go. "I will return on Saturday . . . *Jumamosi.*"

Jomo smiles and nods.

"Do you understand?" I ask, feeling desperate.

He nods again. "I will be here. You will play with me then?"

"Oh, yes. I will bring my own bicycle, and we can go for a ride. Would you like that?"

"You have a bicycle?"

"I'll borrow one," I say, making plans a million miles an hour in my brain. "Please spend as much time around Mama Grace's as you can. I think you are safer here than at the other end of the road."

I ask her if Jomo might earn a few shillings by helping her around the school. I give her a look, telling her I will pay.

"Yes," she agrees, addressing Jomo. "If you are respectful and work hard, I will find a job for you."

"*Asante*, Mama." Standing there in his new shirt, Jomo looks like a bright yellow flower in a freshly turned field. I have never seen a child so radiant. So grateful. He keeps hugging me and thanking me, over and over. I don't have the words in either English or Swahili to tell him how very welcome he is.

"I can spot you a mile away in that shirt," I tell him.

He twirls and giggles and then breaks into a rapid little dance, his feet pounding the ground with the fury of a drum solo.

It is time to go.

I slip a few shillings into Mama Grace's hand and save the rest for my patient *matwana* driver. I then leave my entire backpack with Mama, whispering that there are more sweets for the other children and more jerky. Next time I'll increase my offering.

"One woman cannot support an entire village," Mama Grace whispers.

"You do," I say, giving her a hug.

Jomo takes my hand and gives it three hard squeezes.

My eyes burn with tears of sheer joy.

He looks up at me and studies my face. "Did I squeeze too hard? I am very strong for a boy of seven."

"You are *seven* years old?"

"Yes."

"I thought you were five."

He looks insulted, and his bottom lip slips out. "I have seven years, and I am very strong."

"Yes, you are. Stronger than anyone I have ever known." The weight of that truth settles in the center of my heart, an anchor.

Now his smile returns. I give him one last hug, a quick kiss on the forehead, and it is time to leave.

"I will see you soon, Jomo."

We drive away with me watching as Mama Grace stands next to Jomo, her arm looped around his tiny shoulder much the same way Gavin's was looped around hers that last time I pulled away. I fear to blink; I don't want to miss a single moment. Mama Grace kneels down to scoop a piece of pumpkin off the grill to offer Jomo. His yellow shirt stands out against the muted colors of the village as bright as morning sunshine.

I blink, and the vision is lost. Mama and Jomo become two shapeless shadows veiled behind a wall of whispering gray smoke flecked with copper.

"That boy," the driver asks, "he is your *rafiki?*"

"Oh, yes!" I tell him all about Jomo, how he lives atop the *choo* with his sister. How he loves to ride his bike. How he loves life.

The driver seems keenly interested. "How old is he?"

"Seven."

The driver yawns. "This boy is fortunate to have you for a *rafiki.*"

I rest my head on the vibrating window. I am the one who feels fortunate.

As we enter the second-class district the driver turns to look back at me. There is something different, something darker, about his demeanor. "This Jomo, seven years old, what is your *real* interest in him?"

One eyebrow raises, and the grin he gives me tightens a knot in my stomach.

"What are you suggesting?" I ask, suddenly aware of my position—a *mzungu,* alone with a strange man in the outskirts of Nairobi. I try to sound confident. "I want to help make Jomo's life better. That's all."

He twists around to stare at me. I've seen that look before, and my subconscious reaction is to let out a blood-curdling cry that causes the driver to jerk the steering wheel. A horn blares, and the bus swerves to avoid a car. I lurch forward amid the sound of crushing metal and shattering glass.

The accident is just a fender-bender, no one is injured, but the driver of the car is very angry with my bus driver. Thankfully, the police show up to investigate, and I'm more than happy to accept a ride home with them.

As I leave, the bus driver leers at me. "You owe me money."

I pay him another wad of shillings, and as our hands brush, he grabs my finger.

"Jomo. I will not forget the boy's name." He smirks at me. "I will not forget your *mzungu* face, either."

I am shaken to the core. The man seemed to turn from good to evil right before my eyes. How could I have been so foolish as to get on a bus alone like that? I vow to be smarter, safer, less trusting.

CHAPTER 13

The next morning I purposefully block dark memories from my mind, choosing to focus instead on the life I'm constructing in my dreams for Jomo. I can do it. I *will* do it.

Work keeps me busy. It's lunchtime before I check my personal email and read a message from my father that brings both hope and questions.

How is my princess?

We are doing better. Though we don't have the test results from the biopsy yet, the doc says things "looked good." What does that mean? You know your mom; she's got her hopes up, talking about miracles already. I'm holding back on the party until we know for sure that Laura is going to be all right. She has to be okay. God would not take a mother of six little children, would He?

Speaking of children, it sounds like you're getting very interested in the cause to help them. The need there must be overwhelming. Let us know if there is anything your mother and I can do to help. We'd really like the opportunity to do some good in Africa. I can't tell you how or why, but my feelings about the place and the people are softening, not that they were ever really hard, but as I confessed, I never had a tender spot before. I sure do now.

Princess, I've been doing a lot of research on Blacks and the priesthood. It's a very touchy issue. The truth is, there isn't a clear-cut doctrinal answer why those good folks were deprived the blessings of the priesthood for a span. There is a great deal of speculation, even published opinions, but nothing from the prophets or the Lord. So . . . I'll withhold my judgment and just offer my love.

Did you know that Joseph Smith ordained a Black man named Elijah Able to the priesthood? It's true. He and his wife remained faithful members of the Church all their lives. They even crossed the plains all the way to the Salt Lake Valley. They are buried in the Salt Lake City Cemetery. Besides that, I learned that in 1852 Brigham Young sent the first three missionaries to South Africa. 1852! I've got to do more research. As the Apostle Paul taught: God is no respecter of persons. The prophets are always on target; how could I have gotten such skewed ideas in my head?

The more I pray about it, the more I'm assured that while I don't have the answers, God does. He's fair. He's loving. And He's merciful. We are all His children. All of us.

I'm counting on that knowledge to get our family through this rough time. We all send our best. Laura will be in touch when she feels better.

Dad and Mom

I'm re-reading his email when Nygoya knocks on my door.

"How was your trek to the animal orphanage?" I ask.

She throws her head back and laughs. "The hotel guests got a little more than they bargained for this day."

"How so?"

"There we were, making our way over the boardwalk, when from the opposite direction comes a cheetah."

"It was loose?"

She laughs again. "Oh, yes. It was free."

"Did anyone get hurt?"

"No, *bosi*. The cheetah was just as startled as we were. It darted away."

"How are the baby elephants?" I ask because they are my favorite part of the orphanage. I love to watch them interact with their care-givers. Until I saw it with my own eyes, I didn't realize that elephants are the most intelligent mammals on the planet.

Nygoya's happy mood disappears. "There are two more orphaned elephants. It is a tragedy that continues to multiply. All the poaching. It must be stopped."

"And you're the one to do it."

She huffs and looks down the hallway, her smile returning. "It is not a cheetah, but there seems to be a bit of trouble coming your way."

Alarmed, I stand up and move to the open door. "What is it?"

Gavin McQueen comes down the hallway with his hand extended and a silly grin on his face. "I hope you don't mind that I popped in unannounced."

The pointed toe of my shoe catches, and I nearly trip.

"Very smooth, *bosi,*" Nygoya says. "I'll leave you two alone to talk safari."

In the confines of my office Gavin seems taller. Without his baseball cap on I see that his hair is bleached blond and wild. He looks suntanned and healthy, younger than I recall.

He sits back in a zebra-skin chair, relaxed and confident. "I want to thank you, Lana."

"Thank me?"

"You are a good friend to Mama Grace."

"She's a good friend to me."

"She needs friends . . . especially now."

I fidget with a pencil, twirling it between my fingers. "You mean because of her school?"

He leans forward and loses his smile. His voice lowers. "No . . . because of her illness."

My heart stops, and the pencil drops. "Mama Grace is ill?"

"I'm so sorry. I thought you knew. Everyone knows."

"Knows what?"

"Mama Grace tested positive a few years back."

A sharp pain shoots through my head. "For AIDS?"

"No," Gavin shakes his head. "HIV."

"It's just a precursor, isn't it?"

He shrugs, and I see it; the pain I am feeling is in his eyes, too. It is the exact way I felt when Laura called to tell me she had found a lump in her breast: sick, terrified, helpless. *Oh, God, once again your wrath is directed down the wrong road.*

The air in the room is suddenly hot and dry, like the air in the center of a brush fire. It is hard to breathe. Gavin is saying something; his head moves slowly as if a puppeteer is controlling him.

"But Mama Grace looks so healthy," I blurt out. "Are you sure she is really sick? Maybe they made a mistake. I can pay to have her retested." Then I remember how she coughed, how tired she looked.

Gavin leans forward. "I apologize. I did not mean to upset you."

"You just caught me off guard."

"What do you say I take you to lunch? I know a little place we can walk to where we can have a cup of coffee."

"Okay."

As we pass Nygoya's desk she gives me a brazen wink. I glare at her. Does she know about Mama Grace? Why didn't I know until now? I'm thinking of ways I can get her medicine, treatment, whatever is available.

Outside in the hotel's parking lot, the sun beats down on my shoulders, teasing at the chill, but not chasing it completely away. Gavin slips his arm around me, like a brother protecting his sister. "You're shaking, Lana."

"Why didn't anyone tell me until now? I've known Mama Grace for months, and no one has mentioned a word."

Gavin's tone is kind and even. "AIDS is like the elephant in the room: everyone knows it is there, but nobody mentions it. Mama Grace doesn't talk about her illness, but she doesn't deny it. She's not ashamed."

I wonder how she contracted the disease, but I do not ask. It's none of my business, and it doesn't matter. All that matters is getting her strong and healthy.

We walk out onto the sidewalk and down toward Market Row. Gavin stops in front of a small coffee shop.

"What would you like to drink?" he asks.

"Soda," I say, eyeing the brightly colored bottles; Africa is famous for fruit-flavored sodas. "I'll have a lemon-lime."

Gavin orders himself a coffee, black, and opens my soda bottle for me. The glass bottle is precious, and I'm required to drink the soda there and return the bottle to the seller. We sit on a narrow strip of grass beneath the shade of an ancient baobab tree.

"I'm really sorry about catching you off guard like that. I honestly thought you knew."

I can't swallow for the lump in my throat, and I give the soda back, still half full.

"Are you all right?" Gavin asks, making direct eye contact with me.

"I'm fine."

"You look upset."

I try to picture myself as Gavin must see me. Too thin, too pale, too unauthentic. Even though he's white, Gavin belongs in Africa— and even though I love the land, I'm out of place here. I silently reprimand myself, telling myself to forget about *me* and focus on what *really counts*.

"What can I do for Grace?" I ask.

"You're doing it. She tells me that you are wonderful."

"She tells me that I'm crazy."

Gavin laughs out loud. "The first time we met, I thought you just might be. It was your hair, you know."

I crack a small smile and tell him about the African girls who begged to plait my hair.

As we talk, we slip through an alley where a wood-carver is making an entire family of eight out of a single piece of wood. We stop to watch. His knife twists and turns, shaves off one sliver at a time until an arm appears, then a leg, then the face of a father. Half an hour passes before we know it.

"I'd better get back to work," I say.

We stop at a wall with tall block letters spray-painted across it: *Jesus Saves*.

Gavin nods. "Don't worry so much, Lana. Mama Grace's faith will see her through whatever happens."

I snap like a rubber band pulled too tight. "What is it with all the religion around here? How can people believe in a God who strikes the best woman in Africa with AIDS?"

Gavin is unrattled. "You think *God* gave Mama Grace her illness?"

"I don't know."

"He didn't," Gavin says assuredly. "God had nothing to do with it. Mama Grace got sick from a bad boyfriend."

"Why didn't God protect her?"

"God is our Father. Even the best father cannot always protect his daughter from the dangers of life, from herself." He looks at me with clear blue eyes that seem to see into my very soul. "I suspect you know that."

Every inch of me goes tense. It's like Gavin can read my heart. "Why would you say that to me?"

He smiles. "Just a feeling. No offense intended."

We walk through the city, over ancient cobbled streets, across roads paved and modern. Gavin greets a Muslim man dressed in white. He breaks into fluent Swahili when we are nearly run over by two boys on bicycles. I think of Malik and his village gang. I think of Jomo—of Grace. What will happen to Shanty Village if anything happens to her?

We walk, and we talk about life like we are seasoned friends. I tell Gavin about Laura. I try to describe my parents to him. I tell him I've been married and divorced twice. I have nothing to hide from Gavin McQueen.

He tells me about an older brother who lives in Montana. He tells me of a zealot father who is determined to bring Christianity to the entire African continent, and of a mother who is shy and devoted. They live in the Congo now but will soon head to Sierra Leone.

"That part of Africa is so dangerous," I say. "There's fighting all of the time along the Ivory Coast."

He nods. "My parents are not frightened easily. They're on a mission to bring salvation to the entire continent."

"They sound like incredible people."

"They are."

Feeling like I am with someone who does not judge and who tries to understand me, I fire a thousand questions at him—about Africa, about AIDS, about Mama Grace. It is only after Gavin drops me back off at the hotel, after I am alone in my office again, that I realize the two of us did not once mention the real reason for his visit. Not once did we mention the word *safari*.

CHAPTER 14

The best colors are orange, red, and green. That's what I learn in my research about fighting both AIDS and cancer. I email Laura, who is waiting for her biopsy results. "Eat spinach, whole oranges, and tomatoes. Avoid processed foods. Drink pure water. Rest, and don't stress."

She writes back: "Yes, Doctor Lana. Your fee is in the mail."

I have not been around Laura for years, but now I ache with missing my sister. I miss my parents. All my life I've fought fiercely for my independence—and now that I'm alone, I wish I wasn't.

Friday night Nygoya stops by my apartment to invite me to go out dancing with her.

"You look like a giant lemon," I tell her as I study the flowing yellow pantsuit she's wearing.

"*Asante*. It matches well with my eye shadow, don't you think?" She flutters her eyelashes at me.

"Perfectly."

"So do you have plans with *bosi* Gavin?"

"No."

"How did your meeting with him progress?"

"It was all right. We didn't get much accomplished, but he's helping at Mama Grace's school tomorrow. We'll talk safari then."

"You like him, no?"

"He's very nice."

"Yes he is. Now change your clothes and come with me," she says.

"I can't. I've got a meeting tonight with the manager of The Carnivore. We are working out a deal to get our hotel guests discounts at the restaurant."

"I thought you were a vegetarian," she says. "The Carnivore serves every kind of exotic meat you can imagine."

"I'm not going there to eat; I'm going there to work."

"And you're going alone?"

I nod.

"I'll come with you. I'm not afraid to put away a zebra steak or some ostrich kabobs. A woman can't survive on sweets alone," she says, patting her stomach.

"Okay," I say, grateful for the company.

The Carnivore is a famed Nairobi restaurant known for its exotic meats. The place is packed, and the air is filled with smoke from the meats on the grill.

The manager is very cordial and offers us a table and complimentary meals. While I nibble on grilled pineapple, Nygoya gnaws on a rare piece of water buffalo.

"Taste it," she says, jabbing her fork in the air.

"It's still bloody," I say.

"Blood is good for the body. How do you think the Masi stay so fit? They drink blood. It's a fact."

"So I've heard. I'm just not hungry tonight."

She chews her meat and sets both elbows on the table. "Miss Lana, you are very different recently. You seem sad."

I sigh. "Gavin told me about Mama Grace's illness."

Her fork falls to the table with a clank. "I understand now. You did not know she is sick?"

"No. I had no idea. She seems so strong."

"Mama Grace is strong. She will do much good before . . ."

"Don't say it," I cut her off. Tears burn my eyes.

"You are crying, Lana."

"It's the smoke from the grill."

Her smile is sympathetic. "Yes, that's it. That is what pours tears down your cheeks." She hands me a napkin. "Now wipe them away before the manager thinks it is the food that makes you weep."

Our business meeting is successful. The manager is very helpful, and we forge an alliance between The Carnivore and Hotel Harambee.

"Would you ladies care to go dancing with me later this night?" the manager asks. He's a short African with a goatee, and a tattoo of a giraffe stretches up his arm.

"I would!" Nygoya's arm waves like a school child with the right answer.

"And you?" he asks, giving me a look that causes me to think of the bus driver.

"No. No, thanks. I've got work in the morning."

He does not look at Nygoya, who stands a full head taller and twice as broad. "That is understandable. Perhaps another time."

"Perhaps," I say.

When we get outside, Nygoya huffs like an angry Cape bull. "He's a man with a job. They are hard to come by. You should have accepted his offer."

"I'm not in the mood."

"You are growing dull," she says. "Or have you something against all men?"

I stop in my tracks. "No. I hope not." But a nightmarish memory comes back to me, hitting me like lightning, and I feel sick. It's something I have not allowed myself to think of for a very long time. That's not true; the memory never leaves me. I just haven't allowed it to come to light for so long.

I feel the weight of Nygoya's hand on my shoulder. She leans down and whispers, "You have been injured by a man?"

All I can do is nod and fight back the feelings that threaten to topple me: anger, fear, hatred.

"Should I call a physician? You look very ill."

"I'll be fine."

Out on the street we are immediately met by begging children. They appear from the shadows: hungry, dirty, homeless. The aroma of the restaurant's roasting meat still hangs in the night air. I feel even more nauseated knowing that inside the restaurant there is an abundance of food, but there is starvation just steps away.

I pull out my purse to offer what I can, but Nygoya's trunk of an arm waves the children away. She speaks to them in Swahili and tells them to leave us alone. I can tell they are frightened as they back away.

"It's okay," I tell her. "I can give them a little something."

Nygoya's head shakes. "No, *bosi* Lana. A species must be saved one rhino at a time. If you give to one of these children, the whole pack will charge us, and we will be robbed before we can get a ride out of here."

"I'm sorry," I say, searching for the Swahili word that expresses apology. It doesn't matter. As I look into their dark, retreating eyes, I realize that my apology does nothing to ease their hunger or to soothe their pain—theirs, or mine.

CHAPTER 15

The next morning Gavin meets me at the hotel, and we take his small red pickup truck out to the village. We both make contributions until the entire back is loaded with boxes of books, school supplies, and food.

"What about medicine?" I ask Gavin.

"You mean for Mama Grace?"

"Yes."

"She goes to a local clinic. She has the drugs she needs . . . for now anyway."

I sit back and pull my safety belt around me. "I sometimes overestimate my value. I suppose Mama got along just fine before I arrived. It's just that I want to do everything I can."

Gavin smiles and cracks his window. "You're not like most women. Most women I know would want to get all fancied up and go to Mombassa for the weekend. Not you. You want to put on jeans and a T-shirt and work in the village."

I give him a sideways glance. "I think there is a compliment in there."

His smile widens. "I think so, too."

His truck is old and worn, but clean. I look out the window as we drive through the city.

"It's hard, isn't it?" he asks.

"What?"

"Seeing such overpowering need and not being able to meet it."

"Yeah. Nygoya says you have to save the species one rhino at a time."

Gavin swerves in and out of traffic. Every move he makes is liquid and appears effortless. I suspect it comes from possessing genuine strength.

When the traffic thins, he asks, "Who are you trying to save, Lana?"

I think about his question. "For now . . . Jomo—perhaps his sister, too." There is a special box in the back of Gavin's truck, stuffed with more new clothes, flip-flops, a football, school supplies, and a tube of antibiotic ointment to help heal the sores on Jomo's arms and legs. I've rented a red, rusty bike, the only one I could, to go for a ride with him.

"Jomo is a fortunate little boy to have won your heart."

"I'm the one who is fortunate. Jomo is this powerhouse of energy and goodness. You saw him."

"Yes, I suppose a guy with those big black eyes and all that energy makes it easy to fall in love."

I laugh, forgetting everything but Jomo.

We ride in silence as I take in the colorful sights and smoky smells of Nairobi. There is no wind today, and the sky is a blue so pale it appears almost white. We approach a Masi Mara man in his traditional red clothing standing on a corner, looking lost. Gavin slows to ask if he needs help.

The man only grins and holds out a wooden carving of a rail-thin cow. Before Gavin can respond, another man joins the Masi man, this one dressed in a business suit and tie. They greet each other, obviously acquaintances.

"His broker probably," Gavin says, pulling away from the curb. "Maybe he's here from the Mara to sell carvings. It's unusual to see someone like him here in the city."

"You've lived all over the continent," I say. "I can only imagine the things you've seen and done."

"And you've lived here how long?"

"It will be a year in January."

"And you have not been on safari?"

"No. I've been on a tour through the city game park. I've seen lots of animals."

"It's not the same," Gavin says emphatically. "Moja Outfitters will show you what the real savanna is like, the delta, the whole of Kenya."

"I would like to do that . . . *someday*. For now, my travels take me from my flat to the hotel and back, and out here to Mama Grace's village every chance I get."

"Sounds like you're stuck in a rut."

"Maybe," I admit.

"What are you doing in a few weeks?"

"Working. It's about all I do; why?"

"I start a three-day safari. Why don't you come with me?"

"I'd love to, but I can't get away."

"It would give you a chance to evaluate my company firsthand, see how we do things, experience it for yourself so you can recommend Moja to Mr. C. I could really use the business your hotel could refer."

The idea strikes me that maybe all Gavin and I share is his desire to secure my hotel's business. "I'd like to go, really I would, but this is such a busy time for the hotel."

"I understand, but at least think about it, will you?"

"Sure, but I don't have to go on safari to recommend Moja Outfitters. Mr. C is already sold, and so is Nygoya. I'll just need to get some information from you—some of the details. I'm sure you can provide references."

"Nothing like you'll get if you experience a safari for yourself."

"I'll think about it," I say, knowing that until I'm sure Laura is okay, and Jomo and his sister are taken care of, I won't be going anywhere.

We make one more stop before heading for Redemption Road. Gavin pulls over to purchase some roasted chickens from a roadside vendor. They are whole chickens, only partially plucked, and he carries them back to the truck dangling by their orange-taloned feet. They reek of charred meat and burned feathers.

"Yum," I say, making a face.

"Mama Grace will enjoy them. She can make her famous *supu*." He tosses the dead chickens in the back, and we take off again. "What? Your mother never made chicken soup?"

"Not with chickens that still had feet."

He smiles. "Tell me about Utah. I've never been there."

"It's beautiful. Mountains. Deserts."

"Mormons?"

"Yes, Utah has those, too."

He gives me a quizzical glance.

"How do you know about Mormons?" I ask.

"Remember, my parents are Christian missionaries. I know about a lot of religions."

I go silent, thinking to myself that I don't even know much about my own religion. "So how did you get into the safari business?" I ask, anxious to change the subject.

"I've always loved Africa and her animals. It just seemed like the perfect combination for me. I started Moja back when I was young and dumb enough not to know how hard it would be."

"No regrets?"

He shakes his head. "I'm not big on regrets."

I have a million more questions I'd like to ask him, but when Gavin turns onto Redemption Road the children seem to recognize his truck, and they come running, calling, *"Bosi* Gavin!" He slows and calls to them in Swahili.

I wave and manage, *"Jambo!"*

Already, my eyes are scanning faces for one particular smile. I don't see Jomo, and my heart falls a bit.

Mama Grace is not at her school when we pull up. Gavin goes next door to a small shop where a woman weaves baskets. He asks about Grace.

I cannot understand what is being said, but Gavin interprets for me. "She says Mama Grace is at the medical clinic. She will be back shortly."

"Do you think Grace is all right?" I ask.

"Yes."

We unpack the truck with the help of a few of the bigger children and one little girl who can barely lift a single book. Their eyes go wide when they see the food we've brought.

"Stick around," Gavin says. "When Mama Grace returns we'll all eat together."

We've brought watermelons, kale, and oranges. The good colors for fighting AIDS and cancer.

"Have you seen Jomo?" I ask the children.

They have not.

"Give me a hand," Gavin says, and we stumble beneath the weight of the water buckets he has brought. They are a special treat for Mama Grace. Usually, water comes from sellers who trek miles each day, carrying clean water to the villagers who have no access to wells. For those who can't afford to purchase water, the long trek is made on foot, and buckets are carried on heads.

Gavin chains my rented bicycle to the truck. "It will be stolen the first time you turn around. Bikes around here are worth more than gold."

"Someone gave Jomo a bicycle," I tell him.

Gavin frowns. "Who?"

"His friend Malik. Or Malik's uncle. I don't know, but Jomo sure was happy about it."

Gavin shakes his head, but says nothing more while we work under a sun that is driving up the temperature by the minute.

When we are finished, Gavin sits on the front stoop. "You look discouraged."

"I can't explain it," I admit. "One minute I'm here feeling happier than I've ever felt, then I am hit by the reality of this place and what these people go through, and I'm free-falling."

"I understand."

"I know you do. I keep thinking that nothing I do really matters. A box of oranges or a barrel of water make it easier for a time, but then everything goes back to the way it was."

Gavin swats at a fly buzzing on a stream of sweat that is trickling down his temple. "Don't be discouraged. You're making a difference to Mama, to Jomo. Someday I'll take you to Sauri, where fertilizer is helping bring in the best harvests ever, where wells burp up fresh water, where children receive at least one meal of porridge every day at school. Progress is slow, but it *is* happening."

"Simple fertilizer made that much difference?" I ask, trying to picture a village green and growing.

"The smallest, simplest things often make the most difference."

His smile warms me like sunshine. "I'd like to see Sauri for myself. Is it far from here?"

"It's a journey, but worth the trouble. I could make arrangements to take you there if you'd like."

"Sure. That would be nice, but not now . . . not until . . ."

"I understand." Gavin says, turning away.

I want to stop him and explain that I don't feel as distant as I know I'm coming across, but I don't move. I don't say anything. I just watch as Gavin McQueen walks away.

I keep looking for Jomo. I walk around the school, searching up and down the streets, hoping I'll see him coming at me a million miles an hour. It's still early, and I didn't give him any specific time—I just told him I'd be here Saturday. Maybe he's with Mama Grace. Jomo was supposed to be helping her around here these past few days. I'm anxious to see him.

Gavin is out front when I return, entertaining a group of children with a bottle of bubbles and a fistful of peppermint candy he pulls from his pocket. He requires that each child perform a song or dance before they receive their sweet.

The littlest girl with pigtails like Pippy Longstocking surprises me by drumming on a rusted can. She soon has the other children singing and dancing to a rhythm that has my own feet tapping and has Gavin swaying so that our shoulders touch.

I get lost in the music and the bodies, all of the smiles.

"Well, well, well." We look up to see Mama Grace standing before us. Today she looks strong and healthy. She wears her purple dress and matching bandana. I try not to let on that I know she is ill.

We hug and kiss, and then Gavin says, "I almost forgot something." He rushes back to the pickup, moves the seat forward, and extracts an armload of flowers that I didn't even know were there. The bouquet is beautiful and wild. "For you." He presents them to Mama Grace with an exaggerated bow.

Tears wet her cheeks. "No one has ever given me flowers," she says.

"Never?"

She shakes her head.

Gavin squeezes her. "Then it's about time."

Once we are inside, she seems overwhelmed at the offerings we have brought. The encyclopedias especially move her. She weeps aloud and hugs me until I hear ribs pop. "Okay. Okay. You're welcome."

"I was hoping you'd make *supu*," Gavin says, kicking the charred chickens with the toe of his boot. "With Amanda's recipe."

"Amanda?" I ask.

The two of them exchange an uneasy look.

"My wife," Gavin says. "She was an excellent cook. Mama and Amanda used to cook together."

I feel my cheeks flush as I turn away. "Oh."

Mama Grace clicks her tongue and frowns at Gavin. "One welcomes bad luck by speaking the name of the dead."

"African superstition," Gavin leans over and whispers.

"Um."

Feeling a rush of emotions I can't identify, let alone control, I walk outside. Jomo is nowhere around, and I consider getting on my rented bike to go look for him. But other children are there and ready, so I play a game of catch with them. They've made a ball from wadded-up newspaper. It is torn and filthy. I go inside and find the football I meant to give Jomo. We toss it instead, and the children are overjoyed. I cannot choose just one to give it to, so I say, "I'll leave the football here with Mama Grace so that you can play with it if you help her do chores."

They agree gladly.

"Are you sure none of you has seen Jomo?"

They look at each other, at me, and shake their heads.

I go back inside where Mama Grace is flipping through her Bible. It's worn and tattered, but I know giving her a new one would be an insult.

"Anything worth reading?" I ask, joking.

"Only every word. In this book my *Bwana* supplies answers to all of our questions."

"Does it tell me where Jomo is? I was hoping he'd be here by now."

Her head moves from side to side. "I have not seen Jomo since the day you brought him the yellow shirt. He agreed to come by and help me, but he has not returned. I still have the shillings you gave me for his work."

Worry burns in my stomach, like an ulcer. "Maybe I'll go out and look for him."

"No. It is not safe," says Grace.

"It's the middle of the day. I know how to get there."

Mama Grace's chest rises and falls with a ragged sigh. "Lana, have you forgotten your visit here just days ago? You will not be safe alone."

Gavin steps up to my side. "I'll drive you up the road. Maybe we can spot your Jomo."

Mama Grace relents. "I'll cook while you search. Bring Jomo back, and I will feed him. You have brought enough food today for all the hungry mouths."

We ride slowly up the road. People are out in the streets. When they stare, Gavin honks the horn and smiles. "Most people just want to be acknowledged," he says. "Kenyans are very friendly, kind of like you."

I laugh. "I've never thought of myself as friendly." My arm hangs out my window, waving.

A short, hunch-backed man carries a stick with a dead animal dangling from the end.

"What is that?" I ask.

Gavin slows down and takes a hard look. "Probably dinner for his family."

"Okay, but what is that animal?" It's as big as a rabbit, but without the tail or ears.

"It's a cane rat."

I gag. "That chicken feet *supu* isn't sounding so bad, after all."

We pass a growling, malnourished yellow Lab, and I think of the poor dog that lay dying the last time I was here. The horror of that memory adds to my rising worry. I look at every face. Gavin stops so we can ask if anyone has seen Jomo, but he gets no worthwhile leads. Finally, we are at the *choo;* Gavin seems as appalled as I am that a young boy is forced to take refuge in such a filthy, reeking place.

"Does Mama Grace know Jomo stays *here?*"

"Yes. But I've got a plan: I'm going to propose that I pay Grace rent, and she'll allow Jomo to stay with her. What do you think?"

"I think it's dangerous to meddle in other people's lives."

His reply shocks me. "You don't think living with Mama Grace is an improvement over *this?*"

"That's not what I said. This is home to these people." He gestures out the window. "This is their life."

"But it's so bleak."

He gives me a hard look that reminds me of how Mama Grace glares when she disapproves.

"I'm not judging," I say, feeling defensive.

"Yes, you are."

"You're right; I am."

The truck stops, and I climb out, stepping in a puddle of something brown and wet. Frustration swells inside me, and it's hard to control myself. I want to stomp, I want to scream, to break this place apart and put it back together clean and whole.

Gavin comes around the side of the truck and says, "It's okay to judge; just don't condemn."

I give him a flat look and try to scrape the muck from my boot. "Said like a true preacher's son."

"Amen." He offers half a smile, which I do my best to return.

I'm not angry, not embarrassed, just frustrated . . . and *worried.*

"You're not very religious, are you?" he asks.

"I hope not."

"So I guess you're *not* a Utah Mormon."

"Can we please just look for Jomo? If he's on his bike, he could be anywhere."

In tandem, Gavin and I weave in and out of the snaking line of people waiting to use the public restroom. We stop in front of the four-seat outhouse with no running water. I breathe in, and the smell is enough to make me retch. Flies swarm like small black clouds.

"You okay?" Gavin asks.

My eyes burn, my nose runs. "I'm fine."

He asks, pointing upward, if anyone around knows where little Jomo is. "He's the boy who sleeps up there." Then he breaks into Swahili and gets a few responses.

"They say he hasn't been around for a few days."

"Jomo!" I scream, louder and louder. "Jomo!" People stare and step back like I might be contagious.

We walk and walk. I feel desperate. Where could Jomo be? If he hasn't been sleeping on top of the outhouse, where has he been sleeping?

"What about his sister?" I ask, frantic. "He has a sister named Anyango. Ask about her, please."

Again, Gavin breaks into Swahili.

"They say she lives in Nairobi, that she works there."

"I don't understand. I thought she lived *here,* taking care of Jomo." My heartbeat is wild. My head pounds like an African drum.

Gavin stops in front of an old car, rusted and stripped to nothing but a twisted metal frame. He stoops to talk to a man so drunk he's slumped against the car, a home-rolled cigarette burning in his fingers. The man looks up with ripe tomato-colored eyes and mutters something in an unfamiliar Bantu language. I'm surprised that Gavin can converse with him. When Gavin stands up, he looks past me, like he doesn't want to meet my gaze.

"What is it? What's *wrong?*"

"This fellow says that your Jomo's sister is a sex worker."

"No." My heart sinks. "Anyango is a prostitute? Oh, Gavin, Jomo is only seven years old. How much older is his sister?"

He asks the man more questions, pries answers from him.

"Jomo's sister is about twelve," Gavin says. "She moved into the city some time back."

"And Jomo has been living here *alone?*"

Gavin's lip forms a hard, straight line.

"There's an older boy, Malik, who watches out for Jomo. He's very protective of Jomo. If we can find Malik . . ."

Gavin puts his hand on my shoulder and steers me down a narrow street lined with small, destitute shanties. Raw sewage runs down a little rut like a poison trickle. I cannot help scanning every dark doorway, every dark corner, and every dark face. Jomo is nowhere. My hands won't stop shaking. "He's got to be around here. Please don't give up looking for him."

"We won't. We'll find your Jomo."

I try to think productively. "Malik's uncle owns a bicycle shop."

"That's a start," Gavin says. "Where?"

"I don't know. Another village, maybe."

We go back to the drunken man, and Gavin asks him about Malik. The name brings the man to an upright position. He looks upset and shoots out a thousand slurred words.

"What did he say?" I ask.

"He says that Malik is possessed of evil. He's afraid of Malik and his gang."

Anger spits and hisses inside of me, flames I can't control. "Well, I'm not afraid."

Gavin bites his bottom lip and looks at me with steady eyes. "Maybe you should be."

CHAPTER 16

When we get back to Mama Grace's there is a line of hungry people anxious to be fed. Mama has turned two chickens into a miracle feast. She's managed to provide something for what seems to me to be the entire village.

"Jomo is missing," I say.

"Not necessarily," Mama Grace says serenely. "You should calm yourself, child. You are very upset."

"What if something bad has happened to him?"

She closes her eyes and shakes her head. "Many bad things have already happened to Jomo. He has survived so far."

"But I have a bad feeling."

She touches my cheek. "Lana, perhaps Jomo will show up when he discovers we have food."

"Do you think he is around here?"

"Word of free food travels both far and fast. It is the best lure to coax Jomo here."

"Maybe Malik will show up. He knows where Jomo is, I'm sure."

Mama Grace and Gavin exchange a look that I cannot read.

"Help now, child. Feed those who are here and hungry. Your Jomo will be taken care of."

I help serve. There aren't enough dishes, and Gavin keeps rinsing the few bowls and plates in water that is too precious for washing. I see a woman sneak the bowl of dirty dishwater to give to her children. Before I can leap to stop them, they have gulped it gone like it was hearty broth.

At the first lull, I sit on the tailgate of Gavin's truck, desperate to do something. Anything. Mama Grace joins me. "Child, how is your sister?"

"*My* sister? I don't want to talk about my sister. My sister has a whole family, the best doctors to take care of her. I want to talk about Jomo. What about *his* sister? She's a twelve-year-old prostitute."

From her apron pocket, Grace produces her Bible. "*Bwana's* eye is on the sparrow. He's watching out for that one, your Jomo."

My spine goes board straight. "How can you say that? God can't be watching all that's going on around here. He can't be. He's turned a blind eye to the suffering and cruelty."

Mama Grace backs away. Her voice growls. "Don't you ever do that, Lana."

"Do what?"

She wags a finger in the air. "Don't you dictate *Bwana's* business. You don't know His business because you don't know *Him*."

It feels like she's just slapped my face, and I slink back. "You're right. I don't know God. He gave up on me a long time ago."

Mama Grace's expression goes flat. "Lana, you are like a hyena with an antelope leg in her mouth: she does not bother with the lions surrounding her; all she tastes is the fresh meat."

"I just *have* to find Jomo."

"Why?"

"Because he means more to me than I can tell you."

"Why?"

"Don't ask me. I can't explain. All I know is that there is a precious little boy out there somewhere. He could be hurt . . . lonely . . . or *worse*."

Mama Grace nods. "That is the sad truth."

"Don't you care?"

She closes her Bible with a smack. "I care."

"I'm sorry. I know you do. I've got all this fear and worry inside, and I don't know where to direct it. I feel *so* helpless. Tell me what to do to find him."

"Jomo is but one star in a sky full of stars."

"He *is* a star," I say, not able to stop the tears from cutting a path down my burning cheeks. "He is special." I detest the word *special,* but can think of no other way to describe him. Any word to capture his worth would be inadequate.

Mama Grace presses her shoulder against mine. "You can only break a heart into so many pieces. Your heart was not whole when you first came to Africa."

"My heart is fine. It's Jomo I'm worried about. I think I'll go for a bike ride to look for him."

"And how will you know when to turn around and come back?"

"When I find him."

She stares at me with dark, penetrating eyes.

The task before me is endless, hopeless. "I *have* to find him."

"Then you will."

Her words give me confidence. Jomo has lived in this village all of his life. He has survived against the odds for seven years. There is no cause for worry just because he didn't show up today. Maybe he simply forgot.

Mama Grace wipes her hands on her apron. "Eat some kale. It will give you a bit of strength."

"Really, I'm not hungry." I see dozens of children, mothers, even fathers who linger about, hoping that a bit of food will become available.

Gavin is at the top of the stoop, trying to keep people fed and happy.

"Go back and help Gavin," I tell Mama Grace. "I'll be fine."

I get on the bike and ride to the east, a way we did not search. I ask about Jomo and get no response, but when I mention Malik's name most people know who he is. I keep hearing the Swahili words *janja* and *fisadi* associated with Malik. They are unfamiliar to me, and I try to remember them so I can ask Gavin what they mean.

No one can direct me to Malik's uncle's bicycle shop. Every person I ask points a different way. I ride on, asking, searching, hoping. Nothing. Every corner I turn produces a thousand more doorways, an endless row of poverty.

I stop by a vegetable market where the only item for sale is a withered onion. I give the shopkeeper a couple of shillings, but refuse to take the onion. He tries to hand me back my money.

"No. Just tell me if you know Jomo."

"Jomo Kenyatta."

"No. Jomo. A little boy."

The man smiles to reveal a single brown tooth. *"Mchanga."*

"Yes!" *Mchanga* means "little boy." "Yes. His name is Jomo."

"No Jomo."

I keep pedaling, worry building with every turn of the tire.

A woman steps in front of me and pushes a small child in my path. The child wears only an oversized T-shirt with bare, dirty toes sticking out at its hem. Yellow mucus oozes from both eyes. *Uh-huh,* I think, my heart shriveling, *God is watching all of this.*

"Take my child," the woman says in unbroken English, but in a voice so desperate it makes my throat close over. "Her name is Mary. Take her!"

I open my mouth to explain that I can't, but no sound comes out.

"Take my child and give her a home. Take her to America, please. You do not have to pay. Take her." She gives the youngster a shove so hard the little girl nearly topples. I rush to steady her, but I am not in time and the child falls face-first onto the hard dirt. She does not cry; she does not even whimper, but just stays put where she falls.

When I lift her it feels like I am lifting a skeleton. I hand her back to her mother. Or is it a sister? An aunt? A neighbor?

"I'm sorry. I'm sorry. I'm sorry." It's all I can make myself say because it comes from the core of my heart. The woman situates the child on her hip and turns to go.

"Wait! I have something for you." I reach into my pocket, thinking I have a piece of candy, but all I find are a few more shillings, pennies in American dollars. I hold them out, and the woman takes them gratefully, but I can read the disappointment in her eyes. *Is this all you can offer, a privileged American woman like you?* She bows her head, and her lips brush the top of the child's head. *What more can I give?* I take the earrings out of my ears, a pair I bought from a street vendor. I take a ring from my finger and press the meager offering into the woman's hand. She wraps her fingers around the jewelry as though she's clutching pure gold.

"For me and my child?"

"Yes. For you. I wish I had more to give you."

"Asante. Asante."

I only wish I had more. Even my all is inadequate.

When Gavin and Mama Grace find me, I am sitting there in the road where the child fell. I have not located Malik. Jomo is nowhere to be found. The woman and the little girl are gone. Other people have skirted around me, looking more afraid than curious.

"Did I just lose my mind?" I ask.

Gavin reaches down to help me to my feet. "No. You were crazy to begin with."

Somewhere over Gavin's shoulder I see Mama Grace smile—a sad, pathetic smile—and I know that in my absence, Jomo has not returned.

CHAPTER 17

Days go by with no word from Jomo. The news from Laura is not good, and Mr. C decides he has been working me too hard.

"You need a break from work," he says.

What I need is to hear that my sister is okay, that Jomo has been found.

We are in the workout room of the hotel. Mr. C is not there to work out, but to work; he's dressed in a grape-colored shirt, tan pants, and a black-and-white zebra-striped tie. He is crisp and clean.

Dressed in shorts and a tank top, I'm pumping the elliptical, which is cranked to the most difficult level. Sweat pours down my spine, down my forehead, and into my eyes. It stings, and I blink.

"I understand you sought help from the police to locate your street boy."

"Yes," I huff, "I went to the station last night to ask for help."

"And what were you told?"

"That it is difficult to find an orphaned village boy. I don't even know Jomo's full name or his birth date."

Mr. C shakes his head slowly. "Are you certain the boy is lost?"

"No. I mean yes. I can't find him."

"Perhaps this Jomo does not wish to be found."

"Why? We are friends."

He looks down at the clipboard he's holding. "Lana, when you searched Mama Grace's village, did you check the spool district?"

I stop pumping. "What is the 'spool' district?"

He frowns. "If you pass a doorway and see an empty spool sitting outside, you can be assured that sex work goes on in that house."

"Oh."

"I do not wish to offend you."

"I'm not offended. Jomo's sister is a sex worker somewhere here in the city—and she is just a child."

"Yes. That is a sad fact."

"If you tell me where the spool districts are, I will search them myself," I say.

"Leave that work to the police, Lana."

"I don't know that the police are doing *anything*. I don't know why they aren't more concerned."

Mr. C tugs at his shirtsleeves to be certain they are even. "I am concerned about you."

"I'm okay. My work is all caught up."

"Yes, your work is rated excellent. I am concerned about *you*. Tell me, how is your sister?"

"Cancer. My sister has breast cancer." It's the first time I've said it out loud, and the words burn my throat.

"That makes me very sad, this bad news on top of bad news."

I wipe my face with a towel and try to catch my breath.

Mr. C straightens his already-straight tie. "You and your twin sister, you are the same?"

I laugh out loud. "No. No. It's one of God's little jokes."

"I do not understand."

"We could not be more different."

"Yes. No two people are ever truly alike."

I don't want to talk about Laura. Or myself. "I'm sorry. I've got to go shower and get back to work."

He nods and turns away, but then pivots back and looks at me. "My father was killed by cancer. It attacked his bones first, then his muscles. In the end it ate his brain." He speaks of cancer as though it is a living, breathing, thinking predator—a beast.

I stare at him. This is the most personal bit of information Mr. C has divulged since we met. I don't know what to say, so I just stand there.

"Your sister, she is angry, no?"

"I suppose so."

"Mad can be good. It can help fight the cancer."

"Uh-huh."

"I am sorry for your sister."

"Thank you." The whole conversation makes me antsy.

Mr. C's voice drones on. "You see, if your sister lives, she will be a survivor. If she dies, she will be a statistic. Either way, cancer has marked her forever."

"Uh-huh. I've gotta go shower and get back to work," I repeat.

He steps in front of me. "Lana, I want you to take a holiday."

"I can't."

"You must—if you wish to remain employed with Hotel Harambee."

"Are you threatening to fire me?"

He squints. "Relieve you of your employment responsibilities?"

"Yes. *Relieve* me."

He smiles a smile as wide as a ruler. "I do not wish to 'fire' you. I wish for you to rest. Take some time for yourself. You have not been your usual pleasant self these past weeks."

"Okay," I say. "It will give me the chance to search for Jomo."

His smile disappears. "I have another journey in mind for you."

"What kind of journey?"

"A safari. I wish for you to evaluate one of Mr. Gavin McQueen's safaris."

"I gave you the research and the recommendations. I think Hotel Harambee should give Moja Outfitters a trial run. Let our guests evaluate his safari tour in exchange for a discount. We talked about this in our meeting the other day, Mr. C."

"Yes, I recall."

"Listen," I say, feeling pressure from his stare, "I would like to go on a Moja Outfitters safari—not now, but soon. When I find Jomo."

Mr. C shakes his head. "Mama Grace has the word out, right?"

"To locate Jomo? Yes, she does. She looks for him every day."

"And the police, is it not their job to find this lost boy?"

"They don't seem very motivated."

"That is unfair, Lana. How can you know that?"

"I know. To them, he is just one of countless street children. I am not his family, just an outsider who has no right to show such fierce concern."

Mr. C's expression turns hard. "I am no longer requesting that you go on this safari; I'm requiring it."

I face the truth. I can do what Mr. C requires, or I can quit my job. I came to Africa thinking I might work here a year or two; now I want to stay indefinitely, and Hotel Harambee is the perfect employer. If I leave the hotel, I'll forfeit all of its connections, its influence for good. "I'll go," I say. "When?"

His smile returns. "I will not rush you. You have an entire week to prepare."

CHAPTER 18

Nygoya is drinking *chai* in my office when I return. "So you are going on safari with *bosi* Gavin."

"How did you hear? I just barely found out."

She smirks. "I know more than anyone realizes."

"Then tell me where Jomo is."

"*That* I do not know."

"I have to find him."

"You will. I heard Mama Grace say that if anyone can single one termite out of an entire mound, you are the one."

"Whatever that's supposed to mean."

"It means Mama Grace has faith in you."

I feel a small surge of hope. "Do you think Jomo is okay?"

She reaches for a cigarette in her jacket pocket. "What do you mean by okay?"

"I don't know anymore. I just want to know he's alive and well so I can hold him, take care of him forever."

Her penciled-on eyebrows rise. "You want to adopt Jomo?"

"If that is possible. I know Kenya has all kinds of government rules about adoption."

"You are crazy."

"Yeah, so I've heard."

"There are many orphaned children you might choose from. The slums are overcrowded with children."

"I picked Jomo."

The edges of her wide mouth turn upward. "The way I remember the story, Jomo was the one who chose you."

Nygoya walks out of the room, leaving a plume of cigarette smoke in her wake. I try to sort my thoughts. When I arrived in Africa I was confident, determined, and focused. My past was behind me. Now everything has changed. *Everything.*

Nygoya pops her head back into my office. "I neglected to tell you that while you were exercising, your sister called from the USA. She wants you to call her as soon as you can."

My stomach tightens. I close the door and close my eyes, trying to hone in on a sense of what Laura needs. Twin instinct. I get nothing.

It's evening in Africa, which means it's morning in Utah.

I open my desk drawer and pull out a photograph. It's old and bent at the corner. Dad took the shot of Laura and me when we were six or seven—Jomo's age. The sun is at Dad's back, and I can see his shadow stretched across the grass. Laura and I were dressed for Easter in identical daisy-yellow dresses. She's all clean, and her blonde hair is curled and tied up in a ribbon. Days before the photograph, I had taken the scissors to my hair, and it looked pretty much then the way my hair does now: short, dark, and chopped. The image takes me back in time, and I dial my sister's telephone number.

Laura answers on the first ring. "Hey," I say, "what's up?"

"I miss you," she says.

"That's it?"

"Yeah, that's it."

"Okay."

"I've been thinking," Laura says. "For weeks we've talked about me. I want to know about you."

"You know everything there is to know."

"I know you've been wonderful though all of this."

"We're not through it yet."

A silence hangs taut between us.

"Lana, I am so grateful for all you've done to help me. I just got that nutritional information you sent last night. It follows the Word of Wisdom, don't you think?"

"The only thing I know about the Word of Wisdom is how to break it."

"I wish you wouldn't do that."

"What?"

"Berate yourself the way you do. You're always tearing yourself down."

"No, I'm not."

"You have to forgive yourself, Lana."

"For what?"

"For past mistakes."

"I don't live in the past," I say. "I'm living for the future; you should too."

I hear a catch in her voice, and I realize how insensitive my words are. Laura has no guarantee for a future. "I'm sorry."

"For what?"

"For being insensitive."

"It's okay."

"You sound mad." She doesn't, but I want her to feel something that raises or lowers the line on her barometer.

"I'm not mad," she says.

"Sure you are."

"At who?"

"At me."

"Why would I be mad at you?" she asks.

"Because I should be the one with cancer. I'm the one who deserves heaven's wrath, not you."

"We've been through this before," Laura gulps. "God is not punishing me, Lana. That's not the way He works."

"How *does* God work?"

"He rewards. He doesn't punish."

"Oh, yeah?" I say, unable to hide the sarcasm from my tone. "When was the last time you read the Old Testament? God *created* punishment."

"Whatever."

"If I were you, I'd really be ticked off at God."

"Stop it! That's sacrilegious."

"No, it's not."

"I can't be mad at Heavenly Father. I love Him."

"You love me, too, but you've spent most of your life furious with me."

"Can we talk about something else?" she asks. By the quiver in her voice I know I've pushed my sister too far, but at least she's feeling something besides numb.

"So back to me, huh?" I say with hesitation.

"You've told us about your friends Grace and Nygoya, but who else do you hang out with?"

"Hang out?"

She chuckles. "You can tell I'm around kids all day."

I smile. "Well . . . there *is* this guy."

"Oh, yeah? Do tell."

Suddenly we are back in our childhood bedroom with pink walls and a pink rotary telephone. I am on the top bunk bed, whispering down through the darkness, entertaining and appalling my sister with forbidden tales of my love life.

"Yeah. I don't know him very well," I admit, "but I really like him."

"What's his name?"

"Jomo."

"*Jomo?* Is that African?"

"Yes. Very African."

"Oh."

"He's incredible," I say. I picture Jomo's little face, his ready smile, and I feel his dusty little hand slip into mine. "I can't wait for you to meet him." I speak of Jomo like he is not missing, like I could walk out into the hallway and pull him into the safety of my office. The ache to have him near and safe chokes the air from my lungs.

"You sound over the moon," Laura says.

"I am." There is no point in telling her the truth; even from Utah, my sister would share my worry for a missing little boy.

She giggles into the phone, and I picture her dimples, same as mine, dancing in the depths of her cheeks. Dad used to call us The Four Dimples and would try to get us to perform to Primary tunes: "Jesus Wants Me for a Sunbeam," "Little Purple Pansies," and that "Give Said the Little Stream" song I thought I heard in the village. It is strange to me—disturbing, in fact—how many buried memories float to the top of my life these days.

"Wait till I tell Mom," Laura says.

"Tell Mom what?

Laura laughs. "She's going to pass a kidney stone when I tell her."

"Tell her what?" I ask.

"Tell her that this time you've fallen for a *Black* man."

CHAPTER 19

Mama Grace holds an infant in her arms, a baby girl wrapped in a piece of bright orange material that is one of her scarves. *"Jambo!"* She steps off the stoop and comes toward us.

It's the weekend, and Mr. C has driven me out to the village on a two-fold mission. He is here to build bookcases and benches. I am here to look for Jomo.

"Have you seen him?" I immediately ask.

"No. I am sorry to have to tell you."

"Nothing?"

"Not a word."

She hands me the baby girl. I'm shocked at how light she is, how limp she is.

"Lana, always trust your feelings. God has given us women an inner compass. What is yours telling you?"

"About Jomo?"

"Yes, about Jomo."

"I don't know. I can't get any kind of reading."

Mr. C walks between us. "That's exactly why I am sending Lana on safari with your *rafiki,* Bwana McQueen." He steps inside, carrying an armload of lumber.

She gives me a wide-eyed look. "You and my Gavin?"

I feel my cheeks go hot. "I'm just going on a short safari to evaluate the experience for our hotel. I assure you that business is Gavin McQueen's *only* interest in me."

"Yes," she says with a smirk, "your hotel carries much influence."

I hold the baby close to me, press her against my heart. She does not move, does not whimper. "What's the matter with her?" I ask.

"Just about everything."

"Who does she belong to? Where did she come from?"

Mama Grace rubs her forehead. "I found her outside my doorstep this morning."

My heart stops. "She's *abandoned*? I thought you were babysitting." I press the child even closer to my shattered heart. Laura's babies smell of powder, lotion, and innocence. This child exudes an aroma of sour garbage, dirt, and diarrhea. Mama reaches over to tug the scarf up over the baby's shoulder.

I am aghast. "How could a mother . . ."

Mama Grace's expression goes cold. Her eyes reprimand and remind me that I am an outsider. I remember Gavin telling me not to "condemn."

Mama says, "For all we know, this baby's mother is not the one who left her at my threshold. For all we know, her mother has been claimed by the dreaded disease that kills not for sustenance, but for pleasure." Her eyes glisten, and she turns from me.

Mama Grace is in a fight for her life. "I'm sorry," I say. "I keep making the same mistake over and over."

"You are innocent," she says. "A white woman cannot be expected to know what life is like in the black skin of an African woman any more than a Black woman can know what it feels like to be White. It is not possible."

"But I am a woman. I know what it feels like to be a woman, and that should be more than sufficient to draw us together."

"It should," she says, stepping past me to help Mr. C with the next load of lumber.

I sit on the stoop and cradle the baby. Grace has filled an old, stained bottle with something thick and gray. I do my best to feed her, but the baby's lips are dry. She is too weak to suckle, and I am terrified that she might die in my arms. I swat flies from her eyes and ears.

"You are very natural with a baby in your arms," Mr. C says to me. Guilt hits me like a falling brick. *If only he knew my secret.*

I hum to the baby girl as a few other children gather around. I don't sing the words, but the melody floats out of me as naturally as my very breath.

"Have you seen Jomo?" I ask the children who are rapidly multiplying.

The answer is no. It is always no.

I search their faces. They are varying shades of black, but their clothes are a rainbow of colors, as though someone flung open a closet and the children all held up their arms to let the clothes rain down on them.

One child's face looks vaguely familiar; her slick black hair tumbles down her back in exquisite braids. I smile, and she steps close and begins to hum along. The tune is as familiar to her as it is to me, and I stare in absolute wonder. "I am a child of God, and He has sent me here . . . ."

A levy inside of me cracks, and I feel emotions I have not felt before—feelings I can't even identify. "How do you know that song?" I ask, realizing this is the same little girl who hummed, "Give, Said the Little Stream."

She smiles up at me, uncertain of my question. Just then Gavin's red truck pulls up in front of us. He steps out and is instantly swarmed by the children. Today he has brought them boxes of strawberries. The children are thrilled.

"Hey, what do you have there?" he asks me.

I glance down and am momentarily surprised to see a baby in my arms. She has worked her cracked lips around the nipple and is doing her best to suck.

The sound of Mr. C's hammer and Mama Grace's voice comes from inside the school. Gavin sits next to me, and two children each claim a knee. Holding them and hugging them comes easy for him; he loves them without thinking about it.

"She's sick," I say, looking down at the tiny little soul in my arms. "Mama Grace found her here," I point to the very spot where we sit, "a few hours ago."

Gavin uses the side of his index finger to stroke her cheek with butterfly tenderness; I know, because as he pulls away, his finger grazes the back of my hand, instilling a sense of comfort and warmth. The corner of his mouth turns up. He hasn't shaved for a few days, and the rising sun catches in his stubble, showing red among the blond.

"How can you smile?" I ask. "This baby was *abandoned*."

"Because," he says, leaning so his mouth is next to my ear, "this child has a chance. This isn't the first baby Mama Grace has found on her threshold. Whoever put her here knows Grace and knows Grace's heart."

"What will happen to this baby?" I ask. Children scuffle and shift all around us. They are vying for Gavin's attention and hoping he can produce more strawberries from the back of his truck. The little girl who hummed along with me bends down to kiss the top of the baby's head.

"She'll be all right," Gavin says, sounding confident. "Imagine what would have happened to your Jomo if someone had trusted him to Mama Grace."

A picture of the two of them working in the school, keeping each other from ever being lonely, appears on the canvas of my mind. It is painted in big, bold strokes with vivid colors: reds, yellows, greens.

"If only . . ." I say.

"Yeah, if only . . . ."

"Are you two talking about me?" Mama asks, stepping up behind us. Gavin stands. "*Jambo,* Mama! How are you?"

"I am well. And you?"

Before Gavin can answer, Mr. C is there, and I am left alone with the baby who has fallen asleep with her lips still circled around the nipple. While they talk of safaris I savor the moment, holding this baby so close that I can feel the flutter of her heartbeat.

A white van in unusually good shape for this part of Nairobi pulls up. A short, stout woman climbs out, and she and Mama Grace rush into each other's arms, speaking Swahili so fast even Gavin seems unable to understand.

"This is Mama Dale," Mama Grace says, making introductions all around.

Gavin nods. "Yes, yes. From the unwanted baby center."

"I am a nurse," she says, smiling at Mr. C. "A head nurse at the center."

Mr. C greets her graciously.

Mama Grace introduces me, and Mama Dale takes the baby from my reluctant grip. Immediately, she sets to inspecting the child. She pries into her walnut-sized mouth, examines her ears, looks up her nose. Mama Dale pulls back the orange cloth, and I am shocked at what I see. The baby is naked—no diaper—and her ribs protrude. Her skin hangs in withered wrinkles. While malnutrition causes gas that expands most children's stomachs, this baby looks like an inflatable doll whose air supply has been depleted. Her stomach is concave.

My head pounds. "What can be done for her?" I ask.

Mama Dale smiles at me. "Many things. Our facility is fortunate—generous people fund us so we can give babies a brighter chance."

"Good. Is there anything *I* can do to help?"

Mama Grace touches my shoulder. "Lana wants to save every child in Africa."

"Good, then," Mama Dale says, "we are in agreement. You can come and visit us. We can always find use for a willing pair of hands and a good heart." She turns to the children who have gathered around and calls out in a language I don't understand. The little girl in the pink dress and braids runs up to her. She holds the baby, and the three of them climb back into the van. There are no car seats, no child restraints—just the little girl holding the baby.

"Is that girl Mama Dale's daughter?" I ask.

Mama Grace nods. "Yes, Benda."

Mama Dale stops the van and holds her arm out the window. "I almost forgot—your book."

Mama Grace accepts the gift with a shake of her head and a roll of her eyes. *"Asante."* She then hands the book to Gavin, who has come out onto the landing. "Put this away for me, will you?"

I stare at the book. I've seen the dark blue cover before, but it can't be. I convince myself that I am imagining things.

"Oh, Lana," Mama Dale says, "Mama Grace tells me that you are looking for a boy."

I spring toward her. "Yes, Jomo!"

Her expression falls. "I am talking about a boy named Malik. Are you not looking for him?"

"Yes. I think Malik might know where Jomo is. Malik's uncle has a bicycle shop, but we have not been able to locate it."

"It is east of here, but it is not a bicycle shop. It is a drinking parlor. Bicycles are mended behind the building."

I feel desperate. "What is the uncle's name?"

"I do not know that, but the name of the parlor is *Ona Kui*. It means 'thirsty.'"

Gavin moves to my side. "Can you give me more specific directions?" he asks.

Mama Dale points and mentions something about a filling station and a tailor shop. "Be careful of the uncle," she warns. "He is a foul man who claims the village chief as his *rafiki*."

I'm already on my bike.

"Where are you going?" Gavin asks as Mama Dale pulls away.

"You know where."

"You can't get there on your bike."

"Then will you take me?"

"Now?"

"Yes! Please!"

"Okay."

CHAPTER 20

The *Ona Kui* is a narrow building with bars instead of glass for windows. Men are crowded around, drinking and smoking *banji*—Africa's marijuana.

"See that man dressed in orange?"

"The one playing marbles in the dirt? He looks drunk."

"He is. He is also the village chief."

"You're joking."

Gavin tightens his grip on the steering wheel until his knuckles go white. "I wish I was joking; the man was once useful to this village. He is no good to anyone when he is drunk, and he is always drunk now."

The chief and his drinking buddies look amused to see Gavin and me drive up. Gavin does not stop to ask questions, but pulls his truck around back where Malik is hunched over a twisted piece of metal next to an old slat shed. Dappled yellow light dances down through the leaves of a banana tree. Bicycle parts, none of them new, are strewn around like a hurricane has torn through the shop. No one else is around.

Malik glances up and seems startled to see us.

"Jomo," I say, before I'm even out of the truck. "Where is Jomo?"

Malik wipes black grease on his pants as his eyes take me in. "Jomo is not here."

"Please tell me if you know where he is. No one has seen him for more than a week." I jump down from the cab and rush toward him. "You know where he is, don't you?"

Malik steps back. "You are *always* looking for Jomo. Why?"

I open my mouth to explain, but he cuts me off.

"You do not belong here."

My eyes sting, and I feel my fists clench, my fingernails digging into the flesh of my palms. "I told you before. I am his friend. I just want to know that he's okay. Is he? Is Jomo okay?"

Malik spits dark juice onto the dirt. He eyes Gavin.

"Listen, son," Gavin says calmly, moving closer to Malik, as though he's talking to a vicious dog, "we mean you no harm. We just want to find the boy."

"You want him for what purpose?"

Gavin casts his eyes toward the ground, as though he's making a hard decision. "Tell us, please," he says, raising his gaze to meet Malik's.

Malik bends down to pick up a small metal pipe. Its weight seems to give him courage. "Leave. You are not welcome here."

"Where's Jomo?" I ask again.

"Leave," Malik repeats.

A muscle tightens in Gavin's jaw. "Son, we mean no harm to anyone. Lana just wants to be sure that Jomo is all right. He hasn't slept on top of the *choo* for a week. Do you know where he's been?"

"No," Malik says, flatly. "I have not seen Jomo since the night this *mzungu* woman last came to visit Jomo."

"What?" I demand, blood rushing through my head. If Malik hasn't seen him, where could Jomo be?

Malik's shoulders drag. "My father's brother is very angry with me because of Jomo."

"Why?"

"Jomo did not return the bicycle. It was not mine to give away. It was on loan from my uncle."

"I know that. Jomo knew that, too."

"He promised to return it, but never did. Now I must work off the cost of the bicycle." He spits again, and flies rush to the tiny bit of moisture.

I want to shake Malik's shoulders, knock the whole truth from him. "Are you telling me that you have not seen Jomo since I gave him his gifts?"

"I know nothing of any gifts," he says. "I only know that Jomo disappeared after he met with *you*." His greasy finger points at my chest. The pipe remains in his other hand.

Bile burns in my throat. "Malik, if Jomo hasn't been with you, where has he been? Does he have any other family or friends who might be taking care of him?"

"Only Anyango. She is in Nairobi. Perhaps Jomo stole my uncle's bicycle and rode into the city."

I look at Gavin, who shrugs. "I doubt it, but I guess it's possible."

"How can we find Jomo's sister? Where does she live in Nairobi?"

"I do not know," Malik says, still gripping the pipe. "Anyango has not been seen in the village for a very long time."

"How long has Jomo been alone?"

"He is not alone. He belongs to our village."

"No one knows where he is. I don't think they even care."

Malik looks insulted. "Jomo means much to me."

A small flock of black, yellow-headed birds whirrs above us; they lift in unison, rise and fall, and fall again until they vanish in the thick of the bush. *If a hundred birds can disappear in seconds,* I think, *Jomo may never be found.*

Malik glares at me. "How do I know that *you* did not steal the boy and my uncle's bicycle? I have not seen Jomo since last I saw you."

Confusion swirls inside my head.

Gavin slips an arm around my waist. "Let's go."

"No. Not until I find Jomo."

Malik whistles, a shrill animal call, and within seconds two other boys and a man come out of the back door and stand gawking at us.

"I'm looking for a little boy named Jomo," I say. "Please tell me if you've seen him."

Malik cries something in Swahili and then says, "I think this woman may have stolen Jomo." His finger points at me. "A boy like that would bring a good market price."

"What?"

The circle closes in around us.

Gavin does not budge. He speaks to the older man in Swahili, and then says to everyone, "Listen. We are not looking for trouble. My friend just wants to make sure the boy is safe. Do any of you know anything?"

The man shakes his head and blinks his bloodshot eyes.

Malik's accusation makes no sense to me. The idea that someone has stolen Jomo strangles me.

In a quivering voice I ask, "If *I* stole Jomo, why would I be here asking about him?"

Malik continues chewing on whatever leaf grinds between his teeth. "Leave."

"Malik, *please*. You can help us find Jomo. I know you can."

The man steps forward and wipes his mouth with the back of his hand. "Jomo is not here," he says. "I am the uncle of Malik. His father was my older brother. Malik speaks the truth."

There is no menace in his tone. There is no hope in his words. I rush to him and grab his orange cloak. I put my face next to his and plead, "Jomo is just a little boy; please help me find him. Please!"

He looks to Malik, at Gavin, and back to me. His long, greasy fingers pry my grip from his clothes. His breath in my face is rank. "I can tell you nothing . . . except the boy owes me the cost of a bicycle."

"Please," I beg, my voice sobbing, "tell me anything you can."

There is pity in the way the man looks at me. "I loaned a bicycle to Malik. He loaned that same bicycle to Jomo. The boy was very happy to learn to ride. He went like a gazelle through the village."

"Everything was good until this *mzungu* came!" Malik shouts. "Both Jomo and the bike disappeared after she was here."

"That is your answer," the man says, addressing Gavin, not me. "Leave here now."

Gavin tightens his grip around my waist. "We'd better go."

"No!" I shout, "not until we've found Jomo."

The circle closes tighter, and I sense we are in real trouble. Another group of men, including the chief, have gathered around Gavin's pickup truck. They are eyeing it with envy.

Gavin reverts to Swahili. The uncle replies, and I do not understand anything other than Jomo's name. Whatever he says causes beads of sweat to form on Gavin's forehead.

"What are you saying?" I ask Gavin.

Gavin shakes his head. He reaches into his pocket. I half expect him to pull out a gun or maybe money to bribe Malik and his uncle. Instead he produces a small, folded handkerchief. "You're crying, Lana."

Humiliated, I push the handkerchief away and wipe my face with my hand.

"Please tell me what you are saying in Swahili."

"We'll talk in the truck."

We drive away without any answers and with no sign of Jomo. When I look in the rearview mirror I see Malik standing in the road, the pipe still clenched in his hand.

"What did Malik's uncle say?"

Gavin pulls the truck to the side of the road. "He asked me what business you have with Jomo. I told him that you intend to adopt the boy."

"What did he say to that?"

"He asked me how much you would pay should Jomo mysteriously turn up there."

I feel like my heart has been hit with a hammer. "Do you think it's possible that he has Jomo now?"

"No, I don't. I think the man simply wants money."

"I'll pay money if that's what it takes."

"As you remind me, Jomo is just a little boy, not a commodity to be purchased."

"I know that, Gavin. I'm desperate."

"Malik's uncle knows that. I told him that if Jomo does turn up, he should get in touch with Mama Grace right away. I told him you will pay big money for the safe return of Jomo."

"You did?"

"You just said you would pay."

"I will. Does this mean that they will find Jomo?"

"It means they'll look harder."

Gavin pulls the truck back onto the road. "I hope it does not come to that. A child should not have a price attached to his head."

I don't know what to do. I just rock back and forth, my face buried in my palms.

"What do you know about Jomo's sister?" he asks.

"Just that her name is Anyango. She's about twelve, and she works somewhere in Nairobi as a child prostitute."

"That profile could fit a lot of girls."

"I'm willing to start looking. Jomo might have ridden his bike to be with her."

"He might have, but I doubt it."

We move down a dirt road wider than most. A tall, thin woman with a baby tied to her back and her head burdened with a load of firewood steps in front of us, forcing Gavin to hit the brakes. The woman keeps moving, either ignoring us on purpose or not seeing us at all. I can't imagine what her life is like, and I search her face and the faces of others around us.

"Tell me something," I say to Gavin. "How can God keep track of all His children?" I can't hide the bitterness I feel, and it comes out in my tone.

Gavin slaps the steering wheel. "I don't know *how* He does it, but it's enough for me to believe that He *does*. God knows every sparrow that falls."

"Luke 12:6. Mama Grace gave me that reference when I asked her the same question."

He looks at me. "You don't believe it?"

"I'm not even sure if I believe in God at all."

Gavin shows no reaction to my confession, though speaking the words aloud doubles the knot in my stomach.

We drive through the village, stopping to ask people if they know anything about Jomo. No one does, and my rage soon disintegrates to hopelessness.

"A child can't just vanish and no one notice," I say.

Gavin smiles. "I know someone who knows exactly where Jomo is."

My heart jumps. "You do?"

"*God* knows. Maybe you should ask Him."

"Yeah, right, like God would answer me."

"So you *do* believe in God."

"I didn't say that."

"You do, though."

"How do you know?"

"I just know," he says.

"Can we talk about something else?"

"We can talk about anything you want to, Lana."

"What if I don't want to talk about anything at all?"

"We can do that too."

On the way back to Redemption Road, the sun is radiating a thready light spun with pinks and purples. The air smells of rich earth and wood smoke. The pace of the people has slowed. They are no longer rushing to fetch water or fetch wood. Those fortunate to have located food for the day are now cooking it and sharing it with those they love.

"I'm sorry I've wasted so much of your time," I tell Gavin. "You could have been helping Mama Grace."

"Don't worry," he says, "your *bosi* is there to keep her company."

"I forgot about Mr. C! He's ready to fire me anyway."

"Why?"

"Because I've been so distracted. I think he thinks I'm cracking up."

"He tells me that you're not too excited about our upcoming safari."

"That's not true. I'd just feel better if I knew Jomo was safe before I went." My voice cracks. "Why doesn't anybody seem to care that a little boy has gone missing?"

He does not respond.

"I'm telling you, my heart feels like it's going to explode."

Gavin waits until I meet his gaze. I see his Adam's apple bob. "Lana, what if you *never* find Jomo?"

"I will."

"But . . ."

"No *buts*. I *will* find Jomo, and I'll make sure he's safe for the rest of his childhood."

"You understand the enormity of that task?"

"Yes, I think I do. I don't care how big the challenge is; I have to find him." *How can I make people understand?* I sit in silence, looking out at a man swinging a machete in a field of scrawny green rows.

"He could use some fertilizer."

Gavin nods but keeps driving.

The whole pitiful world goes on without feeling the loss of a child. After a few minutes I study Gavin's profile and say, "I'll do whatever I have to to find Jomo . . . even if it means resorting to *prayer*."

I think the corners of his lips turn upward, but his expression changes to one of worry when he looks in the rearview mirror. "We have company," he says, his eyes fixed on the mirror.

I look back and see that we are being tagged—by Malik and his friends. They're keeping up with us on their bicycles.

"What do you think they want?" I ask.

"I have no idea."

"Stop! Maybe they'll tell us something about Jomo."

Gavin pumps on the brake, but the boys don't stop. They pedal right on past us, so close one of them touches the tailgate of Gavin's pickup truck. He whizzes past my open window in a yellow blur, and that's when my heart freezes. "Let me out!" I scream.

"What is it?"

"That boy! That boy is wearing the shirt I gave to *Jomo!*"

CHAPTER 21

Gavin's hand yanks me back inside the truck, and he stomps on the gas. It is hard to keep up with the bicycles because they don't have to stay on the main road. They dart between people, rush past animals, and maneuver down narrow alleys.

"Malik is lying," I tell Gavin, my heart racing. "He said that he hasn't seen Jomo since the day I gave him those clothes. He claims to know nothing about my gift to Jomo. Malik is lying, Gavin. What does that mean?"

"Maybe Malik is telling the truth, and one of his buddies knows more than he's telling."

"Hurry. Please catch up to them." My head bows, and I do something I have not done since I was a child: I pray. "Heavenly Father, I am not worthy to ask anything of Thee. We both know *why*. I'm not asking for me; I'm asking for Jomo. He's just a lost little boy who has no one to care for him. Please help me to find him. Please, God, please."

Gavin slams on the brakes, and I lunge forward, smacking my forehead against the dashboard. "I'm okay," I say, scrabbling to get out.

The boys have stopped in front of us at the end of a road with trees that butt up against a small stretch of jungle.

I go right past Malik and head directly for the boy who is wearing Jomo's shirt. He's years older, and the shirt is clearly too small for him, but I recognize it.

"That's Jomo's shirt!" I scream. "Where did you get it?"

The boy moves his hat back, and I remember his scars—lines and lines of thin scars down his forehead. His eyes are cold and hard.

"Where? When?" I demand.

He laughs. The others join him, and I feel dizzy.

"Jomo!"

More laughter. Free of the uncle's presence, the boys are more brazen.

A hand grabs mine. I think it's Gavin's, and I spin around to jerk free. I'm wrong; Malik is the one clenching my wrist. "I told you before, you do not belong here. A *mzungu* woman like you is a bad omen. All of his life Jomo was safe with us. You came and made Jomo disappear."

"I didn't! Maybe *he* did!" I jab at the scar-faced boy, wanting to rip Jomo's yellow shirt from his body. "Ask him where he got it."

Malik rubs grease from his chin. "*I* gave him that shirt. Those shoes also."

I look down and see that the boy is wearing the sneakers I gave to Jomo. They are filthy and laceless now, but they are still the shoes I once laced to *Jomo's* feet.

Fear seethes inside of me. "Where? How?"

Gavin steps between us, forcing Malik to let go of my wrist. "You must tell us how you got Jomo's clothes." Gavin's tone is soft and pleading, but forceful.

"My uncle said you offered money for Jomo." His fat pink tongue flicks out like a snake.

Gavin's eyes go cold. "You misunderstood. I said there would be a reward for Jomo's safe return."

"How much?"

Gavin straightens his spine. "Do you know where Jomo is?"

"*Do* you?" I try not to scream.

"No." Malik crosses his arms, and I see that he has traded the metal piece of pipe for his *panga* with its jagged edges. "I will tell you what I know, and I will speak the truth."

I brace myself for anything.

"I found the clothes and shoes in a pile behind Mama Grace's school—the very night this *mzungu* woman came back to our village."

The look he gives me sends a chill up my spine.

"The clothes were in a heap, all new and clean. I gave them to my friends."

His "friends" sneer.

"They were Jomo's," I say.

"I did not know that. When I found them they had no owner, and Jomo was nowhere around."

"When did you find them?" I ask.

"I told you. When I went looking for Jomo and my uncle's bike."

I can picture the whole scene as he describes it. "What about the new jeans?" I ask. "I bought Jomo jeans to go with his shirt and shoes."

Malik shrugs. "There were no jeans in the pile."

"What about his old clothes . . . a gray shirt and pants?"

"I have spoken the truth."

My mind darts in a million directions. "There must be witnesses. Someone *has* to know what happened to Jomo."

"Ask anyone you choose," Malik says, touching the sharp edge of the *panga* with his thumb.

"How about you?" I shout at Malik's friends. "You must know something."

They look to Malik.

"They know nothing. Do not question our honor. You are the one who made Jomo disappear."

His words make me flinch. I remember how thrilled Jomo was with his new clothes. I remember the plans we made. I can still feel his little hand squeezing mine. Why would he abandon his new clothes? Nothing made sense to me.

"Help me find Anyango," I say. "If we can find her, she might know where Jomo is."

"I do not know where Anyango works. Try the cardboard streets at night."

"The cardboard streets?"

Gavin shakes his head. "You don't want to know."

"I want to know *everything*," I insist. Gavin's arm tightens around my shoulders, and I realize for the first time that my whole body is shaking.

Malik puts his knife back in its sheath. He speaks to Gavin. "I am sorry if we frightened your woman friend. I am also worried about Jomo. He is much like a brother to me."

Gavin nods. "Do you mind if we have the police investigate?"

The boy wearing Jomo's shirt ducks his head.

"No," says Malik. "We would welcome the police. Finding Jomo is what matters."

I'm numb as Gavin helps me back into the truck. Hope has drained from every inch of my body.

"I think Malik might be telling the truth," he says softly.

I look out and watch the boys ride away, see the flash of yellow fade down a red dirt road. "That's what I'm afraid of."

CHAPTER 22

The police assign one officer to investigate my missing person claim.

Officer Habib takes meticulous notes. He makes direct eye contact with me. He nods and grunts and seems to care.

"What progress have you made since I made my report?" I ask.

He yawns, showing off a mouthful of teeth that need dental attention. "This is a very difficult case, Mama."

"I have to leave town for a business trip," I tell him, "but I don't want to go before Jomo is found."

For the fourth time this week, we sit in a back office with no window and no air conditioning. His white shirt is stained with half circles beneath his arms. "Would you care for a cup of *chai?*" he asks.

"No. No. Have you actually gone out to Mama Grace's village to search? How about Malik and his uncle—have you spoken with them? I think they know more than they're saying."

"The slums of Nairobi provide ample places for a child to hide."

"Jomo is not *hiding,*" I say, trying to calm my frustration. "He's *missing*. In my country every police officer would be on the lookout."

He leans back and scratches at a scab on his nose. "You are now in Kenya, Mama. Do you mean to imply that our police are inferior to yours?"

"I don't understand why you are not doing anything to help find Jomo—or his sister, for that matter. Have you searched for her?"

"She is not reported missing, this sister. What is her name?" He shuffles through a stack of papers.

"Anyango."

"And how do you know her?"

"She is Jomo's older sister. I have never met her."

"Then how do you know she has gone missing?"

"I don't know that she is missing. I only know that Jomo vanished. Disappeared. Doesn't one little boy matter to you people?"

The scab on his nose oozes a tiny drop of dark blood. "I can see that you are very upset. This child means much to you."

"Very much."

"I am not as lazy as you think. I have ridden out to Redemption Road. I have seen with my own eyes the place where the boy slept. It is very sad."

"Then you understand, *bosi,* that a little boy's life is at stake."

"Yes, so you say."

His belly hangs over his belt, and I think, *At least one African is getting enough to eat.* Now he scratches the inside of his ear with his pinky finger.

"Do you know the spool districts of Nairobi?" I ask.

He rocks toward me on his chair. "What does a *mzungu,* pretty and polished like you, know about Nairobi's spool districts?"

"I know Jomo's sister might be there."

"There?"

"The spool district."

"Oh, Mama, there is not a single spool district, but a spool district in every neighborhood, in every village. Sex work happens on every street."

I rub my throbbing temples and ask, "What are the cardboard streets of Nairobi? Someone said Anyango might be there."

Officer Habib wipes the blood from his nose on his shirt sleeve. "The cardboard streets, they are in the spool districts. Sex workers use large cardboard boxes as their places of business. It is extremely tragic."

A ghastly picture works its way into my head. "You're right . . . it's all very tragic."

"I do have a question for *you,* Mama," the officer says.

"What?"

"What is your interest in this boy, Jomo?"

"I've told you before—I care about him."

"I see that. Why do you care so much about one boy gone missing?"

"If you knew Jomo, you would understand."

He leans forward and clears this throat. "Are you, Lana Carter, in some way responsible for this Jomo's disappearance?"

I catch my breath. It's the same accusation Malik made. "Me?"

"Yes."

"No. Like I've told you before, I only met Jomo a few weeks ago. I played games with him, read to him, and bought him clothes—the clothes I told you about."

"You appear upset."

"I *am* upset. Why would you assume I had anything to do with Jomo's disappearance?"

"Malik and his uncle tell me that you were apparently the last person to see the boy."

I jump to my feet.

He pushes a flat palm at me. "Sit back down, Mama. I am not accusing you of foul play. I am sure, though, that you are in part responsible for Jomo's vanishing."

I feel like my head is in a vise. "How can you say that?"

He glances through his notebook. "You bought the boy new clothes."

"Yes."

"A yellow shirt, jeans, and white shoes."

"Yes."

"Yes, well . . . did you purchase new clothes for any other village children?"

"No." Like lead, guilt sinks to the bottom of my heart.

He slaps the notebook on the desktop. The look he gives me is reminiscent of the look Mama Grace has given me more than once. "You unwittingly made the boy a target for robbery."

"What are you talking about? *How?*"

"What was Jomo wearing before you purchased bright, new clean clothes for him?"

"A gray shirt and pants, worn to rags." The memory rushes back, washes over me like a furious tide. I see Jomo's smile. I see his dirty little hands and feet. I see his sheer joy and feel his arms around me, hugging me tight. The officer is right. He's telling me what Mama Grace tried to tell me: my gift made Jomo a target. How long did he wear that yellow T-shirt before someone ripped it off his back, tore the shoes from his feet? And what, *God in Heaven,* happened after that? Silently, with only my spirit screaming, I pray like I've never prayed. Please forgive me. *Forgive me, and don't punish Jomo for my stupidity.*

Officer Habib slaps his notebook shut. "We could make flyers if we had a photograph of the boy."

"I'm sorry. I don't have a photo. No one does." I had my digital camera at the school that day. Why didn't I think to take a photo of Jomo? It is one of the first things I'll do when he's returned safely.

"What about a sketch artist? I know every detail of Jomo's face. I can describe him, and someone can make a sketch."

Officer Habib sighs. "I will ask my superior if that is a feasible approach. Our budget here is very limited for a single missing child."

Luke 12:6 comes into my mind. *Not one sparrow is forgotten before God.*

"You look ill, Mama." Officer Habib stands up, and with the toe of his shoe he pushes a small black garbage can toward me. "If you are going to vomit, please use the can, go outside, or visit the toilet. I do not want you to vomit in here. There is no window in here, and I do not enjoy the scent of vomit."

CHAPTER 23

It turns out my father's fear for me is justified. Nairobi *is* one of the most dangerous places on earth. Crime grows like grass during the rainy season. Terrorism is bred here. Children who are hungry in both body and spirit, who see no hope for a future, are vulnerable to the shine and clink of evil.

During all the time I've been here, I've only looked at the endless blue skies, the rich red dirt, the lush green foliage, and the exotic wild animals. I've seen the city—but to me, it was not much different from many of the other cities of the world. I have only chosen to see a very small part of Africa.

Tonight I see another side of Nairobi. Nygoya and I are out walking the streets, looking for the girl called Anyango. She might be my only link to Jomo. We know next to nothing about her, and yet we know that she, too, is orphaned, leaving her Jomo's sole surviving relative. At age twelve, she has resorted to selling her body for money. I can only imagine Anyango's desperation.

Nygoya gives me one of her patented stares. "You're out to save this girl as well, are you not?"

"If I can. It's part of my vow."

"What vow?"

"I promised myself that if I find Jomo, I'll do whatever I can to improve his life and his sister's, too. I appreciate you coming with me; everyone else thinks I've lost my mind."

"Just your heart," she says. Nygoya is dressed in a camouflage outfit complete with a beret. I know she's got a loaded gun in her backpack; she showed it to me.

We pass a building off in the distance, and she points it out as the embassy. "It was only in 1998 that al Qaeda bombed it," she said. "That was a very dark day for my country."

"For mine, too," I say, remembering that at least 200 people were killed and 4,000 wounded. It was a precursor to what happened in New York City and Washington, D.C., on September 11, 2001.

"None of this darkness would be here," Nygoya says, "if Jesus was allowed into the hearts of the people."

"I'm beginning to think that's true," I say, feeling my own heart begin to crack.

"Of course it's true."

We make our way down an alley so narrow Nygoya has a difficult time maneuvering. Dark eyes stare. Children whimper but do not cry. They all wonder what a woman as white as I am is doing here. I am as curious as they are.

I hear someone scream and turn to see a woman being dragged by her arm into a building. I try to go help her, but Nygoya's grip jerks me back.

"No."

"She might be hurt."

"Everyone here hurts. Keep moving."

We go past a narrow doorway, and I see my first spool.

"Sex work goes on in there," Nygoya says. "It goes on and never stops."

I pause to ask a woman if she knows a girl named Anyango.

Nygoya has to translate for me.

"She does not know Anyango. Keep walking."

I feel eyes on my back as we make our way into the darkest shadows of the city.

Nygoya guides me by my elbow. "I believe I understand now why you are so driven to save Jomo."

"Help me understand then."

"You are like Jesus."

"Ha."

"Do not mock me, *bosi*. Jesus got his joy in saving souls who were lost and forgotten. You are much like Jesus. It is one of the reasons you wish so desperately to save Jomo."

A man with no legs scoots past us on a piece of cardboard. His forearms are massive, like a body builder's, and I watch him slide up to a group of women and begin a conversation. Another man approaches us and asks if we are interested in purchasing *banji*.

Nygoya towers over him. "Do I look like the kind of lady who smokes dope?" she shouts. She is at least a foot taller than the man, and he slinks back into the shadows like a frightened snake.

We keep walking. "Why else do you think I want to save Jomo?" I ask her.

"Because the secret from your past holds you prisoner."

Her words knock the wind right out of me. It is true that I want to save Jomo, more than anything I've ever wanted before; it is also true that Nygoya's insight holds merit. In saving Jomo, a part of me hopes I'll claim a piece of my own redemption. "Maybe you're right," I say.

She stops and clamps a hand on my shoulder. "You cannot do it, Lana. You will fail in trying to save your own soul."

"Oh?"

"My *Bwana* is the only One mighty to save. Not you. Not me. Only mighty Bwana."

Nygoya is my friend, but I have never shared with her or anyone else the corners of my past. Her insight amazes me. I think about her words and tell her, "You should be a preacher."

Her arms spread so wide she touches both sides of the narrow alley. "I *am* a preacher. I am many things."

The alley opens onto a sidewalk strewn with cardboard boxes and sprawled blankets. The boxes have been converted to tent-like structures—offices. People are everywhere, and I'm sickened by the reality of the world Anyango is said to inhabit.

"The *mazani* do their work right there on the streets."

Prostitutes. Women, men, children. There are no words black enough to describe my feelings.

The street is dark but busy. Cars move slowly up and down the road. Girls and boys alike are where they should not be.

"I don't know if I can do this," I say. My buried memories are resurrecting themselves. With the return of the memory comes fear and pain. "You know something, Nygoya? I came all the way to

Africa to get away from my past, but you're right: it's right here in front of me."

"You want to tell me what you are talking about?"

"Not really."

"So you *are* a woman with a past."

I catch my own reflection in a storefront window. "We all have mysteries."

She laughs, and her earrings jangle. "You can take my arm if you need strength."

"I'll be okay."

"You can carry my gun if that will help."

"I'm okay."

"You paid a great sum of money to have Jomo's sketch made. What are you going to do with the flyers if you cannot pass them out?"

I carry hundreds of small flyers with Jomo's sketch and my cell number. Officer Habib warned me not to offer a monetary reward that would only endanger other little street boys. Finally, I'm beginning to understand.

I pass out a flyer to a pregnant woman with a toddler on her hip. She takes the flyer, studies it, and tries to hand it back.

"No," I say, "please keep it and call me if you see this boy or find anyone who knows him."

The woman waves the flyer in my face. *"Katu!"*

Nygoya grabs it from her hand and says to me, "These people don't know how to read. They don't have access to a telephone. Your pretty white face has no place here."

"I thought you told me to come."

"No. You told me you were coming, and I told you I'd accompany you. I serve as your valiant bodyguard."

I swallow my fear and take Nygoya's arm. As we progress deeper into the district, we manage to pass out most of the flyers. I see sights so vile and heartrending that they will never leave my memory.

No one seems to recognize Jomo. No one.

"This is just one night, one district," Nygoya says, trying to cheer me up. "While you are gone with Gavin McQueen on safari, I will continue to search for Anyango and Jomo."

"It will not be safe for you to come to a place like this alone."

She laughs her famous belly laugh. "So I am safe because I am with *you*? An ostrich feather weighs more than you, Lana."

"I can be tough when I have to be," I say.

"I do not doubt that, but can you lift an elephant gun and blow two and a half poachers away with one shot?"

I stop and stare at my friend. "Did you *really* do that?"

"If you do not believe me, ask the remaining half of the last poacher. His one arm, his one leg, and half of his brain are doing time at the Kamiti Maximum Prison."

"I believe you. I believe you."

"Good—because I might murder, but I do not lie."

"You are a true *rafiki*," I say.

Nygoya nods. "Yes, I am. I told you: I am many things."

CHAPTER 24

Mama Grace's hand weaves long strands of dried grass, around and around, through and over, until her creation takes the shape of a basket. Her fingers are so practiced she hardly glances at what they are doing. Her hands are always busy. Braiding a child's hair, turning the pages of a book, stirring, soothing.

Today the heat is stifling and the air motionless. We have taken a small picnic of fruit and bottled water to the stretching shade of a baobab tree on the jungle side of Mama's village. Its massive trunk is wide enough to house a full-sized sedan.

"There is a forest in California," I tell Mama Grace. "This tree reminds me of the ancient redwoods my parents took my sister and me to see when we were young."

"You must have many fond memories of your childhood."

"More than I ever realized."

She smiles at me, and I am grateful for the respite, even though I feel guilty. I should be out searching for Jomo. But where do I look that I haven't already hunted?

This is a side of the village I'm not familiar with. It is greener and removed from the throngs of people and shanties. A small muddy stream trickles a few feet away from where we sit. Bugs are on the ground and in the air. In the distance dark faces stare, but when children make their way toward us, adults pull them back.

"What's going on?" I ask. "I'm always surrounded by children every time I come."

Mama Grace's fingers slow but do not stop. "Now parents are fearful for their children."

144 TONI SORENSON BROWN

"Why?"

She looks thoughtful. "It could be one of two reasons. They could be protecting the children from me . . ." My mind wraps around the reality that Mama is HIV positive. " . . . or you."

"Or *me* what?"

"People could be avoiding you, Lana."

"Why me?"

"Because the word on the wind is that you are stirring spirits to anger."

"I'm what? How?"

"Your search for Jomo disturbs the refugee spirits that live here." She gently pats the base of the massive trunk.

"Spirits live in this giant tree?"

"Yes." Her voice is flat, and I know she believes what she is telling me. "The spirits of dead village children take refuge here."

"Why do you believe *that?*"

Her fingers continue weaving, and the tone she takes is one of a teacher. "Children who die and are not permitted a proper burial lose their way. Their spirits have no home, so they reside here. Your search for Jomo has disturbed them."

"Please tell me that you're not suggesting Jomo is dead."

She looks at me. "If he is . . ."

"He isn't! Don't even think that."

". . . If he is, Jomo's spirit may well seek shelter here."

I want to leap to my feet and shout, but I manage to stay seated and keep my voice steady. "Mama Grace, Jomo is *not* dead."

"Lana, you must know it is a possibility."

I push back on the heels of my palms and feel the grit of the earth grind into my skin. "Jomo is not dead, and the spirits of children who die do not dwell in trees; they go straight to heaven."

"I thought you were one who knew nothing of heaven."

"I know what happens to children when they die."

"And how do you know?"

Suddenly I'm back in our Utah living room, twenty years ago. My father is teaching a family home evening lesson out of the Book of Mormon. "I just know," I tell Mama, and something inside of me burns hot and true. "Mama Grace, God does not punish little children who die without baptism or a proper burial."

One eyebrow lifts. "Now you know *Bwana*? When did you meet Him?"

"Are you mocking me?"

"Not in the least. I am telling you that there are many spirits here living in this tree, all of them the spirits of dead children. They dwell in torment for eternity because they were deprived a proper burial. This tree is the *only* refuge they will ever know."

"No," I say slowly, a fever burning in my stomach, my chest, my throat, and finally on my tongue.

Mama Grace's eyes go wide. "What do *you* believe happens when a child is eaten by a crocodile, a child whose little body is never recovered?"

It feels like my very body is aflame. "A child's spirit goes straight to heaven. Back to God—to *Bwana*."

"And what becomes of the spirit?"

"The spirit goes to heaven; it never dies."

She scoffs. "And the destroyed body?"

"It turns to dust . . . but only for a time. Then that body, made perfect, is resurrected." I grab two pieces of long grass and weave them quickly together. "Body and spirit . . . they make the soul."

Mama swats at a pestering fly. "You surprise me, Lana. You are very passionate about this idea."

"Yeah, I guess I am. I know there is no limbo for the spirits of innocent children. They go straight back home to heaven."

Her smile is almost condescending. "Can you show me this in the Bible?"

"No. Maybe. I don't know if it's in the Bible, but . . ."

Mama Grace's smile widens. "Lana, what you say is nice, but it is not true."

My words are confused, but not my feelings. "I know what I am telling you *is* true. There are no spirits of dead children trapped in the trunk of this baobab or any other tree."

She pats my hand, smiles sympathetically, and returns to her weaving. "Perhaps we should change the subject. Let's speak of your upcoming safari. Are you not excited?"

"Not really."

That night lying in bed with a beam of blue moonlight streaming through my bedroom window, I fall to my knees by my bedside.

Again, words fail me. What can I say to a God I have ignored, disregarded, and disrespected most of my life? I stay there, unable to come up with anything. At first the coolness from the stone floor seeps up and into me. I am so cold I quiver. But then the warmth I felt before returns, and finally—when my knees hurt and my back aches, when the blue moonlight is all but gone—I open my mouth and out comes a one-word prayer so powerful it says everything I feel.

"Father."

CHAPTER 25

I make the most of the time off Mr. C has given me. He allows me to use my office as a command station to help locate Jomo. Nygoya screens my calls. It seems everyone who has seen my flyer has a little boy they would like me to believe is Jomo. Even though no monetary reward was offered, people hope I will come up with one. I check out every lead. I meet a dozen homeless little boys; each one takes a piece of my heart, but none of them are Jomo.

Still, I write each name down, record whatever vital information I can about each one of these boys. I make sure I take a digital portrait of every child. How I wish I'd done that for Jomo.

"Why are you taking such an interest in *these* boys?" Nygoya asks me.

"So that they can attend Mama Grace's school when it opens. I'll start a perpetual scholarship fund."

"Another very noble idea," is her only reply.

A new day dawns, and Mama Grace asks me for a favor. She wants to ride in the hotel's van to the unwanted baby center. She's anxious to check on the infant girl that was dropped off on her front stoop.

"I've been thinking about her," I say. "Wondering if she's all right. She was so little and so sick."

"I am hopeful that she is stronger now; the center makes miracles of sick babies." Mama Grace leans back and lets the breeze from the open window blow in her face. I have not told her that I know about her HIV, but I can't help studying her. Some days I think she looks weak, but not today. Today she looks well—strong, even.

"Lana, you look very tired. Have I asked you this favor on a difficult day?"

"No. No. I'm happy to do it for you. I'm still taking time away from work, the time Mr. C gave me before my safari adventure. There is no one I'd rather be with."

She smiles. "You are still sure that Jomo is in danger?"

"Aren't you?"

"I've been thinking on this matter. Perhaps Jomo has gone off with other friends or a relative we do not know about. Perhaps where you think there is a problem . . . there is none."

My heart skips a beat. "Do you think that's possible?"

"I think anything is possible."

"I wish I knew for sure."

"What does your stomach tell you?"

"My stomach?"

She points to her belly button. "A woman can know things through a feeling here."

"You mean a gut feeling?"

"Yes. A gut feeling. What does yours tell you?"

I have to take a deep breath and hold it as I build my confidence. "That Jomo is okay. I know I'll find him."

"I pray for you, Lana. I pray for Jomo."

"Thank you, my *rafiki*. I have no doubt that God hears *your* prayers."

"Do you think *Bwana's* ears are closed to your pleas?"

"I hope not."

I'm surprised to see that the building housing the unwanted baby center is new—larger than Mama's school, better equipped and surprisingly clean. Still it is primitive and overcrowded. Three babies lie in a single crib. Four cribs line each wall. The floor is gray, the walls are gray, and the cribs are made of gray metal. Baby nurseries are not supposed to be gray.

With so many babies, I expect the place to be unbearably noisy. It is unnaturally still instead.

"Mama Grace!"

Mama Dale comes running for us and rushes at Grace. The friends embrace and speak in rapid Swahili.

Hesitantly, I walk through the shelter looking for one little girl. It has only been days, but I cannot recall her face. I remember exactly how she felt in my arms. Her sad little whimper still plays in my ears, but what does she *look* like? All of the babies here, all of them, are varying shades of black. All are young and all look hungry to be fed, to be loved.

Mama Grace does not hesitate. She moves directly to a crib across the room and lifts a baby wearing nothing but a cloth diaper. It is the little girl. I see that now—her fuzzy little hair, her small elfin ears, her wide tender eyes. Her stomach is swollen, and I can count her ribs one by one, but her eyes shine when Grace's lips are pressed to her forehead.

"They call her Gracie, in honor of me." Mama Grace beams. "Would you care to hold her, Lana?"

I nod and hold out my arms. This time Gracie smells like a baby—not pink-lotion clean, but bar-soap clean. She is still too thin, but there is life in her limbs and she nuzzles against my neck, molds her frail little body into my embrace. Her baby breath somehow breathes life into me, and I feel my own limbs strengthen.

Nygoya is right about me: I am not the same woman I was months ago. Until lately the sole focus of my life was on me. It feels terrifying to think of someone else, to care more about someone else, than I do about myself, but it also feels *right*.

"You make a very good mother," Mama Grace says, leaning over my shoulder.

She has no way of knowing the pain her words cause me, and I mask my feelings with a quick smile.

"Are you finally happy?" Mama Grace asks.

"For this moment." Thoughts of Jomo enter my head, and I press Gracie to me.

"That is a moment longer than many people receive." Grace wanders off, and I see that women work all around me, caring for babies. They are so outnumbered, it would be impossible for all of the infant needs to be met. One woman, with an ample shape that reminds me of Nygoya, balances two babies, one in each arm. I think how my own mother once managed Laura and me at the same time. I think how she would go insane trying to love all of these love-starved babies. A pang of missing my mother hits me, and I have to bite my lip to keep from tearing up.

Another nurse, lugging something that vaguely resembles a wooden rocking chair, approaches me.

"Sit. Rock." She motions wide and welcoming.

I sit. I rock. I watch as African women, Mama Grace right in the middle, care for African children. It is impossible for me to fathom how these babies, dozens, have been cast aside.

A little girl storms into the room and heads directly for Mama Dale. It is the same little girl with the elaborate braids and pink gingham dress. The "I Am a Child of God" girl.

"Hi," I say, and the little girl smiles. "What is your name?"

"My name is Benda."

"How do you know that song?" I ask, still curious.

"Sing? You know words."

I quietly sing, and she hums along. The lyrics and melody come back to me like a soft, warm blanket.

"You cry?" Benda asks.

I wipe away the tears wandering down my cheek. "Do you know Jomo?"

"Jomo." She smiles.

"Yes! Jomo. He's a little boy about your age from Mama Grace's village."

"Jomo."

"I'm afraid my daughter does not think." Mama Dale is beside me, smiling down at her daughter, stroking her hair. "She does not think like most children do. Her brain is sick."

It takes a moment for me to understand what Mama Dale is saying. Benda is autistic. Her mother hands her a small rag doll, and the girl skips out of the room.

"I'm sorry," I say, because it's the only thing I can think of to say.

Mama Dell is unfazed. "You were asking Benda about Jomo?"

"Yes! Have you heard anything more about him?"

"No, but I can see what Mama Grace says is true: the missing boy means much to your heart."

"Yes. He does."

"Do you have children of your own?"

The question stabs like a knife to my heart. "No. I'm not a mother."

Another nurse, one I have not seen before, approaches Mama Dale with a bottle for Gracie. She hands it to me, and this time Gracie has no trouble wrapping her lips around the soft rubber nipple and sucking down the white milky formula.

Mama Dell stoops over, smiles at Gracie, and asks me, "What have you done to locate Jomo?"

I tell her of the trips through Mama Grace's village. I tell her about Malik and the missing bicycle. I tell her about the flyers and the pleading to get the police motivated.

She sighs. "It is difficult for so few to do so much."

"I suppose."

"Your *rafiki* Nygoya is much help, I presume."

"You know Nygoya?"

"Oh, yes. We have known each other many years."

Mama Dale clears her throat and fixes her eyes on me. "Have you contacted the bishop for assistance?"

At first I am sure I have misunderstood. "Did you say the *bishop?*"

"Yes. Bishop Kaahari. He is a famed Kenyan long-distance runner and has much influence with those in authority."

I'm confused. She could *not* be talking about a Mormon bishop. We are in the slums of Nairobi. "I don't understand."

"My daughter told me that you know our song, 'I Am a Child of God.' Nygoya told me that you claim to be Mormon." Her eyebrows lift. "You *are* a Latter-day Saint, are you not?"

I look away at a small window. Outside, a long line of dingy cloth diapers droop. I look back at Mama Dale and admit, "Not a very good one."

"That is unfortunate for you. I am most proud to be a Latter-day Saint. My father was one of the first Black Africans to be baptized in Kenya. Our family was sealed in the temple in Johannesburg."

I can't believe what I'm hearing. "I can run, but I can't hide," I tell her.

"Pardon?"

"Nothing. I think I remember my own father telling me something about a church in Nairobi, but I had no idea there were Mormons here."

She laughs. "Not enough, but we are working on growing more."

I smile. "So the book I saw you give to Mama Grace—it really was a . . ."

". . . Book of Mormon? Yes. For years, I have been telling Mama Grace that she would make an excellent member of the Church. Do you not think so?"

Little Gracie pulls her mouth away from the bottle and looks up at me with bright smiling eyes. I see the hint of a dimple in her cheek.

"Yes," I say to Mama Dale. "I think she would."

"Would you care for me to contact Bishop Kaahari and ask him to help you try to locate your missing boy?"

I nod. "Yes, please. I would like that very much."

Before I hear anything further from Mama Dale it is time to leave on safari. I feel like I'm running out, running away when I'm needed here, but there are no new leads on Jomo. The police talked to Malik and came away with the same story he told Gavin and me.

Mr. C is insisting that I make a serious evaluation of Moja Outfitters. I don't know how I'm going to concentrate on anything until I know Jomo is found safe.

"I do not understand you, Lana," Nygoya says. She has come to help me pack, and there is little room left in my small flat.

"What?"

"Most women would be thrilled for a three-day journey into the bush with a man like Gavin." She holds up my red bikini. It doesn't even cover half of her chest.

"The only guy I'm interested in is Jomo."

"I think that you are possessed."

I smile. "You mean *obsessed.*"

"No. *Possessed* is the word I want to say. You have a spirit that is evil."

"I do not!"

"You are not the happy woman you were when you first came to Africa."

"I'm beginning to realize that, but I'm not sure that's bad." There have been so many changes inside of me, changes even *I* don't understand.

Nygoya decides against the bikini and tosses it back into my drawer. "I worry for you."

"For me? Why?"

Nygoya clears her throat. She hasn't shaved her head in days, and healthy black stubble is emerging. "I worry that you may have to face down the lion."

"The lion?"

"The lion is what we call the truth. I worry that you will die if you find out that something sad has become of Jomo."

I ease myself to the edge of a bench in front of my window. The monkeys outside are screeching. "I know that something terrible might have happened to him. If it did, it's my fault."

"How?"

"For once in my life, I wanted to feel good about *myself*. I was thinking about how Jomo would look, how he'd feel, in brand-new clothes. I wanted him to know I cared. Once again, all I was really thinking about was myself. In the end, what I did made him a bright-yellow target."

"How could you know?"

"Mama Grace tried to tell me. The police have told me. Why didn't I see it?"

Nygoya shakes her head. "I know you are my superior at work, but here we are equals. I must tell you the truth."

"Okay."

"You are only human, and human eyes cannot see everything. *Bwana*'s eyes alone see everything."

CHAPTER 26

I don't mention anything more to my family about Jomo. They've got enough to worry about, and I'm not sure they would understand the intensity of my feelings.

The morning of the safari there is still no news about Jomo, but I receive an email from Dad:

Dear Lana:

How are you, princess? Africa seems a little closer somehow. Your mother has taken to renting DVDs set in Africa. I am still studying about Blacks and the gospel. Your mother and I attended a group in Salt Lake City—the Genesis Group, Black Latter-day Saints who gather to fellowship. They are the most wonderful people. I've never seen such great faith or devotion to the gospel. Many of them were converted *before* 1978. I'm hoping to forge some new friendships. Your old dad could learn a lesson or two, even now. Of course your mother has no problem adjusting; she has already volunteered to teach Primary. You should see the smiling black faces of those children. They are so precious; but then I guess I'm preaching to the choir. You are surrounded there by those precious faces every day.

I know you've been talking with your sister. She pretends to be so strong, but Laura is having a rough time of it. I'd take the cancer from her if I could. She has so much ahead of her to do, and here I am, healthy and strong as a Cape buffalo. How's that for an African simile?

We are all living on tested faith right now. Nobody around here has your strength, your wisdom, your wit.

We're a bit jealous of your upcoming safari trip. Be sure and send lots of pictures. Laura's kids want you to get them some souvenirs.

We miss you, princess.

Dad

Gavin's enthusiasm for the adventure lifts my sodden spirits. He is like a child getting ready to enter an amusement park. The airplane we take from the city to the bush is not large. I'm introduced to the other guests—two guides besides Gavin, the pilot, and seven other guests besides me. Gavin introduces himself and his guides; one is tall and willow thin, the other shorter, with cheekbones so wide I can't help staring.

The other safari-goers are in groups of families or friends. They come from Africa, England, Denmark, and the United States. Ruby, a loud woman with frizzy red hair, is from Mississippi and has the thickest southern accent I've ever heard.

"Oh, you poor thing," she says directly to me. "Ya'll are all alone?"

"Yes."

"Such a pity for such a pretty girl. A safari is something that should be shared with someone you love."

"I'm an independent woman," I say, trying not to take offense.

"I'm sure you are, honey, but if you get lonely or afraid of the wild animals out there," she swings a flabby pale arm, "just come to us. Me and my son, Heber, we'll take you in. How old are ya'll anyway, hon?"

"Old enough."

"Heber, here," she grabs at her son, a fifty-year-old doughy-looking man with an extra chin so immense it looks like an added appendage, "he's on the lookout for a wife. We'd welcome ya'll's company."

"Hi, Heber," I say, backing up to find my seat. I stare out the window at the tarmac and wonder what I've gotten myself into. The deepest part of my heart feels like I'm abandoning Jomo. Gavin glides past in a hurry but stops long enough to wink at me and mouth the words, "I'm glad you're here."

I smile and look back out my window. When the plane lifts, the land rolls out like a thick, gold carpet. As it whizzes past, the realization hits me that Jomo is somewhere below me. "Please let him be okay," I whisper in prayer, a habit that's beginning to feel more and more natural.

Gavin sits by me and buckles up. "You okay?"

"Everyone seems really excited," I say.

"Except you."

"No. This is a phenomenal opportunity, one I've wanted since before I came to Africa. I *am* excited."

"If you say so."

I know I should be relishing every moment. I should be taking notes for Mr. C's report. Instead, I'm back in Grace's village. I'm back to the afternoon when a wild, worn tire came bounding at me. I look down at my hand and imagine seeing Jomo's little fingers laced between mine. It's a sensation that keeps coming back.

The woman with a Mississippi accent waves her hand and calls to Gavin, saying, "Guide! Guide!"

"Yes, Ruby?" Gavin cranks around and looks down the aisle.

"Is it true that African tribes still practice slavery?"

"Some."

"What kind of slavery?" a voice calls out.

Ruby answers. "Tribes raid each other. They'll capture women and children, young men, and sell them. I read about it in *National Geographic*. I think it was *National Geographic*. Maybe it was . . . "

I yank Gavin's sleeve. "Could that be what happened to Jomo?"

The look he gives me is grim. "I suppose it's possible. Jomo could have been taken from the village; he could be working on a cattle ranch or on a tobacco farm."

The weight in my chest is so heavy it could bring the whole plane down.

"How can that happen?" I ask. "Africa is a civilized continent."

His eyebrows rise. "It is? You've only been to Nairobi, right?"

"Yes. But I know . . . "

"It's okay, Lana. Bad things happen everywhere."

"Yes, but stealing little boys? How could God allow such a thing?"

"That question seems to be replaying in your head."

He's right. How could God allow such good people, such innocent children—millions and millions of them—to starve or die of
disease? How could He not keep one little boy safe? How could He
let Mama Grace suffer HIV? How could He choose cancer for the
righteous sister, the one with six needy children?

All the warm, open feelings I've had are beginning to ice over.

Once the plane reaches altitude and levels out, Gavin stands up
and moves to the front. He fields questions and talks about the land
over which we are flying. I try to concentrate, impressed by Gavin's
knowledge and ability.

"If you'll look to the left, you'll see the snow-capped peaks of
Mount Kilimanjaro."

Everyone but me turns to the left. My eyes stay put on Gavin,
who looks back at me and grins.

I get a fluttery feeling I haven't felt since I was a teenager. It's so
unexpected and so strong, I feel my cheeks blush. How could I be
thinking of Gavin *that way* when I have so many more important
things to concentrate on? Besides, for him our relationship is strictly
professional. He *has* to impress me if he wants the hotel's business.

"How much of Kenya is wild?" someone asks.

Gavin is quick to respond. "If by *wild* you mean game territory,
about ten percent of Kenya is dedicated to national parks and
reserves. We'll be making a rather unusual hop and skip on this safari.
We've got three days to discover what should take three years."

"Will we see lions?" Ruby asks.

"If you keep your eyes open."

"What about elephants?"

"You can see those right now, if you'd care to." As the plane
descends, gray boulders on the ground transform into lumbering
mounds as elephants move through the tangle of acacia trees. I
suddenly have an overpowering desire to show my family this sight. I
wish my parents, Laura and her family . . . I wish Jomo was here.

"Elephants are the most ornery creatures in Africa," Gavin
announces.

Ruby slaps Heber's shoulder. "Hear that? Something ornerier than
you, Hebie."

"I'm not ornery. I'm sensitive."

I see a few people trying not to laugh.

"It's true," Gavin says. "More people are killed in Africa by elephants than by any other animal."

He continues to point out landmarks, name rivers, offer tidbits on culture and history. I am awestruck by the enormity of Africa. It looks endless and nothing at all like the land I've come to know in Nairobi. In spite of my worries, I'm lost in the vastness and beauty of the land.

I make mental notes on Gavin's quick wit and razor expertise. I'm particularly impressed by the way Gavin treats people and how they respond to him. He makes direct eye contact, answers their questions, and makes them feel . . .

A woman with a British accent starts chattering. She sounds as though she's about to hyperventilate. "A leopard! Down there. I see it!"

The rest of us see a dead tree.

Gavin explains, "It's most rare to spot a true leopard in the wild. It is, however, possible. Mostly likely on this particular journey we'll see only three of what we call the Big Five: elephants, rhinos, lions, buffalo, and leopards."

The woman squints and suddenly shoots halfway out of her seat, squealing, "It's a giraffe! Look, everybody! I see a giraffe! No, two! Three!"

Ruby slaps Heber on the back so hard he lets out a whine. "Hebie, look there! That's something you don't spot every day in Mississippi."

Heber doesn't look out at the grazing giraffes. Instead, he looks back and makes direct eye contact with me, his eyes pleading for help.

Our air time is short, and when the plane touches down on a narrow, bumpy airstrip in the middle of the bush, it hits me that I am on a real African safari. Adrenaline pumps through me like a transfusion, and I'm determined to focus on the moment, to enjoy myself, to experience the wilds of Africa. I tell myself that by the time I get back to Nairobi, Jomo will be found safe and sound.

Gavin assists most of the passengers down from the airplane. When our hands touch, I think his grip lasts a bit longer than necessary. I don't let go first—he does, and I feel a twinge of disappointment.

I haven't prepared very well for my safari, and I don't know what to expect. I'm a bit surprised that out here in the middle of nowhere there is a private safari camp with a long, domed structure. It looks like something out of the army. Next to it is a row of crude grass huts and a *kraal* with a thorn fence and a mud-covered domed structure. It looks part Masi, part Navajo.

"Welcome to Simba One," Gavin says, introducing us to his camp.

There are facilities for at least a hundred people. We share tents that are nothing like tents the Boy Scouts pitch. They are more like military barracks. Locals greet us with typical African friendliness. I am shown to my cot, given directions to the "bush bathroom," and invited to dine with the other guests. Roasted antelope is on the menu.

"Home away from home," Gavin says to me. "Hope it's not too crude for your comfort."

"Actually," I say, "it's not much of a stretch from my flat in the city—we share the same lizards." A tiny green reptile is skittering up the wall, its thin tail twice as long as its body.

He laughs. "So you're not afraid of reptiles?"

"I'm not afraid of much."

"Good. Bravery is a quality I find very appealing in a woman."

I feel my ears flush and wish my hair was longer, or that at least I wore a hat to keep my blush from being so blatantly obvious.

"Are there any particular animals you want to see while we're on safari?"

"Lions. Lions fascinate me."

"That doesn't surprise me; you remind me of a lioness."

"How so?"

"You're sleek, strong, capable."

Now my ears are smoking. Where did these feelings come from? I don't need them now. I don't want them now.

Gavin points out at the vastness. "We are not far from the Masi Mari borderland of the lions. Have you ever been there?"

"No, but I've heard about it. I've studied how the Masi worship cattle."

"Cows are their prophets. They follow the cattle to know where to find water in a drought. They gauge their lives around the wanderings of their cattle."

"Is it true they drink blood?"

"Mostly." He sticks his tongue out and shakes his head like he's just swallowed a spoonful of cough syrup. "Nasty stuff, that concoction of blood mixed with milk."

Gavin points to the cracked mud hut in the center of the *kraal*. "Masi women construct their own houses made of grass and cow dung."

A picture of my childhood house flashes through my memory. My mother is fanatical about keeping our home clean. She buys Windex and Lysol by the case. She attacks dust like it is her mortal enemy. Whatever would she do here?

"I used to think I lived in the real world," I tell Gavin, "but this—I mean all of Africa—this is the real world. This is how people live, how they survive and triumph."

He smiles. "Be careful. Africa gets into your blood and you never are the same."

We dine in the open air on a buffet of roasted yams, lentils, and roasted antelope. Not more than a hundred yards away, a small herd of Thompson's gazelles graze, their dark triangular ears up, their white tails twitching. They remind me of baby deer.

"I'm not very hungry," I say, declining the charred piece of meat.

"Ya'll are too skinny," Ruby says. "Men aren't drawn to women who are too thin. No wonder you're still single."

We spend the hottest part of the afternoon in the shade of our tent. The air is baked and dry. I watch lizards crisscross the walls and the ceiling; they are tan, green, and gray. They hang from the posts and cling to the walls.

"Eeek," says Ruby, "they give me the creeps."

"They bothered me when I first moved to Africa. You get used to them."

She shudders and sprays a cloud of DEET. "Honey, I hate to see ya'll so alone. Are you sure you don't want to swap cots so you can be closer to my Heber? You two have so much in common."

"That's okay. I like it here."

"Suit yourself. My Hebie might not look like a movie star, but he's got a real nice personality and good benefits through his job at the post office. When I pass on, he'll inherit my house, seeing that he still lives with me."

"Um."

"You like cats, don't you?"

"Dogs."

"You ever been married?"

I take a hard look at Ruby. She's seventy years old if she's a day. Her head of bushy red hair reminds me of my mother's: one too many home perms. Ruby's skin is also red—red and wrinkled like she's stayed too long in a hot bathtub.

She lowers her voice. "You and our tour guide, ya'll don't have something going on, do you?"

"No. Just business."

Her voice goes even lower, like she's divulging a prime secret. "He looks like Robert Redford."

"Gavin?"

"Yup. The first time I laid eyes on him, I thought he's a dead ringer for Robert Redford. Taller, though. I hear Redford is a midget. He has to stand on a stack of phone books to match up to his leading ladies."

I don't tell her that I'm from Utah, that I got my start in the hotel business working at Robert Redford's Sundance resort. I feel a desire to defend Mr. Redford, but I don't because I'm tired, and Ruby is annoying. The heat is sweltering, and I wonder if Jomo is out in a place like this. When I get back to Nairobi, I'll have Officer Habib look into the possibility of a member of another tribe stealing Jomo.

I feel nauseated and go to the open flap of our tent for air. Armed bodyguards stand at the perimeter of our camp to protect us from hungry predators.

I close my eyes and wonder: Who's protecting Jomo?

CHAPTER 27

There are a couple of deep, dry ruts that Gavin calls a road. We bounce along in our Toyota Land Cruiser, built just for safaris. We have joined a caravan cutting through the lowlands, through endless sheets of waving, scored grass. It feels as though we are riding through a picture-perfect postcard.

Jomo does not leave my thoughts. I imagine him next to me, riding along, listening to Gavin point out thorn trees and all of the animals camouflaged around them.

It is hard for me not to get caught up in the safari experience. This is so different from the Africa I've known. Nairobi and her slums are only a tiny slice of an endless land and her people.

The first animals we spot are Cape buffalo. They are big and black and so far away that they appear to be bears—except for the curved horns that wind over their entire heads.

"Can we get out to get a better look?" someone asks.

Gavin motions for our driver to leave the rutty road, and we cut right through the grass. "You can't get out—it's not safe," Gavin explains. "Cape buffalo are some of the most unpredictable animals in Africa."

We get close enough for some great photo opportunities, but I can't get too stoked up about a Cape buffalo. They are about as exciting as a bull on a Utah farm.

"Don't let them fool you," Gavin says. "They might look docile, but sometimes the things that look most innocent turn out to be the most deadly."

An image blinks in my head. I see the bus driver's face—the stranger I hired to wait for me while I looked for Jomo. At first, he looked innocent enough. At the end, who knows? The memory still gives me the chills, and it triggers another memory, one even darker. One I refuse to let surface.

Next we stop to watch two-story-high giraffes pull foliage from the trees before us, using their long, black tongues with the dexterity of elephant trunks. They move with grace and strength, and even though I've seen giraffes before, seeing them here in the wild makes them different creatures.

All around me shutters are clicking, and I get my digital camera out. When I turn it on, the first image I see is one that stops my heart. I can't believe it! It is a snapshot of Jomo . . . of me and Jomo. I'm kneeling down, and his little arms are around my neck. The image doesn't show my face, but I can see Jomo's—his sparkling eyes, his wide silly grin. I see life and light and utter joy.

I keep staring, wondering who and how and when the photo was taken. It had to be Mama Grace who grabbed the camera and shot the photo. She never said anything, and I never told her how desperate I was for a photo of Jomo. I can't wait to get it to Officer Habib. Now we can make new flyers. Surely someone will give us the lead that will guide us to Jomo.

"You okay?" one of the tourists asks me.

"I'm okay."

"You look as though you've seen a ghost."

I stare at the image of Jomo, grinning from the tiny little screen. My heart is so full it wants to explode.

"I'm fine. Thanks," I say.

The man leans over and asks, "Mind if I take a look at what has you so captivated?"

I show him the tiny little screen.

"A street boy?" he asks.

How can I explain that Jomo is so much more than a street boy? All I can do is nod.

The man looks sad. "It's hard to fathom that there are twelve million orphaned children in Africa."

I squint. "Twelve million?"

"Six hundred and fifty thousand in Kenya alone."

My brain is still calculating twelve million. That's six times the number of people in Utah. Six times!

While the man keeps talking I flip through the other images on my camera, but there is only that one shot of Jomo.

Thanks, God, I say silently, hoping He knows my heart, because "thanks" doesn't come close to expressing the depth of my gratitude for one little smiling face.

Someone shouts, and the Land Cruiser lunges forward, putting an end to our conversation. Crossing the road ahead of us is a mother warthog and two young hogs.

"A face only a mother could love," Ruby says, squeezing Heber's cheeks like he's a toddler.

I keep staring at the image of Jomo. I know if I don't turn the battery off it will die, but I'm afraid if I do turn it off, the picture will be gone when I turn it back on.

Jomo feels closer than ever before, and my spirit soars with hope. We are only hours outside of Nairobi, and I can't help wondering if he has ever seen the wilds of his own country, the expanse and the beauty stretching all around me. Or has he spent his whole life seeing nothing of Africa but poverty, waste, and savageness?

When Gavin moves past me in the aisle, I stop him and show him the photo of Jomo.

"Wow. Mama Grace took that?" he asks.

"I haven't used my camera in weeks," I say. "We were snapping shots that day while we were working on her school. I didn't even know she took it."

"I'll bet you're glad she did."

"You can't imagine. Gavin, tell me something . . . has Grace been on safari?"

Gavin laughs so hard his shoulders shake. "Oh, yes. Mama Grace came with me on one of my first game drives. I thought I would teach her about Kenya, but Mama Grace can name every tree, every plant, and every animal in Africa. She knows tribes and languages and how this land breathes. Mama Grace is first a student and then a teacher."

"Who is Mama Grace?" someone asks, and I realize that other people are listening to our conversation.

"A friend to both of us," I say. "Grace is the most astounding woman. She's building a school in her village."

Gavin grins. "She's the face of Africa."

Mama Grace's face flashes before me, and I see her healthy and strong. I picture her standing on the stoop snapping that photo of me and Jomo.

We move on, slowly snaking through the grass, looking for anything alive and moving. An old, battle-scarred baboon hunches at the side of the road staring at us. Birds rise from the grass in great, dark sheets. Antelope graze wherever there is grass. I can't help getting caught up in the safari experience. But after a time we see no more animals. Gavin and the two guides lope out in front of the Toyota, trying to stir up any sleeping animal.

"What if they come upon a tiger?" Heber asks.

His mother smacks his shoulder. "Don't ya'll know nothin'? There are no tigers in Africa—only lions."

Heber grunts. "What if they stir up a sleeping lion?"

His mother laughs. "Then we'll be able to check off another of the Big Five."

"Tell me again, what are the Big Five, Ma?"

"Lions, buffalo, rhinos, elephants, and leopards."

The man I showed Jomo's picture to pipes in, "If you go on one of Gavin's ten-day safaris, he guarantees you will spot all five."

I crank around and ask, "Have you been on one of Gavin's safaris before?"

"Yes. This is my third safari with Moja Outfitters. Gavin's wife used to give anthropology lectures along the way. Fascinating. Very fascinating."

I look out to make sure that Gavin is still jogging in front of our Toyota. "What was his wife like?" I ask.

"She was very beautiful. Exotic. Serious."

"Oh." I can't seem to quell the emotions Gavin brings out in me. I keep telling myself our relationship is strictly business, but it doesn't always *feel* like business.

The caravan stops, and Gavin and the guides motion for everyone to be still.

"Lion tracks," he says, climbing back into the cruiser.

I suddenly realize that we are in an open-air vehicle with bars to keep us from falling out, but nothing to protect us from a charging lion.

"Where?" some of the people whisper.

He swings his muscular arm, and the thought strikes me that Ruby's observation is right: Gavin *does* resemble a younger Robert Redford.

"Ya'll are up in the night," Ruby says loudly. "Those are not lions . . . they're zebras."

Off in the distance a small herd of zebra graze. I see no lions, only tall dried grass and a few small antelope.

Gavin's excitement is obvious; his energy level has soared. He's passing out high-powered binoculars and explaining, "Wherever there are zebra, there are lions close by."

He invites us to climb out, and most do, though Heber refuses to leave the safety of the cruiser. Gavin points out huge paw prints in the dried dirt road. They are the size of a small cantaloupe.

"Holy moley!" Ruby says, "Lions walked down this very road."

"Not today," Gavin says. "It hasn't rained here in weeks. These tracks are old."

"Whew! Then there are no lions around now," Ruby says.

Gavin shakes his head, and his tone turns serious. "Don't kid yourself—wherever there is prey, there are predators."

A moving image flickers across the screen of my mind. I see Malik. I see anger burning in his black eyes—anger toward me because my presence in the village put Jomo in harm's way. At least that's the theory that won't leave my mind. I wonder about Malik. I know virtually nothing about him except that he leads a village gang of boys, and he's the appointed protector of boys like Jomo. When I get back from safari I'm going to seek him out and convince him that I am not his enemy. If we work together, we'll find Jomo. I look at the picture again, hope surging through me every time I see that smile.

Ruby is trying to coax Heber from the cruiser, but he's afraid to come out. He looks like a fifty-year-old man, but acts like a three-year-old boy.

The lady with the British accent gives me a sideways glance and laughs. "Men. They're all babies."

Most safari-goers, including me, want to see a lion. We wait there hoping to catch the flick of an ear, a part in the grass, the twitch of a black-tipped lion's tail, but all we see are zebra, docile and unconcerned.

We continue to wait, and I spot more antelope than I can count, a family of giraffes, and a lone swooping vulture whose shadow passes over me like a heavy cloak.

"You're shivering, dear," the British woman says, putting an arm around my shoulder. "It's scorching out here. Are you afraid of coming face-to-face with a lion?"

Nygoya's words come back to me: "The lion is what we call the truth."

Another chill runs through me, and I turn in a full circle. If there is a lion out there, it's nowhere in sight.

That night we sleep beneath an endless sky of black scattered with twinkling silver stars. It makes me feel so miniscule but glad to be alive. Glad to be where I am. How I wish the people I love could be here with me. It would be medicine to Laura's soul to see a sky like this. It would be medicine to my soul to share this wonder with Jomo.

When it's time to turn in, I go into the giant tent and bunk next to Ruby. A thin-coated piece of mesh hangs above each cot to keep the mosquitoes out.

"Aren't you afraid?" Ruby asks, "I keep thinking something is crawling on me."

"The nets are sprayed. You'll be safe."

"I'm on double dosage of malaria medication. People die of malaria; I guess you know that."

"Uh-huh." I try to drift off, but Ruby doesn't seem to be sleepy.

"Do you hear all those noises?" she asks.

"They're just animals. The fire will keep them away."

"Hebie, are you okay?" Ruby calls so loud, it sounds like she's using a bullhorn.

"I'm okay, Ma," he shouts right back.

I lie there with mosquitoes buzzing in my own ears, thinking how a tiny bug like that poses more of a threat to me than a lion or a rhino. Mosquitoes infect humans with HIV and malaria—and who knows what else.

In time Ruby's not-so-soft snores rattle the rise and fall of the African night. Then another sound rumbles in the darkness, loud and snarling—and so close every strand of hair on the back of my neck stands erect. A shadow passes between me and the flickering campfire. I freeze, still as a corpse in a coffin.

"It's only me," Gavin's voice whispers. "I just wanted to let you all know that the old devil is close by, but I've got my boys posted around camp, armed and anxious."

"What are you talking about?" someone asks.

"I'm assuring you that there is nothing to worry about."

In spite of all the noise and chaos, Ruby's snores rip the air.

"What made that sound?" I ask. "It sounded like a crazed animal."

"It's a rouge lion; an old fellow, maybe wounded, maybe sick."

The lion makes a deep, raspy coughing noise. It sounds as close to us as Gavin.

Someone lets out a yelp. "It's terrifying!"

Gavin remains calm and assuring. "We're here to protect you, though the old bloke is a little too close for comfort." The sound of metal clicking makes me grip the edge of my pillow.

"Nothing will happen to you; I give you my word of honor."

"Are *you* safe out there?" I ask, concerned.

"One mistake, and it's all over."

"One mistake," I repeat. "One mistake."

"I'm just joking with you. I've been doing this for sixteen years; never once have we had to shoot a lion."

"There's always a first."

He chuckles. "The big cats usually hunt in groups and don't go after people. Instead they pick out the young, the weak, the old. They kill for survival, not for entertainment."

I snuggle down in my sleeping bag. "Whatever you say."

"Are any of you afraid?"

Ruby's snore answers him, and then the lion coughs and coughs, brutal and deep. Voices sprinkled through the camp ask Gavin a barrage of questions, but Ruby sleeps on.

"Ma!" Heber calls out as the lion's cough becomes a full-throttled roar.

"None of you move, no matter what!" Gavin bolts like a frightened animal and disappears into the darkness.

My heart pounds.

Another roar rips through camp. Then another—this time so close I swear the beast is in the tent with us. I hear someone crying, someone else praying.

Another deafening roar, and then a single gunshot cracks through the night. Time goes still and black.

I lie motionless.

"Ma?"

Ruby bolts upright. "What? What's going on? Hebie, is that you?"

"No, Ma. It's a lion!"

She scrambles to get out of her sleeping bag and almost falls.

"Everything's okay." Gavin's voice is even and strong. "We scared the old fella away. He ran off with his tail between his legs."

"Are you sure he won't be back?" someone asks.

"Not likely. We're posted outside, so you'll be safe even if he does wander back this way."

There are more questions, and Gavin has answers to all of them. His calmness settles everyone—even Ruby, who demands to know what excitement she missed.

As Gavin turns to leave, his hand brushes my foot. "Good night, Lana. Sleep peacefully."

"Thanks, Gavin. Thanks for protecting us."

"It's all in a day's work."

"Gavin?" a man's voice whimpers. Heber has crawled into our tent to be closer to his mother.

"Yes, Heber?"

"That . . . that . . . was very scary."

"Yes, but the lion won't be back to bother anyone."

"Gavin?"

"Yes, Heber?"

"Would it be possible to get some dry bedding? Mine seems to be a little damp."

I manage to fall asleep only to have a nightmare. Something Gavin said has wedged its message into my brain: *One mistake and it's all over.*

I'm nineteen years old again, returned to a place I vowed I would never revisit.

One mistake.

It's all over.

The cinder-block walls are tan, the paint fresh. The air reeks of rubbing alcohol. I am not alone; my sister is with me. Her face is pale, and her hands tremble violently. She can't speak. She can't even cry. I both resent her being with me and appreciate it.

"It'll be all right," I say, my bare feet hanging off the side of the examining table. A thin layer of white sterile paper protects me from whatever spoor other patients have left before me.

"Are you afraid?" Laura asks me.

"No."

But so many years later I wake up trembling, the mosquito netting tangled away from me so that my bare flesh is exposed to the morning air when the mosquitoes are thick and their appetites for blood are primed. I toss and turn and do my best to free myself of the netting as well as the memory.

Faint pink light breaks over the flat horizon. I dress quickly, breathing in wood smoke and a dry cold that hurts my lungs. Most of the others, including Ruby, are still sleeping, except for a few who are stirring the coals, preparing food for breakfast.

The small trail I follow to the "bush bathroom" makes me wary, and I look this way and that, curious about what hungry animals might be lurking nearby. Is last night's lion really gone? I make as much noise as I can, something Gavin told us to do to scare away any wild beasts.

On the way back I meet up with Sirus, one of Gavin's guides. He is a willowy African who is padding over thorns and grass barefooted and silent. His neck rests on his shoulder like it's broken.

"Good morning," I say in Swahili. *"Jambo."*

His neck pops up and his smile is fast and wide. He says something in Swahili, but when he realizes I don't understand, he deftly switches to English. "You slept well, Mama?" He flicks a small plastic lighter and sets the tip of a black cigarette aglow. He is thoughtful enough to blow the smoke away from my face.

"Except for *simba.*"

"Yes, *simba.* He was loud. He is gone now. You are safe."

"He scared me a bit," I admit.

Sirus's eyebrow lifts. "Me too, Mama. Old *simba,* he scared me, too."

I laugh, then ask a question that I had not intended to ask. "You are a tracker, no?"

"Yes. My father is Masi. I am an excellent tracker. What is it you wish to track: a buffalo, a black rhinoceros? They are very elusive and dangerous."

"A boy."

Smoke billows from both of his nostrils, and he gives me a look of utter confusion. "A *boy?*"

"Seven years old."

"A boy? *Mbulana.*"

"Yes. He is my *rafiki,* and I cannot find him." I tell Sirus what I know of Jomo.

Sirus puts out his burning cigarette on the heel of his hand and puts the unsmoked portion in his shirt pocket.

"His name is Jomo."

"Jomo Kenyatta was Kenya's first president after we won our freedom from the British."

"Yes. I know."

"Your Jomo, he is Black African?"

"Yes. A very handsome little boy." I show him the photo from my digital camera.

"Yes, a happy child. I can see that."

"Can you help me track him?"

"You think your boy has gotten lost in the bush?"

"No. I think he was lost in the village, or the city. *Bosi* Gavin says that there are tribes who steal boys to make them slaves out here in the bush."

"For farms and ranches, yes; that is sadly true."

"I must find Jomo."

"He means much to your heart, Mama?"

"Very much."

"It is easy to get lost in Africa."

"That's why I came here," I say more to myself than to Sirus. "I thought I could run away, but no one can just disappear."

He looks at me but says nothing.

I ask, "If Jomo was your friend, how would you find him?"

"I would follow his tracks."

"Jomo left no tracks."

"That is impossible. We cannot move through a place without leaving tracks."

I think about what Sirus says and realize he is right. Jomo's tracks were the stolen yellow shirt, the shoes, and his missing bicycle. It has to be somewhere. If I can find the bicycle, I might find Jomo.

Gavin bursts into camp with his arms waving. "Wake up!" he calls out, but I see that almost everyone is awake and moving about. He speaks to Sirus in rapid Swahili.

"What is it?" I ask.

"One of our spotters has a leopard in sight, twenty kilometers from here. It's unheard of to see a leopard in the bush. We must go!"

The entire camp moves in frenzied chaos, grabbing sleeping bags, backpacks, and camera gear. We take off at a roar, and I can't help thinking that we will frighten the elusive beast away before we ever get to it.

"Poli, Poli!" Gavin calls out, which means "slow."

A troupe of baboons frolic a few meters away, and many of the safari-goers want to stop and take photos.

"We can always find baboons, but even I've only seen a wild leopard three other times."

Gavin's excitement is obvious, and I find myself sharing his enthusiasm.

We locate the magnificent cat by the vultures circling overhead and by the traffic jam of Land Cruisers stopped to get a glimpse of the cat, which is perched on a low branch of a dead tree. It is so far away, it's impossible to see without binoculars.

Gavin is ecstatic, and hunches down in the grass to peer through a custom lens made for honing in on such a sight. "You've got to see this," he says, waving for me to take my turn. The cat is smaller than I expect. Narrow and sleek. I see its spots and fresh blood around its whiskery mouth; I see the flick of a wide pink tongue.

"She's carried her prey up the tree," Gavin says. "It's what leopards do."

I squint and see a small piece of fresh meat. "What is it . . . . I mean, what *was* it?"

"The foreleg of a gazelle."

In spite of a hundred cameras shooting pictures, the cat looks unconcerned at our presence.

What would Laura's kids think of this? What about Mom and Dad? I wish I had a way to share so much of Africa with them.

I take one last look at the freckled face of the leopard. It snarls, and I see its yellow fangs, its matching yellow eyes.

Gavin is like a little boy spying the tree on Christmas morning. I am happy for him.

Ruby and Heber bicker over a small pair of binoculars. Gavin turns to motion for them to be quiet, but another man from one of the other Land Cruisers carries a camera with a lens longer than his arm. He moves toward the cat and has to be pulled back from his own stupidity.

Too late.

The cat looks up and spots the man. It yawns, showcasing a mouthful of impressive razors crafted for destroying. Its long tail whips up and down, the end curling like a leaf in the African sun. Stretching, the leopard unmoors itself and in a single leap is swallowed by the gold-flecked grass. I realize that I failed to take a single picture of the cat's sleek perfection.

CHAPTER 28

The day unfurls as splendidly as it began. Across the savanna we see grazing zebras, lumbering giraffes. Gavin points out two young giraffe bulls that appear to play a game of Twister.

"Actually," he explains, "they are necking."

This gets a spattering of laughter; Heber laughs loudest.

Gavin passes him a pair of high-powered binoculars. "See how they are pushing each other?"

"Shoving like teenagers," Heber says.

"They are practicing for battle later on. It's always a fight around here. May the best male win."

I wipe my mouth because the air is continually spitting insects. The heat is steady, but nothing I am unaccustomed to.

As we make our way to the lowlands, birds become more bountiful than even the antelope. Gavin knows most of them—and Sirus knows the ones Gavin can't name. There is a man seated at the back who has a book about East African birds, and he enlightens us with their names in English, Latin, and Swahili. I attempt to identify them, but all I see are purple, blue, red, and yellow wings rising to paint the canvas of the sky.

"God loves color," Gavin says, pointing out a small bird that is an entire palette of color.

The man with the book tries to identify the bird, and Gavin takes a seat next to him so they can study the guide book together. I can't help but notice that Gavin has a knack for making people feel valued. He has a knack for a lot of things, and I find myself watching him for no reason at all.

A family of elephants can be seen in the distance. I stare at them through binoculars. Maybe if they were closer, their impact on me would be greater; as it is, they seem so far way and so small, they feel unreal.

A small pack of hyenas tromp through the bush, obviously on its way to a predetermined destination. They are spotted and thin. Ugly.

"They look like mongrel dogs," someone says.

"There are wild dogs out here," says Gavin, "but hyenas are more tenacious, even ferocious. They can intimidate a lioness from her kill."

Every question that is posed is answered with patience and respect.

We bounce past more zebras. More antelope.

"Why haven't we seen any lions or elephants?" Ruby asks. "I thought we'd at least see a Cape buffalo by now."

"Have patience," Gavin says, an uncomplaining smile working at his mouth. He hasn't shaved since we left, and his stubble has a definite red cast to it—like Robert Redford's.

The caravan ahead of us claws dust from the road and pounds dried grass into powder. A fine coat of soot covers everything and everyone. I sneeze and swat at a fly the size of my thumbnail.

We stop for lunch at a small village where the houses remind me of intricately woven birds' nests, turned upside down. They are made of grass, mud, and twigs, not tall enough for a lanky Kenyan to stand straight-spined. We are met by women and children in brilliantly colored traditional clothing and smiles to match.

"*Samburu,*" they greet us.

Gavin explains, "These are pastoral people who usually live closer to Mount Kenya but have traveled here to plant a garden for a single season. The rain or lack of it determines everything in Africa." He directs us to the left of a hut where withered stalks of corn bend, where squash and other vegetables lie wilting, choked and covered with dust.

The children, younger than Jomo, seem shy but eager to please us. They perform a simple, beautiful play about a bird who sacrifices itself so that it will rain. One child lies on the ground, cloaked in a tattered costume made to resemble feathers. Other children, who represent rain clouds, dance around him. A piece of the bird's costume is lifted into the air like it is borne on wind. The bird is reborn and joins the others. Then other children rage forward, pretending to be lightning. They strike the bird dead, and the rain clouds retreat.

"That's just plain sad," Ruby says, loud enough that every head turns and looks at her.

"These children are all girls, aren't they?" someone asks.

"Yes," Gavin says.

"Where are the men and boys?"

"If they are old enough, they are off with the herds of cattle."

The women offer wares, including jewelry and woven baskets that remind me of Mama Grace's handiwork. I buy a necklace carved from animal bone. It is shaped like an elephant. I'll give it to Jomo when I see him. I buy a bright-blue pair of hoop earrings for Nygoya and a carved wooden bowl for Mama Grace. I buy souvenirs for Laura's children—carvings, spearheads, and a hand-carved chessboard.

"Go easy," Gavin says, whispering in my ear. "We'll be stopping at other places to shop."

"Look what I got for Jomo." I show him the elephant necklace.

"You never cry uncle, do you?"

"I'll never give up," I say. "I've got a feeling that when we return, Jomo will be back safely. When I pull up to Mama Grace's school, I'll see Jomo there riding his bike or playing marbles. I keep picturing the scene in my head."

"I hope you're right."

I grip the elephant necklace in my hand, and my brain rewinds. I can't give the necklace to Jomo, not after what happened the last time I gave him a gift. Still, I hold the offering in my palm and tell myself there has to be a way . . . .

After a lunch of soggy sandwiches and warm sodas provided by the lead Land Cruiser in our caravan, we head to the river. The closer we get to the water, both the air and vegetation thickens. Pink flamingos, something I'd expect to see in Florida, flutter across the blue sky.

I get my camera out to take a picture but stop and stare at the smiling face of Jomo. Looking at it gives me hope.

Gavin advises everyone to recoat themselves with DEET and reminds us how important it is to take our malaria pills. As I'm coating myself against the invasion of mosquitoes, I wonder if Jomo has ever been protected by modern medicine against the diseases that prey on the young and the weak. I wonder if he has ever been to a doctor or a dentist.

With the force of a raging rhino, a new revelation slams into my heart. Jomo's parents—at least his mother—died of AIDS. What are the odds that he, too, is a carrier?

My head aches. The warm soda I drank threatens to rise like bile.

It doesn't matter. If Jomo *is* sick, I'll find a way to take care of him. I'll adopt him, make him my own. Anyango, too, if we ever locate her. It is all so unfair, unjust, cruel. Why do people like me have so much when so many millions of others have nothing?

I pull out my camera and stare at the happiest smile I've ever seen. The battery is blinking low, but I can't stop staring.

"Do you need a drink?" Gavin holds out a bottle, cracks the lid, and hands it to me.

I slip the camera back in my bag. "Thanks. I'm feeling a little queasy."

The water is warm and bitter from being treated for those microscopic bugs Africa is infamous for. It drips down the back of my throat, washing down the rising soda, the dust, and the pain that is always with me. It comes back up, choking me.

Both Ruby and Heber pound my back until I insist, "I'm okay. Really, I'm okay now."

Gavin leans down close to me, so close his face is next to mine. I try not to breathe on him, embarrassed by the bitter taste in my mouth. He smells of dust and sweat. A muscle twitches in his jaw.

"You don't look okay."

"Gee, thanks."

"Are you ill?"

"No. Not in the way you think."

He pulls back. "You haven't been stung by anything, have you?"

"I'm fine," I say, a little defensive. "It's all in my head."

He leans down again. His lips brush the top of my ear. "It's all in your heart. You haven't quit looking at that image of Jomo since you discovered it. I promise you that when we get back to Nairobi, I'll help you find Jomo. We won't give up, and we won't give in until he's safe."

Tears spurt from my eyes, and I don't trust my feelings. It seems like the weight of an elephant has been lifted from my heart.

There is truth in the depth of Gavin's eyes, blue as the sky above us. I have an overwhelming urge to throw my arms around his sunburned neck, pull him to me, and hold him until his confidence seeps into me and restores my hope.

The river is teeming with open-mouthed, grunting hippos, so many I can't count them. They splash and climb over each other like kids gone wild in a muddy pool.

"More people in Africa are killed by hippos than by any other animal," Gavin tells us.

No one appears overly interested in what he is saying. We are too entranced by the river scene at the base of the escarpment. Besides the hippos, there are gray-green crocodiles in the water and on the banks. For all I know, they are crawling in the grass around me.

"You're safe," Gavin tells me.

"What do they eat?" I ask.

Ruby laughs, a nervous twittering laugh. "Each other."

"If you were here during the wildebeest migrations, you'd see the crocs store up on all the fresh meat they can grab." Gavin motions for the crowd to gather around him as he explains, "Wildebeest migrations are legendary. A million or more of the animals join with other herbivores to cross this river into the grasslands of Kenya."

Ruby's hand goes up. "Where do they come from?"

"Tanzania."

The man who has been on three safaris with Gavin says, "It's spectacular. Isn't your migration safari one of your most popular?"

Gavin nods and then launches into a lecture about frogs that bury themselves in the mud of the escarpment wall. I try to listen—I have notes to take for Mr. C—but my thoughts keep pulling me back. A voice inside my head, a voice I thought I had quieted years ago, keeps taunting, *One mistake and it's all over.*

When the camp settles, I get a folding chair out of the Land Cruiser and sit down to take in the unbelievable sight before me: hippos, crocodiles, and the muddy, winding waters of Africa. I pull the bill of my baseball cap over my eyes and think back. I came to Africa looking whole, acting healthy, and needing no one. I wore my confidence like a warrior wears his shield. The truth is, there is a hole in my heart where there should be happiness. Sometimes I fill it with other emotions, mostly guilt, but in the end the hole is empty, throbbing, and bottomless.

I remember an old adage Mom taught me, wisdom from Abraham Lincoln: *When you do good, you feel good.*

I want to feel good. I'm tired of hurting.

I want to fill that hole with something besides guilt and pain.

I flew six thousand miles to get away from everyone and everything I knew. I wanted a new start with nothing familiar. Now I find I'm emerging like one of the frogs Gavin taught us about. They wiggle themselves deep in the earth and stay virtually buried in the sun-baked, rock-hard earth for nine months, the entire gestation of a human fetus. Then the long rains come, and with them, a season of resurrection. What was once dead and buried bursts forth croaking and celebrating the glorious business of life.

How I want that second chance at life!

We set up camp at the top of the escarpment. Gavin hands me a package of batteries for my digital camera, and I shoot pictures until my finger grows sore from pushing the button. I can't wait to email them home to Laura and her children. I imagine myself showing them to Jomo, frame by frame.

Then the reality hits me. Laura has cancer. How is a photo of splashing hippos going to benefit her? Jomo has vanished, and I'm not sure anyone really cares except me.

No. I will not give in to the dark thoughts that cloud my head.

I force myself to appear more cheerful than I feel. I chat with people, take notes for Mr. C's report, keep an eye on Gavin, and fight my way free from the invisible force that always threatens to pull me back in time, to tow me under, to tie me to the anchor of guilt that I've dragged around for so long.

Without warning, a round-faced monkey armed with an attitude descends on us while we're chopping vegetables for our meal.

"Oh, that's Bobo," says one of the camp cooks. "He's a frequent visitor here."

I toss Bobo a wedge of sweet potato, which he grabs and throws right back at me.

"So you're looking for a challenge," I say, tossing the potato at him again.

The women around me laugh, but Heber backs up, afraid of the chattering, teeth-baring primate.

Bobo climbs up a tree, screeches at me, and then hops to the roof of our Cruiser. I take a larger piece of potato and wind up. I don't mean to, but my aim is accurate, and I hit Bobo dead-center in the head.

The poor creature shrieks and topples backward.

Ruby's hand claps over her gaping mouth

I feel terrible. "I didn't mean to hurt him, I swear."

By now the entire camp has gathered to stare at me, at the dead monkey, and back at me.

But the monkey isn't dead. Bobo springs up, shakes like a little wet dog, looks for the piece of sweet potato, and then looks for me. He flings the wedge and it sails past me, right into the pot with the other chopped vegetables.

"Yuck!" Heber says.

Gavin is doubled over.

"Keep laughing that hard and you'll burst an artery," I say.

He laughs harder. "You should have seen your face when you thought you'd murdered that monkey."

Everyone has joined Gavin's laughter. Even Bobo. He's hopping on top of the Toyota, cussing me out.

I laugh like I haven't laughed in years. And for a moment, the hole in my heart fills up and overflows with sheer happiness.

CHAPTER 29

"What do you know about Africa?"

Gavin asks me the question as we sit on a couple of dented folding chairs overlooking the hippos and crocs, gazing down the majesty of the escarpment. The grunts and groans and sudden splashes are a perfect symphony for this time and this place. The sky, the ground, even the air around us holds a purple cast. It's all magical.

I breathe in the smell of damp earth, musty and rank. Bullfrogs the size of footballs, hippos the size of Volkswagens, crocodiles the size of Gavin bump and splash and sleuth all around. I've never been anywhere so foreign or unfamiliar, and yet I feel at peace.

"What do I know about Africa?" I play with the string on my hoodie and look at Gavin. He seems to grow more handsome every time I see him.

"In a single word, describe all of it." He leans back, and the sun seems to focus on his face. An artist could have carved the lines there. He is the picture of rugged masculinity.

I wish that I could stop myself from feeling the way I'm feeling. Gavin is only being kind and helpful because he wants Hotel Harambee's business. Thinking anything else is going to lead to a broken heart for me. Besides, what would a man as strong and solid as Gavin see in a weepy woman who is so . . . "Neurotic," I say aloud.

Gavin snorts. "You think Africa is neurotic?"

"No. Not Africa. Me. I was thinking about me."

"You seem more driven than neurotic."

"Yeah, well, you don't know me."

"Tell me about you."

"What do you want to know?"

"What size boots do you wear?"

"Seven . . . okay . . . eight and a half. Why?"

"You may need a better pair of boots if we go hiking."

"I'm not hiking anywhere near hungry crocodiles."

He laughs. "You said that you'd been married."

"Twice, actually. And I failed both times."

"*You* failed? It takes two people to make or break a marriage."

I shrug. "And you? You lost the love of your life when your wife died."

His eyes glisten, but he does not take them from me. Gavin leans toward me until our shoulders touch. "Back to Africa . . . if you had to describe what you know of her in a single word, what would it be?"

"One word?"

Black shadows sweep and dive in front of us.

"Bats," Gavin says. "They keep the insect population down."

I jerk, and Gavin's arm loops over my shoulder. The weight is heavy, protective, and welcome. I have to fight off an urge to rest my head on his shoulder.

"Biblical."

"Huh?"

"*Biblical.* That is the single word I'd use to describe Africa."

Gavin goes silent, giving my contribution consideration. His arm slips away, and he looks at me with wide eyes. "That surprises me."

"Why?" I ask, "This land is ancient, it's sacred, it's fierce and unforgiving. It's beautiful. We've got the Indian Ocean, the Cape, the Congo, the pyramids, deserts, and mountains."

"You sound like a travel agent."

I kick the toe of my boot into the ground. "I know you already know this: right here in East Africa the oldest fossils and fragments of life were discovered."

He looks pleased. "You've done your homework."

"Before I ever accepted my job, I studied everything I could about Africa. One day, somewhere out here, two adults and a child took a walk across a mud pan. Three million years later scientists discovered their fossilized footprints and made a case for evolution."

"Do you believe in evolution?"

"No," I say quickly, "not in the sense that life came from a big bang. I know there is a God behind all of this chaos." That warm feeling in my chest returns.

"So you are religious."

I laugh. "No one has ever said that about me."

"Why not?"

"I'm not religious. I mean, I was raised with religion, but I've always been the black sheep, the rebellious one."

"The rebel Mormon," he says, smiling.

"I was. I mean I am. I mean I probably shouldn't be."

"You don't have to apologize for what you believe."

"I'm not apologizing." I hug my ribs and have an overwhelming urge to push the heaviness from my heart. I want to leave it in a heap at Gavin's feet. "I really don't know how I feel or think. Everything was fine until my sister got cancer and until Jomo . . ." My voice cracks, and I'm angry with myself for being so emotional, so weak.

Gavin stands and hugs me. I mean he really hugs me, tight and unrelenting. The top of my head barely brushes his chin, and my ear listens to the steady pound of his heart. My own heart isn't fluttering, but slows to take this new feeling in. It is one of safety, of surety. Good thing: my own legs threaten to buckle.

Gavin tightens his grip and whispers in my ear. "The day I saw you working at Mama Grace's school with your arms all scraped and banged from carrying chunks of concrete, your knees bloody, and that contagious smile of yours, I thought, 'Now here's a woman strong as a Cape buffalo.'"

"Gee, thanks."

"No, it's a compliment. I knew then that I wanted to get to know you."

Now my heart flutters.

He leads me away from camp, down a narrow overgrown path. I don't think of crocodiles or snakes. I don't think of anything except how right it feels to be next to Gavin. We stand there looking at the sun sink, at Africa turning a page of eternity.

"I wish I was Joshua," he says.

"Joshua who?"

"From the Old Testament. He had the faith to hold the sun steady. If I could do that, this moment would not end so soon."

There is a mighty splash in the shadows below, and I jump.

"This is one of the best vantage points from which to watch wildlife come to the drinking hole. You can see just about everything if you've got night vision equipment."

"Do you?"

"No. It's on my Christmas list."

Another sound, this one of something moving in the grass not far from us, gives me a creepy feeling. "What was that?"

"Could be anything."

"Maybe we should go back."

"Do you want to go back?"

"No. But I don't want to be eaten by a lion or a crocodile."

"I promise I won't let anything happen to you."

The tenseness in my neck eases.

"I mean, what would Mr. C say if I had to tell him you'd been snapped up by a croc?"

I smirk. "So your only interest in me is business, right?"

"I wouldn't say that. I want to get to know you."

"Tell me about you first," I say, feeling a bit threatened. "What was your wife like?"

"Amanda was Scandinavian. Blond, bullheaded. She was a biologist."

"So the two of you had a lot in common."

"We shared a love of animals, but on the deepest level, we found we stood at opposite ends."

"What do you mean?"

"We got married too fast. We only knew the basics about each other, but not the things that really matter."

"Like what?"

"Faith. Amanda did not believe in God."

"Oh. I've got to be honest; I've had my own doubts."

"Not like hers, I'm sure. Amanda was an anthropologist. Science was her religion."

"That would be nice . . . to have all the answers. Lately, all I've got are questions."

"The God I know *likes* questions." Gavin's eyes glint. "I don't think it's weak to ask questions, to have doubts. But to deny that there's a Supreme Creator when—well, just look around you. I swear to you, Lana, I know *here*," he pounds his heart with a thud of his fist, "there's a God in heaven, and He does know every sparrow that falls."

My spine tingles, this time with a searing bolt of truth. "You're right, Gavin. There is a God, and I know it, but I'm so angry with Him right now."

"You're mad at God?"

"I am. Look at Grace. How could God allow her to get sick?"

"God didn't infect Mama Grace; her boyfriend did. She slept with an infected man. *He* gave her HIV, not God. We've had this conversation before."

"I still don't have answers . . . only questions. What about my sister? She is good and strong and true all the way to her core. Yet she's the one, not me, who finds her life strangled by breast cancer."

He is silent.

"And Jomo. Tell me what kind of God allows a boy that wonderful to get lost, just swallowed and forgotten?" My fists ball up.

"You don't know that Jomo is lost. And *you* certainly haven't forgotten him."

I take a deep breath. Words don't come.

Gavin touches my cheek with the back of his fingers. "I know you've heard this question before, but *why* does Jomo mean so much to you?"

"I don't know. I didn't plan it that way. He just showed up and stole my heart."

"You're so passionate, so driven. Jomo is a lucky little boy to have you on his side."

"Did you and Amanda have kids?"

"No. I always wanted a big family, but kids weren't her thing."

"I'm sorry."

Gavin swats at a hungry mosquito trying to land on the back of his hand. "Don't be. If you don't want to have kids you shouldn't have them. It was another one of those deep issues we should have been clear on before we ever got married." He tugs the zipper on his jacket;

the air is turning colder. "How about you, Lana? Have you got kids back home in America?"

"No." The weight of that word makes my knees weak.

Suddenly Gavin's arm is around me again. He pulls me tight against his chest so that my brain pounds with the beat of his heart. I want him to kiss me, and I tilt my head back and wait, sure he wants to kiss me.

He does.

On my forehead.

He presses his lips, full and warm, against my skin. It's not the kiss I'd hoped for, but it gives me comfort and something more. Even after Heber's voice calls for Gavin to come back to camp, even after Gavin moves away from me, the feeling stays, seeping through me.

I never thought I'd feel this way about a man again. All of my defenses are crumbling, and I'm terrified.

And with good reason. I guess the past never really goes away.

According to Sirus, the Great Rift Valley that cuts across Kenya is the result of an argument between Mother Nature and her first children. Mother Nature claimed to have the greatest power because hers was the ability to create. Her children boasted they were even more powerful because they had learned the art of destruction.

Slowly, the argument caused an irreconcilable separation: fault lines in the earth's surface moved apart, causing the land to sink to a valley low of 3,281 feet below the escarpment on either side of it. Shallow lakes like Nakura and Bogoria that dot the valley are where tears from both Mother Nature and her children have pooled. The millions of pink flamingos that gather there are messengers from God Himself, sent in hopes that Mother Nature and her children can find a way to mend the great rift that has separated them to this day.

Looking out at the stunning scene, I think the lake is pink and not blue. The birds rise in one giant pastel sheet, tossed on the wind.

Sirus points a rippled black arm at the moving vision. "Look! A symbol of God's love."

I search the crowd for Gavin but can't see him. I've been thinking a lot about God since we spoke last night. I've been thinking a lot about Gavin, too.

Sirus has the crowd entranced. His voice is as deep as a gorge and as smooth as a rising flamingo. "God, the power of both, looked down and wept. His tears pooled into lakes. But God is not a god of sorrow; He is a god of joy. Just as He sent Noah a rainbow, He sent Africa flamingos. God's hope is that one day Mother Nature and her children will reconcile."

Gavin's khaki baseball cap moves through the people. He is taller than almost everyone else. "Great story, Sirus," he says, smiling as wide as the valley.

We have paused near the town of Naivasha, near a lake that bears the same name. There is a beauty and peacefulness that reminds me of Heber Valley in Utah. Laura and Dad and I used to float inner tubes down the Provo River during the hot afternoons of July and August. We'd stop along the shoreline, eat lunch, and dive off rocks into the deep areas of the river. Memories keep coming back to me, one by one.

"Has anyone ever seen the Grand Canyon?" Gavin asks.

My hand goes up, along with those of several others.

"Well, this is Africa's version of the Grand Canyon."

This is the last day of our safari, and Gavin seems wound a little tight. We still have a lot to cover before we return home. I'm anxious too. Has Jomo been found safe? How is Laura doing? It's hard to concentrate, although as we drive through the sun-baked land, I'm surprised at how fertile Naivasha is. Farms are laid out in neat, green squares. Most of Africa is bone-dry, but here, whenever the land grows parched, it can lap from the nearby lake.

The main industry here is flower farming: roses, lilies, carnations, all commercial flowers.

"My mother is a gardener," I tell Ruby. "She'd go crazy here."

"Are ya'll close?"

"Mom and me? Not as close as I wish we were."

"That's a pity. A woman your age should have ironed out any wrinkles of her youth. There is nothing more precious than the bond between a mother and her child. Isn't that right, Hebie?"

Heber is seated next to his mother. He has a nasty bug bite on his cheek that looks red and inflamed. Someone has smeared pink lotion on it.

"Calamine?" I ask.

Heber shakes his head. "All we had was Pepto-Bismol."

"Um. Let me know how that works out."

We stop to tour a flower farm. It is immense. The colors are brilliant, and the air is thick with perfume. While the guide gives us a lecture, I seek Sirus out. "Is there a pay telephone I could use?"

"Is there a problem?" he asks.

"No. It's just that we've been out of communication for three days, and I'd like to call my hotel."

"Technology has reached the far corners of the earth," Sirus says, producing a small silver cell phone from his pocket. "Go ahead and dial."

"Did you have this the whole time?"

He nods. "This is the first place we have had good cellular reception."

"Asante." The reception is scratchy, but I make contact with the front desk and ask to be connected to Nygoya.

"Jambo!" I'd know her voice anywhere.

"It's me. Have you heard anything about Jomo?"

The silence between us answers my question, and my throat swells.

"I am sorry to tell you that Mr. C spoke with the police this morning. They have no new information."

"What about Mama Grace? Maybe she's heard something."

"Perhaps. We have not spoken with her since you've been gone. I have gone searching for Anyango. No one knows of the girl."

All the happiness I've been feeling drains out of me.

"Tell me of your safari, Lana. How are things?"

"Great . . . until now."

"Hold on to your hope. Now tell me more about your safari." There is lightness in her tone, a teasing, and I have to tell myself not to resent it. Nygoya has every right to be happy.

"There's not a lot to tell," I say slowly.

"How is Gavin?"

"He's fine. Very professional." I feel protective of whatever it is that Gavin and I shared. I'm not even sure we *shared* anything. Maybe all of the feelings are mine alone.

"Did you spot any poaching?"

"Nope. Oh, yeah, we saw a leopard."

Nygoya huffs. "No. I do not believe you. A cheetah on a termite mound, yes, but a leopard in the wild? No."

"It was a leopard."

"I'll believe when I see it."

"That reminds me. I found a photo of Jomo on my digital camera. Mama Grace must have taken it."

I hear her gasp, and I can almost see her jumping up and down like an excited child. "Oh! Oh! Oh! It was *me*. I shot the picture of you and your Jomo. The two of you looked so happy that day."

"Why didn't you tell me? You know how desperate we've been for a photo of Jomo. This is a terrific one of his little face."

"I am most apologetic," she says. "My mind did not recall the incident until this moment. When will you be back to Nairobi?"

"Not soon enough."

CHAPTER 30

I have spent much of my life emotionally shut down. Now the feelings, the thoughts, the memories surge through me like little stabs of electricity.

I'm dead, brought back to life, one feeling at a time.

We drive back to Nairobi instead of flying because Gavin wants to take us along the more scenic route. I don't care about the scenery. I just want to get back to Nairobi to find Jomo, no matter what I have to do. I want to check on Laura. These past days I've made a mental list of things I must do to put my life in order.

I lean back and close my eyes. The ride is too bumpy for a nap, and when I look out the window I'm surprised to see that the green of Naivasha has dried to gold. We are back along a strip of savanna.

"Zebra!" someone squeals, like we haven't seen four million zebras in the past three days.

"Could you look a little more bored?" Gavin asks me.

I straighten up and blink a smile at him. "I'm tired."

"Good thing I didn't take you on our two-week safari. Imagine how much fun you'd be at the top of Mount Kilimanjaro."

"I just have a lot to do when I get back to Nairobi."

"I told you I'll help you find Jomo. I mean it."

"Good, because I'm forming a plan."

Someone calls out, "Gavin, we still haven't seen a lion. I thought you said we'd see the Big Five."

"We heard a lion," Ruby says, though I know for a fact she snored though the entire hawking, coughing, gun-firing episode.

Our driver slams on the brakes, slapping us forward. There in the middle of the day, in the center of the rutted road, a pair of sinewy lionesses saunter. The females are thin and not much wider than a dictionary. They are the color of the dried golden grass around us—except for the tips of the tails, which look like they've been dipped in black oil.

Heber moves to the center of the aisle, blocking the view. "I think they're twins," he says, "sisters."

"Yes, sisters!" Ruby says. She's got her camera to her eyes, clicking away.

It's true; the lionesses are perfectly matched and step in sync. Of all the sights we've seen on safari, this one is my favorite.

We stay and watch the lionesses. They seem unconcerned and move so close to our Cruiser that I'm sure I can touch one if I stick my arm through the bars. Everyone around me is taking photos, but I don't want to take my eyes off the animals.

Zebras and antelope graze tranquilly all around us. The lionesses pose no immediate threat, and life, for the moment, goes on peacefully.

We watch these sinewy carnivores move in tandem. I think of Laura, my own twin.

The man who sits at the back of the van, the one who has a guide book for everything, says, "Lionesses do the hunting. The males feast from their spoils."

Ruby stands in the aisle and calls back, "And that's supposed to be news?"

Everyone laughs.

The man continues reading from his book, "Only one in ten attempts at a kill is successful."

Something unseen and unsuspected startles the lionesses and they shoot off, one to the right and one to the left.

They vanish, just like that.

I can no longer see them, but I know they're there, just like I know Jomo is out there somewhere in the camouflage that Africa so deftly offers.

It is dark when we finally pull into the city.

"We didn't get to see a black rhino," Ruby says, sounding dramatically disappointed.

"I really wanted to see a black rhino," Heber says, his mother's elbow wedged into his ribs.

"Next time I'll invite Nygoya," Gavin says to me. "She knows where every black rhino in Kenya is."

"No kidding?"

"I might be exaggerating, but Nygoya's first love is the black rhino. She'd kill to protect the species."

"I know the feeling."

As we make our way into the city I feel a growing anxiety . . . there's so much to do.

"Ya'll will have to stay in touch," Ruby says, passing out little flowered cards with her telephone number. "Hebie would love to come back to Africa and visit. Wouldn't you?"

Heber smiles at me and nods. "Not without you, Ma."

"Of course I'll come along. Next time we'll climb Mount Kilimanjaro with ya'll."

"It's a date," Gavin says. "And I'll bring my friend who knows how to spot a black rhino."

"Do Hebie and me get a discount next time around?"

"Sure, why not?"

I give Gavin a look, hoping that he'll offer me a ride to my flat, but he lets all of us off at the airport, and I'm forced to take a taxi.

I'm a little embarrassed and a little hurt. Everything between us is business as usual, and we part with only a handshake.

"Hope you'll give Moja Outfitters a favorable review," he says as I climb into the taxi.

I don't give him the satisfaction of a straight answer, just a fast smile.

During the ride home I realize that every muscle in my body is sore. I can't stop yawning. It's good that it's so late; if it wasn't, I'd drive out to Mama Grace's village tonight.

In the small enclosed courtyard of my apartment compound, a male peacock struts full-blown under the glow of the blue moon. Monkeys chatter in the branches above.

I love Africa.

The first thing I do is check my email. I can't get a connection so I shower and shave my legs, grateful to be rid of the safari grit that clings to every inch of me. I have to brush twice to get it off my teeth. What did I look like, smell like, to Gavin? It doesn't matter, because whatever I imagined was between us, wasn't. A part of me is relieved—I know where my heart was headed, and that road always dead-ends for me.

My icebox is the size of a suitcase. I find a piece of cheese and slice the mold off the end. I drink a Fanta blackberry soda. A cockroach scoots out when I open the cupboard door. It doesn't faze me, and I find a sleeve of crackers to go with my cheese.

I'm worn out, but sleep won't come.

I check my telephone messages: nothing. There's still no Internet connection. I shower again and shampoo my still-wet hair. The water is uncharacteristically hot, but I can't steam away the anxiety that is building inside of me.

Neurotic. Wasn't that the word I used to describe myself? On Sundays when I was young, Mom boiled potatoes in a pressure cooker. One day the little round gauge rattled until it came off and the whole thing blew, spewing boiling water and chucks of scalding Idaho russets all over our walls and ceilings.

I am that pressure cooker, rattled and ready to blow.

If it wasn't so late, I'd go to the hotel and run off my anxiety on the treadmill. I turn on a radio and get nothing but static. My bare feet pace the small, cramped space.

My neighbors to the left argue, and I hear their heated voices through our paper-thin walls. They yell in Swahili, and then everything goes still.

I still can't sleep; wearing shorts and a T-shirt, I step outside into the chill of the night. The whole city seems unnaturally calm; even the peacock and monkeys are asleep. I see no one, but I smell cigarette smoke and hear someone move close to me.

"Jambo," I say into the darkness.

A voice laughs, deep and growly. "Who's there?" I bolt back through my open door, which I quickly lock and deadbolt.

I grab my *panga* from the kitchen drawer and wait. My hands won't quit shaking as my fingers tighten around the blade.

The seconds tick . . . tick . . . tick.

Who's out there? Who would want to harm me? If it was anyone who really wanted to injure me, they could have. I tell myself that I'm fine.

The truth is that I'm not fine. For more than a decade I've been injured. I bandaged the wound. I nursed it. I ignored it until it festered and infected my very blood.

Will it kill me, or can I be healed?

I crawl into bed with a notepad and write to my parents.

Dear Mom and Dad:

I just got back from safari. I saw some animals and some beautiful sights. I took some photos and got some souvenirs that will make great show-and-tell items for Laura's kids. When she's well I want you all to come and visit. I know a fabulous safari outfitter who will show us a great time.

Mom, you won't believe the flowers they grow here. And there's an unwanted baby center in a nearby village that could use some of those little quilts you're so good at making.

Dad, I want you to know that you are not a bigot. You never have been and you never could be. I have a long list of tough questions, but I know there are answers out there. I learned something while I was on safari: I learned that I have the start of a testimony. I know God lives. I know that cancer can be cured. I'm sorry for all the pain I've caused you. Please give my love to Laura, Ethan, and the kids.

Someday I hope you'll be proud of me.

Love,

Lana

P.S. There are Mormons in Nairobi. I'll tell you more later.

I fold the letter and slip it into an envelope. I should feel good—better, at least—but I've never felt so alone in my entire life.

At some point I drift off and dream that I am holding Laura's hand. She is lying on a hospital bed, and, without anyone telling me, I know that her breast is gone. Did the cancer go with it?

She's my twin; I should feel something for her loss, but all I feel is my own pain and fear—and guilt, because guilt is an old, familiar friend, a part of me just as sure as my shadow.

Laura lets go of my hand, and I cry out in prayer, "Help me!"

My head fills with a memory from when I was nine years old. Our family dachshund, Fudgy, got cancer. We'd had her since before Laura and I were born. We all loved her, but Fudgy loved *me* best. She'd stay at my heels whenever I played in the neighborhood. She'd be at the front window watching for me when I came home from school. She'd wag her tail for Laura, but for me, she'd wag her whole body.

For nine years she slept at the foot of my bed. Then one morning instead of bouncing off the bed, wagging and licking, she just lay there. We took her to the veterinarian that afternoon, but he just shook his head and said, "I'm sorry." We took her home, tried to make her comfortable, but all she did was lie around and whimper. When she stopped eating we took her back to the vet, just Dad and me, because Mom and Laura were too emotional. I held Fudgy's head and looked into her eyes. I was looking into her eyes when the doctor put a small needle into her vein.

She didn't even have time to close her eyes.

One second Fudgy was alive, and the next, she was dead.

I wake up and curl into a tight ball, draw my knees almost to my chin, and weep like I did when I was nine years old. I don't cry; I wail. I don't care if the neighbors think I've gone mad. I mourn for Fudgy, for Laura, for Jomo, for Mama Grace, and for every other loss of my life. I cry until my eyes burn and my throat and eyes swell. I shake and sob and shudder.

"Please, God," I beg aloud, "I'm sorry."

And then the real sorrow comes. I weep for a sin that cannot be excused or forgiven. I weep for the worst moment of my life, the single decision that defines who I am and what I'm worth.

I weep for a baby that I did not want.

And though I'm wide awake, I'm back there on that cold, metal examining table in a clinic where good Mormon girls never go. Laura keeps touching my bare feet, trying to comfort me. Her eyes are red, and her hands shake. "Are you sure?"

"No."

"Then let's go while we still can."

"No. You can go if you want to," I say, "but I've screwed up all of my life and this is where I have ended up. Maybe I deserve to be here."

"That's crazy. None of this is your fault."

"Yes, it is. I *married* Nick."

"You divorced him—more than a year ago. He's remarried and has a baby."

I flinch at the word *baby*.

"Please, Lana, this is *wrong*. I know you know it's wrong."

I lift up my thin, stained examining gown. "This is what's wrong," I say, revealing dark black and purple bruises on my thighs, beneath my arms. I lift my hair that I wore longer at that time, and I show her the bruises where Nick's fingers clamped around my throat and tried to choke the life out of me. I don't tell her of the other evil he's inflicted on me, acts too vile and vicious to describe.

"I think you should call the police," she says.

"I did call the police. I warned them Nick was going to do this. They couldn't stop him."

"They'll put him in jail."

"He'll get out and come after me . . . after Mom and Dad . . . you . . . he swore to me that he'd kill his own baby. We both know he'll do it."

Laura's arms wrap around me and hold me tight while I sob.

"I did go to the police," I whisper in her ear. "I went, and they didn't do anything. They said I have no proof."

Laura looks stunned. "Didn't you show them the bruises? You could have had one of those tests."

"I waited too long. Nobody believed me. It was so humiliating, so infuriating."

"I believe you."

"You can't let Mom and Dad know anything about this," I say, pulling back. "Dad will go after him, and Nick will kill Dad."

"Or Dad will kill Nick," Laura says.

Time passes like poison through us. Every second brings me closer to a choice that will forever feel wrong.

Laura grabs my hand again. "You should talk to a bishop. You can always give the baby up for adoption."

"And I might," I say. "I haven't made any decisions."

"Then why are we here?" she demands.

"You didn't have to come. But I have to find out what my options are."

"*This* should never be an option."

"I don't want his baby," I say.

Her eyes shift to the cold, concrete floor. "It's *murder.*"

My head feels pinned in a vise; an invisible hand cranks it tighter and tighter. "I didn't say I'm going through with it. I just have to find out about it."

"Are you sure Nick doesn't suspect you're pregnant?"

I shake my head. "He told me he'd kill me if I tried to trap him."

Laura looks as desperate as I feel. "There have to be options," she says.

"And *this* is one of them. I'm just here to find out."

"You can't go through with it. I know you can't."

"I don't know what I'm capable of," I say, loathing myself. "I only know I won't let Nick hurt anyone I love." My hand rests on my stomach, and I know in that instant that my sister is right: I can't go through with it.

She looks at me with utter terror in her eyes. "Please, let's go."

The vise loosens, and my head clears. I nod. My feet swing off the side of the table, and I'm ready to run when a woman walks in. She does not wear a white medical coat or a stethoscope around her neck. She's dressed in jeans and a button-up shirt left untucked. Why would I notice such an unimportant thing when I'm about to ruin my entire life and the life of . . . I think of tiny wrinkled feet, newborn and pink. I think of soft baby fingers circling a mother's finger. *My* finger. I think of all my childhood dreams of becoming a mother.

"Hello, I'm Doctor Flander."

"I'm Lana Carter."

"It's courageous of you to be here," she says in a flat voice.

"I don't feel courageous," I say, seeing Laura's ashen face in the corner, begging.

The doctor rubs the side of her face like she, too, has a headache. "I'm afraid there's been some mistake, Lana."

"Yeah, that's exactly what I was just thinking. I shouldn't be here." I'm standing now, my bare feet cold on the floor. I want to put my clothes back on, to take my sister's outstretched hand and run as fast and far as I can.

"You're not pregnant," Dr. Flander says.

My heart turns upside down. "What?"

She holds a clipboard of my medical report, papers I've filled out. Her finger taps it.

Her words make no sense to me. "I took a test," I say. "I'm pregnant, eight weeks. I know the exact date."

Laura runs her fingers through her hair. Her eyes are wide and moist. "I was there with Lana. The test was positive."

The doctor's voice is kind and consoling. "I'm sorry. Your sister is not pregnant."

"Don't be sorry," Laura says.

The doctor goes on to say, "I understand, Lana, that you've suffered some other physical trauma, psychological as well. We have an excellent medical and counseling staff. I can give you an immediate referral."

I am adamant. "I took the test three times! It was positive; I know it was." I search Laura's face for confirmation but see only a budding smile on her lips. Her face looks upward, and her lips whisper words I cannot hear.

The doctor clears her throat. "Drugstore tests aren't always reliable; they can be skewed by a number of factors," she says, writing something in red pen across the top of my chart. Then she turns to leave and gives me one simple flicker of a smile. "I'll be right back and we can examine you thoroughly. But Lana, I have your blood test results. You are definitely *not* pregnant."

The room starts to spin, the doctor's face blurs, and Laura's voice goes foggy. Her hand reaches out for me, but before she can get hold of me, I go limp and pass out in a heap.

More than a decade later, I am a continent away and a lifetime apart from that horrific memory. I suffer for a sin I never committed; in the deepest part of my heart, I know I never could have committed it. Yet here I am crumpled on another concrete floor, feeling the very same pain I did then.

For hours I lie on the floor, begging for utter and complete forgiveness.

Has God heard?

I don't know. I only know that I feel a new resolve to let go of the past and get on with the future.

I take a taxi to the hotel and get there while the cleaning staff is still polishing the floor, and the food staff is preparing the Sunday brunch. I have 151 emails, most of them junk, some pertaining to work; one is from Mom.

> Dear Lana:
> How are you? How was your safari?
> I'll get right to the point. Laura is still in a lot of pain. She's opted for reconstructive surgery. Your thoughtfulness to her has meant so much.
> I know you're all the way over there on the other side of the world, but I swear, there are times when I feel you are right here next to me. You've always been the strong one.
> When all of this blows over and Laura is well, your father says we are getting on an airplane and coming to visit you in Africa. I can't wait to meet your . . . oh, what do you call them . . . *radikies . . .* you know what I mean. Besides, I admit I'd like to see animals that aren't trapped behind zoo bars.
> I love you, Lana.
> Mom
>
> P.S. I don't want to upset you, but you're going to find out one way or another. Nick was arrested in Las Vegas. It was all over the news here. Reports say he ran over a woman with his car. Apparently, it was intentional. Who would ever have thought him capable of such violence? You never know.

I read her email over and over.

The information about Nick should make me feel vindicated. It doesn't. I just feel sad.

CHAPTER 31

There is no new information about Jomo. It's early and it's Sunday, so Officer Habib is not in his office. Sundays are a big deal in Nairobi. Christians here take the fourth commandment very seriously, and most of the markets close. I wonder if Mama Dale has talked with Bishop Kaahari yet. I am raring to go look for Jomo if someone will just point me in the right direction.

It's still only six-thirty A.M. when I finish reading and answering my emails. I plug my digital camera disc into my computer and print out an 8x10 photo of Jomo and me. I'm looking at it when I receive a new email. When I see who it is from, I'm stunned.

> Hey:
> You probably won't get this until Monday. I just wanted to thank you for your company. Three days never went so fast.
> Next time I take you on safari we'll go to the Masi Mara. You'll see more lions than you can count. And Kili. I know you're a fitness freak, so you'll enjoy the weeklong hike. From the top of Mount Kilimanjaro you feel so close to heaven, it seems like God can just reach down and shake your hand.
> You'd like that, wouldn't you? To know for absolute certain that He's up there? A handshake from Him would remove all doubt. You've started me thinking a great deal about God. Thanks for that.
> Lana, someday I'd like to take you to the white sands of Mombassa, where you can ride a camel. I want you to take a

canoe ride to fish for tilapia in Lake Victoria. We can watch
whales off the shores of Watama. Don't let me scare you away;
I just want you to know that even if you give me a failing
mark for Moja Outfitters, I would like to see you again.

  Gavin

I rest my head on my desk. My heart is fluttering like it's brand-
new and somebody just wound it up. I don't know what to do with
myself. It is still insanely early, and I can't focus my thoughts.

I sit down and write the report for Mr. C. I give Gavin's company
an A- because I don't want to appear too partial. The minus is for
feeding us too many hard-boiled eggs.

I answer more emails and reread Gavin's until I have it memo-
rized. I fantasize about doing the things he suggests—together.

Then I see it. On the table in the corner, propped against a lamp,
is a note with my name on it. I recognize Nygoya's block handwriting.

"Call Mama Dale as soon as you can. She says it's important." A
local telephone number is scribbled at the bottom. I immediately
think of Jomo. She has information on Jomo!

Even though it's insanely early, I dial the number. A woman's
groggy voice answers.

"I'm sorry for calling so early. This is Lana Carter. I've been out of
town, but I'm told you're trying to contact me." I take a deep breath
and say a silent prayer that her news is good news.

"Oh . . . yes. Yes, Lana, Mama Grace's girl. Yes. I called your hotel
to invite you to attend church with me today."

"You're inviting me to church?"

"Yes. Church. The Nairobi First Ward."

I stare at the telephone. "Nairobi has more than one ward?"

"Oh, yes. There are four wards and two branches in the city. We
meet at nine on Kungu Karumba Road. You will enjoy it."

"You're inviting me to attend church with you—that's your
urgent message?"

"Yes, Lana. I told Nygoya that I will introduce you to Bishop
Kaahari. The elders will be present also. I am sure everyone will be
anxious to assist you in your search for your lost little friend—what is
his name?"

"Jomo."

"That's right. Jomo."

It comes back to me, the promise Mama Dale made to ask the bishop for help.

Mama Dale clears her throat and asks, "You haven't found him yet, have you?"

"No. No. I've been away on safari. I was hoping Mama Grace has heard something."

"I was in Mama's village last night. She said nothing of the boy except that you have a motherly concern for him. Mama Grace is very fond of you, Lana."

"I love Mama Grace. I'll be grateful for any help your church can give me."

Mama Dale laughs. "Oh, Mama, it is not my church, not your church. It's the Lord's church. Help is what we do."

"Okay."

She rattles off an address. "Do you need assistance getting there?"

"No. I'm familiar with the area." My throat threatens to close over. I have not set foot inside a Mormon church building in almost twenty years. I shift my weight and stare out the window at the stars twinkling against the morning darkness. "How is baby Gracie?"

Mama Dale squeals. "Oh, her HIV test came back negative!"

"That's terrific news." I'd never considered the probability of Gracie being an AIDS baby. When will I focus on the reality that is all around me?

"I'll look for you by the main door of the church," Mama Dale says.

I feel anxious and afraid. My feelings are not all negative. Something inside me *wants* to go to church—not just to ask for help, but because . . . because I want to be there.

What is happening to me?

I lay the jewelry I bought for Nygoya on her desk. There is so much about her that I admire. She has a cause and stands up for it. Gingerly, I touch the barrel of the elephant gun hanging on her wall. It is time I develop that kind of conviction in my life.

I type up my report, eat breakfast, put on a skirt and top, and adorn myself with African jewelry. I keep a small closet of extra clothes at the office for needed changes, but I don't own any outfit my mother would deem appropriate for church. My ear is pierced three times, and I have a tattoo of a four-leaf clover on my ankle. I got it long before skin ink separated the sheep from the goats. I am a goat. I've always been a goat.

I go easy on the makeup but spray myself with a bottle of perfume I bought last year in Paris. Then I sit at my desk, an hour and a half to go before church time.

Impulsively, I reply to Gavin's email. I don't expect him to get the message in time, but I invite him to attend church with me. The idea of going alone is gloomy.

Thirty minutes before it is time to leave my telephone rings. It's the direct line to my office, and I expect to hear Nygoya's voice on the other end. Instead I hear Gavin say, *"Jambo."*

My heart leaps like a startled gazelle.

"Hi." So much for conviction; I've already lost my nerve.

"I just got your email," he says.

"Oh, that. I shouldn't have . . . "

"No. I'm glad you did. I've been awake all morning, going a little stir crazy. I'd love to attend church services with you."

My heart won't stop pounding. "Have you ever been to an LDS . . . a *Mormon* church service?"

"No, but how different can it be? You're Christians, aren't you?"

"Absolutely. But I should warn you that I haven't been to church in years."

"I think you mentioned that before."

I tell him about Mama Dale and the goal to get Bishop Kaahari to help us find Jomo.

"Okay, then," Gavin says. "Should I meet you at the church or pick you up at your hotel?"

"Pick me up," I say quickly, before I change my mind.

I'm surprised at how much the Nairobi meetinghouse looks like my childhood meetinghouse back in Utah.

Gavin and I walk toward the building side by side. I think how handsome he looks in his khaki shorts and white shirt.

"You look nervous," he says.

"I am."

"Don't be. What are they going to do, stone you?"

I laugh. "So you *do* know about Mormons."

His blue eyes squint. "They can't be that bad; you said they're Christians."

I straighten my spine and brace myself to be judged by every person there.

But they don't judge. They rush to welcome me. Mama Dale is the first to take me in her arms and kiss my cheek. Then she scopes out Gavin. "Good for you, Lana. You have landed yourself a man."

I blush flamingo pink.

"Gavin McQueen," he says, reaching out to pump her hand. He possesses Nygoya's confidence, and a part of me envies him.

She claps her hands and squeals. "Oh! You are Mama Grace's Gavin. Of course, I recognize you now. Welcome, *marafiki*." She slings an arm around each of us and ushers us inside. Part of me fears the roof will fall in or the building will be struck by lightning, old jokes about what happens when a sinner steps on holy ground. Nothing happens except what changes inside of me.

Fear and insecurity melt, and all I feel is welcome, like I've come home after a very long time away.

People stare at us, two white faces in a flowing river of dark beauty and strength. We are introduced to Bishop Kaahari, the tallest African I have ever seen. While some people here wear traditional native dress, colorful patterns and prints, the bishop is dressed in a long-sleeved white shirt, gray and worn at the collar, and black dress pants too short for a man of his stature. His tie is something that Mr. C would covet—the head of a rhino, painted in brilliant blue and purple.

The bishop grins and shakes our hands. His fingers are long enough to wrap all the way around my palm.

"It's an honor," says Gavin, clearly recognizing the local running champion. They chat about sprints and races.

When he turns to me his dark eyes are soft and gentle. "I understand you have a request."

"Yes," says Mama Dale, speaking for me, "Lana is looking for the lost boy I mentioned. A child named Jomo."

"Oh, yes. You requested help in locating him."

"I would appreciate any help I can get. Jomo seems to have simply vanished. I have to find him."

Bishop Kaahari touches my elbow. "You are a kind and caring woman. We will do what we can to help you."

"We are a great force for good when we work together," Mama Dale says.

Gavin nods. "We all want to help Lana find Jomo. Whatever it takes, we're willing to do."

"Then we'll find him," Bishop Kaahari says, and his words bring a calm to my soul, a feeling I haven't known since Jomo disappeared.

A large portrait of Jesus hangs in the foyer. The image is familiar to me; it depicts Christ ministering to a group of children. One smiling boy is Black.

I stare at the portrait, recalling a scripture my father mentioned to me. It's in the Book of Mormon—the one about Christ loving all God's children, the bond and free, the black and white. I can't quote it—I can't even find it, but my heart knows it's true. Skin color does not regulate God's love. Not even sin regulates God's love.

I feel it, and my heart seems to expand.

"You okay?" Gavin asks.

"Oh, yeah."

"So is this like your childhood memories of church?" he asks.

"This is so different . . . and yet the same." My memory of Sunday mornings is a sea of white shirts and pale dresses, but here there is an explosion of color—reds and oranges, purples and greens, and sunshine yellows. There aren't as many people as I'm used to seeing, but the river of black faces radiates joy. I've never seen so many smiles. As far as I can see, Gavin and I are the only white faces in the building.

Like everywhere I've traveled in Kenya, the children flock around us. *"Mzungu."*

They grab my hands, whisper and stare. They want to touch my skin. They touch my heart. A little boy with huge dark eyes takes my hand, and I look down, half-expecting to see Jomo, but the boy is much younger and fuller.

Before I realize what is going on, Gavin is swept down the hallway beneath the umbrella of Bishop Kaahari's arm.

"Don't look so worried." The bishop laughs. "I'm not kidnapping your man, just taking him to priesthood meeting."

I give Gavin an apologetic look, but he doesn't appear worried. He looks perfectly calm—happy, even. He grants me a signature wink and melts into the throng of priesthood bearers shaking hands, slapping backs, and hugging each other. I wish Dad was here to see this.

When I first came to Africa, all the hugging surprised me. African people by nature are overt and tactile. I picture my father here with his spiritual comrades. He would fit right in.

Mama Dale guides me into a room that very much resembles every other Relief Society room I've ever seen—except for the beaming black faces and vibrant dresses.

There is no air conditioning, and between the temperature and the crowd, the scent is very earthy, but not unpleasant. I'm made to feel welcome right away and suddenly find myself the focal point of the room.

When Mama Dale tells the women that I'm originally from Utah, the entire room gasps. "How is our prophet? Do you visit the Salt Lake Temple often?" Their questions leave me with no answers, and I'm anxious to take my seat on the front row next to a woman introduced as Sister Sunshine, the Relief Society president.

A woman at the piano pounds out a familiar tune that I cannot place.

"Welcome our visitor," Sister Sunshine says, clapping her hands together like a child.

It takes me a second to realize that every eye in the room is still on me. My throat goes dry. My legs feel like rubber bands gone limp. I don't feel judged; I do feel like these women have expectations of me that I cannot meet.

"Jambo," is the only thing I can think to say.

The room sputters with greetings, in both English and Swahili.

"What city in Utah do you call home?" someone asks.

"Provo."

I'm surprised that these women know Provo.

"BYU."

"Yes." I nod and smile.

"What ward are you in?" someone asks.

I force my smile to be more confident than I feel. It's so phony my mouth hurts. I can't think of my childhood ward. "My parents live in Grandview," I say. "My dad was the bishop many years ago."

More ooohs and ahhhs.

"Welcome, Sista," the Relief Society president says.

I love the ways she says *Sista*. The way she lifts me off the hook and lets me wriggle free of the questions.

The opening song is sung with gusto that I've never heard in another church. "We are all enlisted till the conflict is o'er . . . happy are we . . . happy are we."

They *are* happy. These beautiful African women all sway and tap their feet. They don't just sing the lyrics; they believe in the message of the words.

The sister who says the prayer limps to the front. She has one crippled foot and only one arm, but when she prays in her native Bantu tongue, I peek to see if Jesus has come down from heaven. *Never* have I heard a prayer so heartfelt, so beautiful—and I don't even understand her words. I *feel* them.

"What did she say?" I whisper to Mama Dale.

"She gave thanks to the Lord for all of our bounties."

What bounties? The people around me are some of the poorest people in the world . . . and yet they define gratitude.

The lesson is about service, and I feel like I'm the only one in the room who needs it. The teacher is introduced as a faculty member at one of the highland Harambee schools. She has some type of skin infection; her eyes are swollen, and bumps the size of marbles protrude from beneath her skin. "It is paramount," she says, making direct eye contact with each woman in the room, "that we share our blessings, that we use our talents to assist those in need. If you are a sister gifted with a reading talent, you must share it."

She passes the manual to a sister at the back row who stands to read a quote, but stumbles on many of the words. I want to rush to her to help, but Mama Dale holds me back. "No."

When the reader finally finishes, the entire room bursts into emotional applause.

The woman beams. "I have been practicing that passage all month long. *Asante sane.*"

By the end of the lesson I realize that I am in the company of the Lord's chosen—his most humble, most grateful daughters. I am seated among angels.

"You are crying," Mama Dale says, touching my cheek with the back of her fingers. "Tears are needed to cleanse the soul."

The sisters come to greet me one by one. They shake my hand, say my name, and hold me in their arms.

"Would you and your man care to stay for Sunday School?" Mama Dale asks me. "It is held in this very room."

"I would like to visit Primary, if that would be all right." I did not plan on making this request. I didn't even think about it; it just tumbled out of my mouth as my heart split open.

"Yes, you are a woman who loves children."

I meet up with Gavin in the hallway. He is the one pumping hands and giving hugs. If I didn't know better, I'd take him for a long-standing member of the ward. When he spots me, his smile stretches.

"Would you like to come to Primary with me?"

"What's Primary?"

"My favorite part of church."

The Primary room is cramped and crowded, but right away I feel my spirit move to an even higher level. We are introduced to a member of the bishopric, who sits at the front on a banged-up folding chair. The president is a short, stout woman named Mama Osanga. As far as I can tell she has no counselors. Gavin and I sit at the very back of the room, and every child there twists around to stare at the two white strangers who have come to visit.

There are at least two dozen children; most of them look as if they walked here straight from Mama Grace's village. I can tell that someone has made an effort to dress them in their Sunday best and provide them clean clothing, but some of the children don't even have shoes.

Two or three are scrubbed and shined. They stand out as the fortunate ones; Mama Dale's daughter, Benda, is one of them. She sees me and offers a fast wave. It's impossible to tell that she is autistic just by looking at her.

Some of the children have probably never been scrubbed or shined in their lives. Their clothes are filthy, their feet bare, their eyes hungry. The majority of the children are average, if *average* means "poor."

Still, the room glows, not from the sunshine streaming through the windows, but from children. Each one is a light.

They never stop smiling. Neither do I.

They sing loud and strong. They sway. A trio of boys cannot stop themselves from slapping out rhythm on the back of folding chairs. "Jesus Wants Me for a Sunbeam." There is nothing irreverent about their behavior; on the contrary, these children are worshipping with all of their hearts, their bodies, their spirits.

Gavin is getting into it. He doesn't have a clue about the words, but he's humming and swaying and grinning like he's one of the kids.

After the song, Sister Osanga introduces us to the children.

I remain seated, but Gavin stands as though he is official. "Jambo!"

"Jambo!" a chorus of children sing.

Gavin points to me and speaks to the children in Swahili. Whatever he says brings a spattering of laughter from them and a look of astonishment from Sister Osango.

"What did you say?" I ask when he sits back down beside me.

"I told them you are my one-cow wife, and that I left my two-cow wife at home."

I roll my eyes, knowing that tribal men do indeed purchase wives with cattle. After a moment I turn back to Gavin, my cheeks burning. "Only one cow?"

He laughs out loud.

Sister Osango goes on to explain that I work at the hotel but that I am originally from Utah.

"Do you live by the prophet?" a little girl asks.

"No," I say.

"Do you live by a temple?"

"Yes. My parents live very close to the Provo Temple."

"What a blessing," Sister Osango says, and I feel guilty because the only time I ever went to the temple was to do baptisms for the dead when I wasn't much older than most of these children. I never realized what a blessing the temple is—not until now, when I can see in Sister Osango's eyes the longing to have the blessings of a nearby temple.

I have never realized a lot of things.

The children lose all interest in me when they learn that Gavin is a safari outfitter. He talks to them, and we learn that most of the children have never been outside of the city. I make a mental note to see if the hotel can sponsor a trip to Ambrosia National Park, the closest reserve. It would garner good publicity for the hotel, and I'm already formulating my proposal to Mr. C.

So many ideas and feelings are flooding through me, washing away old ideas and embedded feelings. There is something truly holy about this Primary room, simple and sacred.

My heart aches, wishing Jomo were here.

Instead of splitting into classes, we stay as a group. We sing, and then a woman about my age gives a lesson on the Atonement of Jesus Christ.

"Who knows what the word *atonement* means?" she asks. Hands shoot into the air, and one young boy is called on. He is the tallest and the oldest-looking boy in the class, almost as tall as Gavin. He speaks slowly and distinctly. *"Atonement* means to be at one with God."

"Very good, Charles. What would separate one from God?"

"Sin."

"And how do we come back to God after we sin?"

"We repent."

"Very good. What does it mean to *repent?*"

The same boy's hand waves. "It means to break our hard hearts. To fall to our knees. To beg God for a new chance."

"And what do we do when we get up off of our knees?"

"We forgive ourselves and go on living life better than before."

The lesson, so simple, sinks to the very bottom of my broken heart.

"You know something," I say to Gavin as we make our way out of the Primary room and into the chapel for sacrament meeting, "I went to Primary for years but learned more in that hour than I did my entire childhood."

"I know what you mean," he says, taking my hand with ease and confidence. I feel like a teenager on a first date.

At the start of sacrament meeting Bishop Kaahari calls us to the front, where we are introduced to the congregation. I search the

214 TONI SORENSON BROWN

crowd and see a few other white faces. One belongs to a missionary in a white, short-sleeved shirt, whose freckled face makes him look like he could be from Utah or Idaho.

I feel so grateful to be part of something bigger and better than myself. I feel hopeful that together we will find Jomo, that one day he will know the happiness that is swelling in my heart.

When we sing, the whole congregation sings; every mouth is open. *Because I have been given much, I too must give . . . . "*

I look around. The chapel is clean, but scant. It is less than half the size of my childhood chapel. Instead of padded benches, we sit on dented and battered folding chairs.

Because of thy great bounty, Lord, each day I live.

The clothes of the people are colorful, but as I inspect them more closely, I notice that they are threadbare—even torn and mended. Pants are shiny at the knees, and shirts are stained where ties do not cover.

I shall divide my gifts from thee With ev'ry brother that I see . . . .

I sit in the midst of people I do not know, but feel a kinship with them that I don't quite understand. Gavin sits next to me with his fingers still laced through mine.

Warmth and wonder pulse through me.

The music swells, and so does my heart. To a privileged person unfamiliar with Africa, a glance through the chapel windows would reveal some of the poorest people in the world.

They are poor, and yet they have everything.

. . . thus shall my thanks be thanks indeed.

My whole body goes flush, starting from the inside out. I know tears are rushing down my cheeks. I know I have been ungrateful; I just didn't know *how* ungrateful until I feel gratitude. I know I have been self-destructive; I just didn't know how much damage I've done to those who love me. I know I have been wrong; I just never felt such burning sorrow.

I am so, so, so sorry.

When the sacrament is passed I try to explain the ritual to Gavin. He seems to understand. The prayers are the same words I've heard on hundreds of Sundays, but the broken bread is served very differently. It is not presented in tiny silver sacrament trays, but instead is served in large, woven, hand-painted baskets, much like the ones Mama Grace weaves. Part of the bread is broken into small, bite-sized pieces, pushed to one side, while the rest—great, organic hunks of bread big enough to serve an entire meal—are stacked in the basket. The reason why becomes clear to me. For many of these men, women, and especially the children, a handful of bread is all they will have to eat for the entire day.

After the service, Bishop Kaahari introduces Gavin and me to the missionaries, who'll be helping us look for Jomo: Elder Mercer from Soda Springs, Idaho, and Elder Cherry from Botswana.

Elder Mercer tells me that his father grows potatoes. I smile to myself as I look into his sun-baked, freckled white face and hazel eyes. I think how proud I would be if he were my son.

Elder Cherry is quieter and keeps his head bowed much of the time.

"We're here to help," Elder Mercer says, squeezing my hand just like I expect from a farm boy. Powerful and sure.

Bishop Kaahari leads us down a narrow corridor, through a door, out into an open-air classroom by a lemon tree. I am surprised to see that the sky is blanketed with dark, potbellied clouds. The air is humid and ripe with the scents of the city.

"I haven't seen it rain in weeks," Gavin says.

"That is because it has not rained," Bishop Kaahari says, looking up. "That will change today."

I don't want to talk about the rain; I want to talk about Jomo.

"Oh, yes," says the bishop, "Sister Lana and Brother Gavin are friends to Mama Grace."

Elder Cherry grins for the first time. "We know Mama Grace. There are times we do work in her village."

So I wasn't crazy when I thought I saw Mormon missionaries walking down Redemption Road.

"Yes," says Elder Mercer, "Mama Grace has fed us roasted pumpkin more than once. She is a very traditional woman."

I think of Grace's conviction that the spirits of children haunt the trunk of a tree. "Yes, Mama is traditional. But it's not Mama Grace who needs our help. A little boy has disappeared, and I was hoping you might be able to help look for him."

"Tell us what we can do to assist you," the bishop says.

Gavin looks at me, and I can tell he is anxious to speak. I nod for him to go ahead.

"Jomo is a street boy, as you know. We have no surname, no real family information. Lana has a photo."

I reach into my bag and produce a copy of Jomo's smiling face. The sound of thunder rumbles in the distance.

"He's a handsome boy," Bishop Kaahari says. "Tell us all about this Jomo."

Between me and Gavin, we cover every detail we know. I wish we could offer more.

"I am very sorry your friend is gone," says Elder Cherry.

The word *gone* strikes me like a closed fist to the stomach.

"With your help, we'll find him," I say, forcing a smile.

Gavin asks, "Any ideas?"

The bishop has been taking notes. "Yes, many ideas already. We will search the village; our members will help. Locals are more likely to speak with someone who is not a stranger."

"Mama Grace is the heart and soul of the village, and no one has told her anything. Maybe no one knows."

"Even the trees have eyes," the bishop says. "The police have not provided the assistance you had hoped for?"

I shake my head.

"I have connections with the police department. I have connections with the politicians. I will use them as the Spirit directs." Bishop Kaahari purses his lips. "Tell me more about this boy—Malik."

"I think he is like a big brother to Jomo. He is very upset that I meddled in Jomo's life."

"You mean by giving him new clothes?"

I nod. "I made Jomo a target."

Mama Dale puts her arm around me. "You cannot blame yourself for everything evil and tragic. The good Lord knows your heart, Lana. He knows that you only wanted to help your little *rafiki* Jomo."

The idea that the Lord sees past my sins and reads the thoughts of my heart gives me a surge of new hope.

Light rain begins to fall, but no one goes back inside. Instead, Mama Dale joins us along with more people she has gathered. They all seem eager to help.

Bishop Kaahari turns to the missionaries. "I will talk to your mission president. He may spare your service to go and search for Jomo's sister."

I think back to the night that Nygoya and I trod the cardboard streets, the spool district. It is no place for young, impressionable elders. Bishop Kaahari seems to have the same revelation as I do and he says, "On a better thought, perhaps the missionaries should work in the village."

He passes out assignments to Sister Osango and the Relief Society. The elders quorum and high priests also agree to specific tasks. I can't help thinking that if Officer Habib had the bishop's drive and organizational skills, Jomo would be safe now.

"By the time we are finished, each and every house in the village will be searched."

"I can't tell you how much hope you're giving me. I know a child can't just disappear."

"Keep in mind that you do not know for certain if this boy has met with foul play."

"And I pray he hasn't," I say quickly. "I just have to find him and be sure Jomo is safe."

"We all understand."

It is agreed that tomorrow morning we'll meet at Mama Grace's school. I dread having to ask Mr. C for another day off. None of the Church members are whining about having to forfeit a business day to help, and I'm sure Mr. C will understand.

If he fires me, so be it.

We set the time early, and I thank everyone repeatedly. Part of me does not want to leave, but Bishop Kaahari excuses himself; he has meetings. "We will meet tomorrow. For now, safe journey."

When I look back, Elder Cherry and Elder Mercer have Gavin cornered. "So," says Elder Cherry, "we understand that you're not a member of the Church."

"No, I'm not."

Elder Mercer grins so wide, I can see his molars. "We can fix that."

CHAPTER 32

The clouds grow heavier, and a steady rain wets everything—steamy rain, thick and sauna-like. Gavin and I ride back to the hotel for lunch. I feel completely at ease with him, but we don't say much. I wonder what he's thinking and feeling. I am so grateful for all he's done to support me.

"Your church is different," Gavin says.

I take pride in hearing it called *my* church.

"How is it different?" I ask.

"In just about every way. For starters, nobody gets paid. They give their time and service for free. Do you know that your bishop is a genuine celebrity?"

"I didn't know that. I'm just glad he's got connections that might be able to help find Jomo."

Gavin falls quiet. "You said you haven't been to church in years."

"That's true, too."

He sets down his fork and looks at me. "The same with me. I was trying to count backwards. I guess it's been, let's see, seventeen years since I've been inside a church."

"I had the impression that religion is really important to you."

"Faith is; I don't know about religion. When I was a kid we *lived* religion. While my friends read Dick and Jane, I was required to read Habakkuk."

"Excuse me?"

"It's a book in the Old Testament," he laughs. "When Amanda and I got married, my life went in the opposite direction; *religion* became a curse word."

"So now you're searching your soul?"

He nods. "You told me that you have a lot of questions—hard questions about poverty and suffering and injustice."

"I do, but these past days I've come to know for myself that God has the answers."

Outside, thunder growls and coughs. "That reminds me of that angry lion on safari."

Gavin smiles and reaches across the table to touch my hand. "You're an amazing woman, Lana."

I'm caught off guard by the compliment, by the way Gavin is looking into my eyes, as if he can see to the very center of my soul.

"Not really. If you knew the real me . . ."

"You're so hard on yourself. Don't be. I'll tell you something I've learned about God."

"Tell me."

"It's not so difficult to get God's forgiveness; what is really difficult is forgiving ourselves."

Something catches inside of me. "You're talking from your heart."

"I'm to blame for my wife's death."

"What? I thought she was struck by a bus."

"She was. Amanda was upset; we'd had an argument, and she stormed out of the house angry, angry at me."

I can feel Gavin's pain. I guess I'm not the only one packing around guilt. "Gavin, it wasn't your fault. You have to know that."

He taps his temple. "I know it here, but not here." His finger taps his chest, and I understand better than he can imagine. Someday maybe . . . maybe I'll tell him about my own self-appointed perdition.

"I felt better after church, didn't you?"

He nods.

"I know I can't just show up once and expect to be forgiven, but I used to hate church. It wasn't like that at all today."

"I know what you mean."

"Oh, I'm sorry about the missionaries. I should have warned you that their job is to zoom in on potential converts."

He laughs and tosses his napkin onto the table. "Don't worry. Missionary zeal is nothing new to me."

I look over at the clock and realize it is still early. "Let's go see Mama Grace. I'll buy her a meal from the hotel."

Gavin frowns. "I wish I could, but I've got to get back. Besides, if it keeps raining, the village roads will turn to soup, and there's no way my truck can get through."

"Do you think it will stop raining for our search in the morning?"

"Yes. It will clear up in an hour or two. It's unusual for it rain like this out of season. It won't last."

"What about tomorrow? The muddy roads won't hamper us, will they?"

"Tomorrow the sun will shine, the Mormons will come, and Jomo will be found."

I leap up and throw my arms around Gavin's neck. His lips are on mine, or mine are on his. We are kissing right there in the middle of the banquet room. I don't care who sees me or what they say. I've found a friend, maybe something more. I've found someone who makes me feel like I can do anything.

We walk back to his truck beneath a blanket of clouds knitted into black squares. As we walk, I want the rain to wash away every sin I've ever committed. I want to be strong like Mama Grace, helpful like Mama Dale, brave like Nygoya, and genuine like Gavin.

I tell myself that next week, with Jomo in tow, I'll go back to church. I'll make a private appointment with Bishop Kaahari; I'll bare my soul, deal with the consequences, and start again. When it's all over, I'll be one of the strong ones, the giving ones. I see it all like it's already real.

Gavin leans down and takes me in his arms, pulling me to him. I want him to kiss me again, but he plants his warm lips on my forehead like he did when we were on safari.

"I'll see you bright and early tomorrow morning."

"I'll be there."

CHAPTER 33

My head is spinning when I return to my office, damp from the rain, happier than I ever remember feeling. Ever.

I call Officer Habib and leave a voice mail for him, telling him that we're organizing a thorough search of the village. I drop Bishop Kaahari's name just in case it carries any clout with him. I write a check to pay for the office supplies I've taken from the hotel, and use the copy machine to make more posters of Jomo to pass out tomorrow.

It's only three o'clock in the afternoon. I haven't had any decent sleep in twenty-four hours, but I'm not tired. I'm eager to do something more.

I check my email. No messages since morning. I walk back outside and spot a bit of blue sky. I go back in and pack restaurant containers with leftover buffet food: fresh spinach, sliced mangoes, fresh pineapple, grilled chicken, and boiled eggs.

When I give the cashier my credit card he raises an eyebrow. "You just ate, Miss Lana."

"This is for my friend," I say. "Do you have any of those fruit tarts left?"

I grab a package of cookies, too; Mama Grace can share them with the children.

I change my skirt and blouse for jeans and a pink hoodie. I keep on the same flip-flops.

I intend to catch a bus to Redemption Road. I'm pushing the revolving front door of the hotel when I remember my last bus ride to the village.

The driver turned out to be a creep. I can still see his big head and beady eyes. The details come back to me at once. He asked me all about Jomo, and I told him everything: I told the man Jomo's name, where he lived; I told him that Jomo was an orphan.

I keep pushing through the door, feeling like I'm going to vomit.

The hotel concierge looks up from her desk. "Are you ill?"

"I'll be okay, but I'm going to borrow the smallest hotel van— *matwana*—to ride out to Mama Grace's village. I'll be back before dark."

"You should not travel alone, Miss Lana."

"I've done it before. I'll be fine."

First, I stop by my office and call Officer Habib to leave another message. "I might have a new lead," I say. "I don't know the man's name, but he's a local bus driver, and he was in an accident the evening he gave me a lift to Mama Grace's village. Please call me as soon as you get this message, and I'll give you more details. I'm headed out to the village now."

The van bounces down along the dirt road as I think about the bus driver's questions and his interest in Jomo. Is it possible that he went back to the village? Did he have something to do with Jomo's disappearance? What if . . . ?

I have no idea how to find the driver. I don't even remember what his *matwana* looked like. It was small and battered. Blue, maybe.

Wait! Mama Grace saw him while I was with Jomo. She'll know if the driver showed back up in her village.

I feel sick at the thoughts that race through my head. My stomach turns over and over. My rapid breathing is steaming up the windshield. "Please don't let the rain start again," I pray aloud.

It rains. In buckets. Sheets. Torrents. The water comes down so fast and furious that the windshield wipers are worthless, and the back end of the van fishtails as the road turns from baked hard dirt to, just as Gavin warned, soup.

My heart leaps, and my fists clench on the steering wheel. I roll down the window and try to see outside. The air fills with steam, smelling like wet, raw sewage and sodden garbage.

Adults run for shelter, while children make a game of the mud and the muck. Inching along, I slip and flop slowly so that I don't hit something or someone.

I should not have come. It was impulsive and stupid. I can't do any good here—not today. I just felt so helpless sitting around doing nothing but waiting.

Through the blur in front of me I spot the sign: Redemption Road. I think of Mama Grace: I've forgotten to bring her a book.

I lay on the horn to scatter the children. The sight of Grace's school gives me assurance. I should be here, after all. The school looks a little more complete; part of it is still roofless, but there's been progress made while I was on safari. No doubt Mr. C and Nygoya worked while I was gone. I grab the bag of buffet leftovers and make a beeline through the rain for Mama Grace's open door.

"Mama!"

No answer.

"Mama Grace! It's me, Lana."

The muddy yard is packed with soggy children, staring at me. Do they still think I'm a bad omen, come to disturb the spirits of dead children? They don't look too fearful of me now—only curious.

Mama's door doesn't exist, but out of respect, the children stand in the rain rather than coming inside. It is customary for African people to stand out by the gate and call rather than approach the door and knock.

"Come in!" I shout above the storm, waving them in. The school is dark and shadowy; rain is puddling over the concrete floor. I'm used to being here during bright sunlit days. It is eerily empty of the woman whose presence fills it so completely. Lightning flashes and thunder booms. Apricot-sized raindrops pound against the corrugated metal of what exists of the roof. The sound is as deafening as war drums. I keep blinking, trying to get my eyes to adjust to the sudden shadows. My foot hits something: a book. I pick it up and see then that Mama Grace's classroom has come under attack. Books are everywhere, open with broken spines and torn pages. A glass bowl is shattered.

My heart stops. "Where's Mama Grace?" I demand of the children.

One tall boy wipes his muddy face with the back of his muddy hand. "She go."

"*Where* did she go?" I shout, feeling a new type of panic rise, like bile in my throat. Grace is not well. She should not be out in this rain. She should be here.

"She go to fight," the boy says.

"Mama Grace? Fight who?" Panic chokes me. What if the bus driver came back? What if Mama Grace put the missing pieces together and found herself in harm's way?

I groan and shout. "Have any of you seen Jomo?"

"No Jomo. Jomo go too."

I freeze. "Is Jomo with Mama Grace?"

"No," says the boy.

The children fall back, huddled; they are afraid of me. The food falls out of my arms, crashes to the floor, then I kneel hard, knowing that something horrible has gone on here.

"What happened?" I ask the tallest, oldest boy. "Did a man come and cause trouble for Mama Grace?"

Even as I ask the question I remember the night Nick came back to our apartment and attacked me. I remember it, but the memory no longer holds me hostage. I am no longer a victim. I survived, and Mama Grace will, too.

"No man," says the boy. "Malik."

"Malik." My brain burns. "*He* did this?"

"Malik and his gang."

I grip the boy's wet shoulders so tightly he jerks back in pain, but I do not let go. "Tell me. Did they hurt Mama Grace?"

The boy laughs and wiggles free. "No. No. She hurt them. They want to wreck her, and she wrecked them."

"What do you mean? What happened here?"

The rain pounds harder. The little girls have fallen to their knees to help gather the food. It is precious and must be saved at any cost.

"Malik mad at Mama," the boy says, lifting wilted leaves of spinach from the floor, handing them carefully back to the girls.

"Why?"

"Mama Grace says Malik and his gang not welcome at school. They have bad manners."

I sob. A clear picture of what has happened here plays in my mind. Why didn't I see Malik for what he really is?

The boy is growing very animated; his arms are flailing as he recounts what transpired. "They bust up things. Mama Grace gets mad. She gets gun and shoots."

"Mama Grace shot somebody?"

"No. She aimed at sky. She scared Malik."

"I didn't even know that Mama Grace has a gun."

The boy smirks. "Everybody knows that Mama is a crack shot. Her gun stays in her Bible box."

"I didn't know." Terror threatens to drown me. "Tell me, where's the gun now?"

"With Mama. She fired many bullets."

"When? When did all of this happen?"

"Before rain came."

I look the boy right in the eyes. "This is very important. Where are Mama Grace and Malik now?"

"Malik and gang, they take off pedaling, throwing threats at Mama Grace."

"What did she do?"

"She fired into the air. Mama laughed. Malik stopped; he got real mad. He said, all crazy, 'Shoot me.'"

I'm afraid to hear what happened next.

"He grabbed gun and BANG!"

"Mama Grace got shot?"

"No."

"Where are they NOW?" I am screaming, scaring the children. "Where is Mama Grace *now*?"

"Malik pushed her down. He came in here and stole her Bible. Her Bible is most precious to Mama Grace."

My heart sinks. My head pounds with the unrelenting rain. "I know." My knees threaten to buckle, but I have to be strong. Mama Grace needs me.

"She got more bullets," says the boy. "She will get her Bible back."

I stagger, realizing that Mama Grace's life is at stake. "Which way did she go?"

Twenty little arms point left, to the top of Redemption Road.

"You will go get Mama Grace back?" someone asks me in a small, desperate, begging voice.

I look around, but there are no adults in sight, only children. "Yes. I will get her. You children stay here. Stay safe. Eat the food."

I cast a frenzied glance at the van but opt to make my search on foot. Then I run, slipping, brazen and blinded, out into the rain. The mud immediately sucks me down, and I stumble.

I have to save Mama Grace. I have to.

The storm has rolled up its sleeves now, and it, too, is prepared for an all-out fight. Water deluges me, wind whips garbage and scraps of corrugated metal into the air. I'm nearly knocked off my feet into the rolling river of mud.

"Grace!" I scream into the wind. "Mama Grace!"

The few drenched faces that have not taken shelter stare at me in disbelief—or is it shock? One old woman with a sunken, toothless mouth and a baby bundled to her hunched back peers out through a narrow doorway. She motions for me to take refuge with her.

"Which way did Mama Grace go?"

The woman shakes her head, and when she turns I can see that the baby is screaming, but I can't hear its cries over the roar of the storm.

I *have* to save Grace. Why can't I get any help? The village might have discarded Jomo, but Mama Grace is their very heartbeat. "Help me!" I scream, "Somebody, please help me!"

The narrow village streets are always packed with people, curious, hungry, homeless. Now they are empty and deserted.

"Mama Grace!"

Water and dirt flood my eyes. There are no longer streets—only red rivers of mud and human waste. The stiff corpse of a dog floats past me as I slosh my way up the road. I don't know where Grace and Malik could be in this brutal weather. I only know I have to keep moving.

Bewildered eyes look out at me from the shelter of shanty windows and doorways; I am a crazed white woman fighting her way upstream. They've never had to fear me before, but they do now.

A voice inside my head, familiar and dark, screeches, "You will never make it."

"I have to," I say aloud.

The sky is growing darker. The smells are beyond sickening. Only inches divide one shanty from another. Which one hides Malik? Where is Mama Grace?

Thunder pounds in my head. Somewhere I lose a flip-flop, and I stop to remove the remaining one. Mud and rocks, filth and metal slosh around my bare feet.

I am ankle-deep in death.

I trudge ahead, feeling that every step I take robs me of my strength. I might as well be walking through quicksand.

"You're going to fail," that old voice says.

"Leave me alone, Satan!" I scream. "I know you now; all you do is lie!"

Halfway up Redemption Road my strength completely drains from me. I turn my face to the growling, spitting sky. My knees buckle, and I am half-buried in mud. I pray with my whole heart. "Father, I'm sorry. I'm sorry for everything. I'm not asking for me; please help me find Mama Grace and Jomo. Give me the strength and wisdom to do this for them."

I struggle to stand. I'm crying for help, but the fury of the wind rushes at me, blowing my words back at me. A man stands outside of his shanty. I cry out to him, but he only stares at me like I'm an evil sprit.

So that's why no one will help me.

Time passes torturously slow until my entire body fails me. My knees buckle, and I fall, this time slamming face-first into the slop. I choke. Muck fills my mouth, my nostrils; it coats my eyes. I choke on the waste of Africa's bowels.

The metallic taste of blood fills my mouth. My tooth has cut through my bottom lip. I spit blood. I vomit mud.

"I can't do it, God. I can't." My voice falters to a pitiful whimper against the storm. The swirling ground around me froths, foams, and threatens to suck me under.

Someone laughs at my defeat, loud and cruel and victorious—someone I cannot see, but who I know sees me.

"Father, I can't do it," I say, pushing and pulling myself along, inching my way forward with my arms. "I can't save Mama Grace. I can't save Jomo. But *you* can. You are strong; grant me Your strength. You are wise; grant me Your wisdom."

"Mama Grace! Jomo!"

The laugh sounds again, biting against the wind and the water. I go so cold I quake. "Father . . . " It's all I can say, and I remember a night not so long ago when that was my entire prayer. *Father.*

And then a miracle happens. His strength is sufficient. His mercy is mine.

My broken spirit is restored. Strength surges into my legs, and I stand. As a cowering African audience watches me, black eyes from black places, I lift my arms above my head. I let the rain wash the mud from my eyes. I allow it to puddle in my ears.

"Thank you, Father."

I am not rescued from the storm, but granted strength to outlast it—to traverse its destruction.

I move forward, broken and yet whole at the same time.

The road does not veer, and I tramp on and on and on.

"Grace!"

"Jomo!"

That's when I hear the laugh again. A dark silhouette appears through the thick gray rain curtain.

"Grace!" I rush forward and fling open my arms.

But the figure is not Mama Grace.

Malik stands before me.

"Where is Mama Grace?" I demand.

He pivots away from me, only a matter of steps, and I follow him through a low, narrow opening into a shanty. It is enclosed, but so small neither of us can fully stand. The rain thunders down on the roof.

I blink and blink. "What have you done to Mama Grace?"

He laughs again, showing teeth as white as bleached bones. "Mama Grace is safe."

"Where is she?"

He leans down so his face is next to mine. His eyes are even older and harder than I remember. Hatred burns in them like glowing embers.

I see evil when I look at him. I feel it. I have never known such fear, and it threatens to stop my heart forever. *One mistake and it's all over.*

My prayer has not ceased, and when I open my mouth, confident words spill out. "Malik, you *have* to tell me where Mama Grace is."

He spits in my face. I flinch. "I do not have to do one thing you say. You are a crazy *mzungu,* a mutt, sniffing around here where you are not wanted."

"I came here trying to help."

"I told you, your help is not wanted."

Lightning flashes blue, and that is when I see it—the *panga* Malik holds, a blade six inches in length. It looks chipped and stained dark. In that instant I also see figures, hunched and dark in the corners along the walls. Hyenas in waiting.

Then the room goes pitch. I suck in a breath of rancid air. There is no light on a day like this, in a place like this. But another bolt of lightning permits me to see that one of the figures wears a bright yellow shirt.

"That is Jomo's shirt." My voice cracks. My heart crashes. Why couldn't I see the truth before now?

Malik laughs, and a cloud parts, allowing a stream of pale, white light to illuminate the shanty. In that second I see Malik not for what he appears to be, but for what he really is: an African boy robbed of childhood.

What unspeakable horrors has he suffered to bring him this far down Redemption Road?

"Please tell me where Jomo is."

"I thought you were looking for Mama Grace."

"Please . . . please . . . please."

"Jomo is gone for good," he says. "All that is left of the boy are the clothes you gave him."

"What do you mean? Please tell me the whole truth."

Malik's lip curls back in a snarl. "I sold him."

A portion of my very life leaves me. I know his horrible revelation is true. "Who bought my Jomo?"

"He was not *your* Jomo. He belonged to no one. I sell them all."

"Where . . . where is he now?" My teeth chatter, my bones go cold.

"Madagascar. Sierra Leone. Who knows? Men who buy boys sell them again and again." He laughs, and this time the other boys step out from the shadows, circling me with hate and murder seeping from their very pores.

I reach for something to hold on to, but there is nothing to grip—only empty space. I stumble, crumble to my already bloody knees. Now I know Jomo's fate. I am too sad to feel afraid.

"Did you sell him to the bus driver?"

Malik gives me a blank stare.

"The *matwana* driver—did you sell Jomo to him?"

"No."

"What have you done with Mama Grace?"

He laughs and laughs. "That old diseased woman got her Bible back. She is probably at her stupid school by now, teaching stupid children."

The circle closes in, and I struggle to stand. "I *will* find Jomo," I vow.

One of the boys lights a handheld torch of dried, wound grass. It smokes at first, then bursts into blood-red flames. I see that the boys, six or more, have painted their faces striped and savage. They want to terrorize me.

Through flickering light and shadows I look at each one, making direct eye contact. "I *will* find Jomo." I step backward toward the open rectangle of the door, toward the still-pouring rain.

Malik steps toward me. "You will find him dead. He is a stupid boy, grinning all the time. A boy like that does not survive for long."

Someone steps to block my escape.

"I'm leaving now," I say.

No one moves.

"Jomo is gone," Malik says, laughing. "If you want another little boy for your pleasure, I will sell you one."

I spit at Malik, hitting him in the forehead with a mixture of saliva, blood, and mud. "Is that what happened to you? Did someone sell you once?"

He lunges at me, and I think he might kill me, but he stops short and wipes his forehead with his forearm.

"Get out of my way. I'm leaving," I say.

They all laugh.

"You can't keep me here."

"Yes, we can."

"People know that I'm here."

Malik's voice is the deadly growl of a beast. "No one cared about Jomo. No one cares about you. You are a crazy *mzungu* who stirs up the ghosts of our dead children. The whole village will say that they never saw you."

"Mama Grace knows that I am here."

Malik's wide tongue flicks out to moisten his lips. "Mama Grace cannot tell anyone anything if her tongue is gone." He holds up his *panga* so that I get a good look at its deadly blade.

"Jomo, the happy boy, is dead," he says.

"Jomo is *not* dead." I fight the tears that boil behind my eyes. I will not allow them the vision of me crying, helpless, and weak. "Move," I say to the boy blocking my way.

More laughter.

"We will carve your dead flesh and feed you to the village dogs," Malik says. "Your bones we'll burn to ash and scatter through the streets. No one will miss you."

"Jomo is *not* dead," I say, stepping toward the doorway.

"Fool!"

There is a war cry, a flash of blade, and a sudden sharp pain in my stomach, deep and deadly.

The rain stops, and the sun comes out smiling.

You'd be surprised at the things you think and see and do when you are dying.

I think of the color black. It is beautiful. I see myself standing in a sea of African faces, measuring my pale complexion against the richness of their dark skin. I feel small, smug, entitled. I feel inadequate.

I think of my father, a man who thinks of himself as a reformed bigot. I think of all that he has taught me, especially in these past months, about humility and change. He will be sad that I am gone. I see his weathered, gnarled hands and think of all the work they've done in sixty years. I see his ashen face; even his lips have gone gray at the news from Africa. Maybe God did claim the sinful twin after all.

My ears ache with the sound of Daddy's heart breaking. I reach out to hold him, but my arms go right through his shoulders, and he does not know that I am with him, even though I am.

I picture my mother's garden. I see it pink and blooming. I smell her flowers and feel warm sunshine on my neck. I cannot see my mother's face—her back is turned to me—but I see the fruits of her labors. "Mom!" I call. She does not turn around. How I'm going to miss her.

And Laura: I see her at that horrific clinic. She's nineteen, whole, and cancer-free. "Please, let's go," she begs me.

I'm glad I listened to her.

Dying brings no white light, no tunnel, no heavenly guide to show me the way through the veil. Where is the veil? All I see is dark—dark red. I feel my body moving, jerking uncontrollably. I am in excruciating pain, yet I feel nothing.

I am dying.

It's over.

No! It is *not* over. I have unfinished business. I'm not afraid to die, but I can't let go because I have one final task to accomplish.

I do my best to swallow the blood that bubbles in my throat. I try to spit it out. I choke on my own blood.

I must find a way to say the words. My lips move. I choke.

Voices around me mutter, foggy and fearless. I hear a scream. It ricochets from inside a cave. I am cold. My body shivers.

A distant voice orders, "Let go."

Not yet, I think. *Not yet.*

I cling and clutch and manage one final feat. "I am sorry," I say aloud. I've said it before, but this time it has to cover a multitude of sins and sorrow, a lifetime of regrets.

"Forgive yourself," a gentle, piercing voice whispers. "I have already forgiven you."

Two arms wrap around me, enfold me in a love I could never imagine. They lift me, and I can breathe.

Again, I repeat, "I am sorry."

And in my heart and head I hear, "I know you are."

I let go.

CHAPTER 34

I do not die.

I lie in a hospital room; white sheets, soaked red, wrap me now, like a wounded mummy. Strangers rush around me. They wear black faces and white coats. Mama Grace stands at the door. Her hand is at her mouth, and she looks worried.

"Don't worry," I want to tell her, but when I try, powerful hands hold me down.

I think of African parasites, the ones that are so small they can fit into a human pore. I think of AIDS and infection.

I feel a pain so blinding it brands me like a searing iron, from the inside, pulling outward.

Swahili. The doctor is jabbering in Swahili.

I think of Laura. Sister, I did not feel pain when a scalpel hacked off your breast. Do you feel my pain now? Oh, Sister, I hope not.

I close my eyes to rest, but rest is not possible. Mama Grace comes to me and takes my hand in hers. She squeezes. Tight. I squeeze right back and look at her, but they are not Grace's eyes that stare at me.

Jomo!

His perfect little smile blazes. His presence lights up the entire room.

"Jomo! You're okay. Oh, thank God."

"Yes." His little fingers lace around mine and he squeezes with all his might. I force my heavy eyelids up to be sure this glorious moment is not a dream. I inspect Jomo for injury, but his eyes are dark reflecting pools, full of light and joy. I have never seen him so clean. His usual cuts and scrapes are healed. No scars.

I pull him to me; newfound strength surges through my arms. Jomo smells of pink baby lotion and shampoo.

"Where have you been?" I sob.

A shadow flickers across his smile. "Away."

"I was so worried. I looked all over for you."

"I am here now."

My own pain is gone, and I stroke his head, touch his wooly hair, and press him to my heart. "I will never let you go again. I love you, Jomo."

"I love you too, Mama Lana."

Unfiltered joy swells inside of me. My mind, as always, races ahead, making plans for our future. Jomo will live with me at my flat. I'll send him to Mama Grace's school. I'll do whatever I have to do to make it official. I'll take him to church every Sunday. He'll learn all about Heavenly Father and Jesus Christ. He'll grow up strong and healthy, happy and safe. In my mind, our future unfurls clear and unending like the morning sun lighting the whole Serengeti.

"Please do not cry," he whispers.

"These are happy tears. Good tears."

I use my index finger to trace his features, to touch his eyes, his eyebrows; I trace around his nose, so wide and proud, his lips, full and tender. Everything about Jomo is perfect, and now that I know what I did not know before, I cannot wait to teach him of the things that matter most.

"Do you remember the day we met?" he asks me.

"Every second of it."

"Do you remember how I held your hand?"

"Yes. You thought I was crying because you squeezed too tight."

He squeezes me now, and my fingers pinch together. "You are so strong," I say.

He smiles. "I am stronger now."

"There is so much I want to do for you, so much I want to teach you."

"You have taught me much," he says.

"No, you're the one who has taught me . . . " I struggle with the words to make him realize how my life has changed since he came along.

"You rest now, Mama Lana," he says.

"I don't want to rest. I don't want to blink; I'll miss you. I want to hold you, to play with you. Please don't ever go away again, Jomo."

My head feels heavy. It hurts to draw a breath. I look toward the door for Mama Grace, but she is gone. The doctors in the white coats are gone. And when I look to Jomo, I see that my limp hand lies on a blood-stained sheet.

The room goes blazingly bright.

I stare at my lonely hand. My palm lies flat and pink except for the places where Jomo's fingers have left perfect little indentations, white places where he squeezed my hand . . . until he had to let go.

Days later, Gavin and Mama Grace come to tell me. Mr. C and Nygoya are here too.

"I'm sorry," says Gavin, fighting back tears. "The police found Jomo's body in Mombassa. He was identified only because of all of your efforts, Lana. If the authorities hadn't been aware of your flyers, no one would have recognized him."

My mouth opens, but I cannot form a single word.

Gavin glances down at the gray tile floor. "They don't think he suffered. Jomo died from a single blow to the head."

"The hotel funded a very nice burial," Mr. C quickly adds. "We are sorry you were unable to attend. It was very nice."

How? Who? *Why?* The questions throb in my brain and pound in my heart.

I try desperately to comprehend what they are telling me, but they are wrong.

All of them.

Mama Grace kneels by my bedside. "We buried him properly in the village.

"Jomo's spirit is not trapped in the trunk of the baobab tree. He lies along Redemption Road in the children's burial ground."

"No. *No.*" I struggle to sit straight, and my lips turn upward in a soft, sure smile. My heart thunders like a herd of running elephants. A fire burns within my chest, and I have never been so certain of anything in my life.

"Jomo is not in the village. I know where he is; Jomo is with Jesus."

In time, my wounds begin to heal. There is recurring pain, and the doctors say my scars will never completely fade, but will serve to remind me of how close I came to losing my life. When I look in the mirror I see how close I came to losing even more than my final breath.

Father. The prayer comes easier now. And more often.

Dad emails me and sends scriptures "to attest to the fact that the gospel is bursting forth in great light, shining down on all of God's precious children. All of His children. Remember Ammon? He was in line to take over his father's kingdom, but once converted, chose to leave his own people, to travel to a foreign land, to a foreign people, to bring them the light and truth of the gospel. He reminds me of you, Lana. Go look up Alma 26:37."

I do, and though I don't tell him, I soon have the scripture committed to memory. God is "mindful of every people, whatsoever land they may be in; yea, he numbereth his people, and his bowels of mercy are over all the earth."

It brings comfort to know that both Jomo and I are numbered, not forgotten. I have been a recipient of that mercy, and it makes me want to give back, to share that love with others the way my friends here in Africa do, the way my family does.

Dad writes that he sold the boat he rebuilt. He's going to use the money to fund a trip to visit me in Nairobi. As soon as Laura is done with chemo, he tells me, they are all coming to Africa.

My sister is doing well, as well as can be expected for someone who has gone through what she has. Sometimes the two of us talk about our scars and all they mean to us. To someone listening in, we might seem crazy, but we understand each other without having to explain our words.

I stand in continued awe of Nygoya, who has launched a one-woman war against child prostitution in the city. She's teamed up with Bishop Kaahari and they've vowed never to quit. "One day we'll bring Anyango home," she tells me, and I don't doubt it.

Officer Habib took great pride in rounding up Malik and his uncle. Several village men and young boys were charged with running a child abduction ring. They have not located the person who "purchased" Jomo and ultimately killed him. Gavin tells me that it doesn't matter if they never find out; God knows.

I smile and nod. Some days the smiles come easier than other days.

People tell me that it was Malik and his uncle, not the yellow shirt, who made Jomo a target. I still struggle with the guilt—for that and other mistakes—but slowly, I'm learning to let go and let God carry those burdens for me.

I don't allow myself to dwell on the horror of Jomo's last days. I choose to stay focused on a beaming little boy whose grip still holds my mind.

Jomo is gone—for now. His little life was pure and innocent, and he did nothing to deserve the suffering and tragic end that came to him. My heart is broken, but remade by the fact that I know without doubt where Jomo is, and in whose care he now is.

Today is the opening of Mama Grace's school. She has named it Redemption Learning Center. On the wall hangs a giant sign boasting the Ten Commandments.

People come in droves—children dressed in yellow shirts, the color Grace has decided on for her school's uniform. Yellow, in honor of Jomo.

It's difficult for my mortal mind to wrap around the fact that heaven could be a shade brighter than this little corrugated metal-and-concrete school stuffed with smiling faces and full hearts.

Gavin stands in the bed of his truck, tossing oranges like baseballs to eager, hungry children. I watch as the older children peel the fruit, section it, and share it with the younger children.

Sharing is the African way.

Mr. C has taken it upon himself to build matching bookshelves, benches, and chairs for the school. Nygoya has painted the entire alphabet around the top of the ceiling. She has also hand-painted African animals on the walls. It's difficult for me to differentiate between Nygoya's zebras and her giraffes, but that doesn't deter her enthusiasm.

"I am a woman who does many tasks," she says proudly, show-casing her work to a group of young students. "Painting is the newest of my many skills. All of you can one day also be skilled and know a better life. Listen to Mama Grace, and your futures will be so bright you will have to wear sunglasses to look at them." Her belly shakes when she laughs, but the children just stare at her, not understanding her joke, not understanding her hope for them.

I watch her in wonder and long to be more like Nygoya.

Mama Dale is here with Benda. In the girl's arms is a baby, happy and smiling—Baby Gracie.

"Look at the book I've brought for your library," Mama Dale tells Mama Grace.

Mama Grace takes the familiar blue book and rolls her eyes. "Lana, come see something." She motions for me to follow her.

"It got so bad I had to request Mr. C to build a special shelf for my collection." She pulls back the cover from a bookshelf, and I see a row of books . . . all the same.

"Mama Dale insists that I read the Book of Mormon. She is not the only one; your LDS missionaries keep bringing the same book over and over. Soon I will have a copy for each of my students. Perhaps we will read it together someday."

"I'd like to read it with you," I say.

"It's translated into Kissi," she says. "You will have to learn a new skill."

"I can do that."

She winks and laughs. "I will loan you a copy. I can spare one."

"Mama Grace, I have a gift for you . . . for this special occasion."

"Not another Book of Mormon?"

"Not exactly, but it would be appropriate for you to put it on this shelf."

"Oh? What is it, my *rafiki*?"

"It's something I asked my father to make for you."

She beams. "Your father in the USA made a gift for me?"

"Yes." I hurry out to Gavin's pickup truck and bring back a small, heavy box wrapped like a birthday present.

Mama Grace opens it slowly. She stares at it for a very long time.

"It is the photo of you and Jomo. I will treasure it."

"Please read the inscription below the photo," I say. "Read it out loud."

". . . he doeth that which is good among the children of men; and he doeth nothing save it be plain unto the children of men; and he inviteth them all to come unto him and partake of his goodness; and he denieth none that come unto him, black and white, bond and free, male and female; . . . and all are alike unto God."

Tears glisten in Mama's eyes as she takes me into her arms. "I've heard those words before," she says. "They sound to me like an old memory returned."

"To me, too," I whisper in her ear as I tighten my arms around my dear, dear *rafiki.*

Grace takes my hand, winds her beautiful black fingers between mine until we are linked. Dark and light. Best friends holding on for dear life. I give her hand a faint squeeze, and she squeezes back with such strength that her grip takes hold of my heart.

"I have a gift for you also," she says. "It is one that is wrapped in words. May I tell you a favorite African tale?"

"Please."

"A water bearer once made two identical pots for holding precious water.

"They balanced perfectly until the day one was dropped and cracked. Still, it held water, and so the bearer went each day to the river along a barren, dusty trail to fill the pots and return to his parched village.

"By the time he got back, the perfect pot was still filled to the brim, while the cracked pot only carried a portion of its measure."

Mama Grace squeezes my hand again. "Lana, to me you are the cracked pot."

I cannot help but laugh.

"You see, that pot felt so bad it was broken. It wished with all of its might that it could be perfect and whole like its identical sister. Then one day the water bearer grew weary and stopped to rest. As he did, the pots realized that they were resting in a green, lush clump of grass. Grass had grown where once there had been nothing but barren, dry dirt. Flowers, too, and ferns had sprung to life all along the path.

"All that time the cracked pot had been leaking precious droplets of water, springing forth life where there was none, sprouting seeds that would have withered beneath the scorch of the sun if they had not received life-giving water."

Mama Grace lets go of my hand to reach up and wipe a tear from my cheek.

"So you see," she says, "where your broken heart has traveled, good things have grown."

Asante sana does not come close to expressing my gratitude.

Everyone wants time with Mama Grace, and eventually I slip away from the celebration, outside under the umbrella of a cloudless, blue sky and blazing sun.

How I wish that Jomo could be here. I fight away my sorrow, reminding myself that he is in a better place.

Gavin puts his arm around me. "You okay?"

"Better than new. I'm redeemed."

He smiles, and for an endless moment we stand beneath the African sun, basking in all that this word—*redeemed*—has come to mean to us.

About the Author

Toni has always had a deep interest in and love for the African continent and people. When her daughter Taylor completed a summer service mission to Kenya, Toni vowed to get involved in helping the "street children" of Africa, as well as children from every corner of the world. A small foundation was established to do just that, so a portion of the proceeds from *Redemption Road* will be donated to the real Grace and her school.

Toni is the mother of six children and a dog named Kenya. She is motivated in life by her love for people, her desire for gospel scholarship, and a passion for brownies, still warm from the oven.

She has authored a number of best-selling books for Covenant, including *Behold Your Little Ones*.